Until I Do

T.I. LOWE

Copyright © 2017 T.I. LOWE
All rights reserved.
ISBN-10: 1546870709
ISBN-13: 978-1546870708

DEDICATION

To Bernie Lowe
Happy 20th Anniversary!

OTHER BOOKS BY T.I. LOWE

Lulu's Café
Goodbyes & Second Chances
A Bleu Streak Christmas
A Bleu Streak Summer
Coming Home Again
Julia's Journey
A Discovery of Hope
Any Given Moment
Orange Blossom Café
Until I Don't
Until I Decide

ACKNOWLEDGMENTS

A special thank you to my honey, Bernie Lowe. What a journey we have been on. Can't wait to see where it leads us next.

Thank you to my Lowe, Stevens, and Healy Family for loving me and supporting this dream.

Christy Anderson, thanks so much for putting up with my medical questions. You always have great answers! Love ya!

My beta readers and for keeping my ramblings in check.

Christina Coryell, thank you for cleaning up my stories and keeping me on track!

Most importantly, my Heavenly Father for allowing this dream to come true in His time and in His way.

Prologue

Weathered tombstones and shrouds of mournful black surround the substantial congregation, gathered on this dreary evening is to celebrate the life of Mia Calder. Such a beautiful life to celebrate. The murmuring of the somber group quietens as the pastor stands before them, bereavement creasing his forehead and down-turning his mouth.

"We all knew the young woman Mia Calder—always full of spunk and enthusiasm. Everyone can attest to her youthful dedication to her patients." Pastor Chase pauses as an amen here and there echoes through the group. "No matter, today we have to mourn the loss of that youth taken too soon."

"Way too soon," Mia's dad bellows as he wraps a consoling arm around his wife's shoulders. Heads nod in agreement.

"Yes, Richard. Way too soon indeed." Pastor Chase settles his attention on a group of teenagers. "Let Mia be a reminder to us all of how precious life truly is. Young folk, you are wise to remember you are not exempt. None of us are. Mia is proof of how quickly our time goes."

"Why her?" Mia's little sister sobs while leaning her head heavily against her friend Parker's shoulder for support.

"Yes, Neena. Why Mia? Why? It was inevitable..." He clears his throat and continues. "Perhaps some Geritol and a cane can help our old gal out." A roar of laughter flickers through the crowd as gazes drift to where Mia stands in their midst, a black glittery crown nestled on top of her brown locks.

"That's not funny!" Mia sasses, arms folded, trying and failing to produce a scowl. She gives up and laughs along with the party goers.

The fortieth birthday is one not to be taken for granted. Another decade complete— four in total. An important milestone in one's life, and Mia finds herself amongst a grand crowd happily celebrating her milestone. The gleam on the birthday girl's face broadcasts the fact that she is well aware of just how blessed she is to have each one of her guests in her life.

"Happy birthday, Mia," Chase concludes with a boisterous voice as the group chants out their own birthday declarations.

Enthusiastic energy ignites the Calder family's spacious basement/game room as the impressive number of family and friends create a symphony of laughter and friendly chatter. The guest of honor circulates through the crowd, thanking each guest personally for taking part in her day.

Metallic streamers and balloons, in moody shades of black and silver, elegantly dance around the robust party. The birthday girl bats a wayward balloon out of her path as she heads toward her husband. Bode reaches for Mia's hand and pulls her to the bar in the small kitchen where the fluffy two-tiered confection sits. The tombstone topper declares, "Here lies Mia's Youth." She rolls her eyes at the silliness of the statement while swiping a finger through the gray icing. Bode snatches her hand and steals the sugary dollop before she can successfully make it to her mouth. She playfully pops him in the stomach, igniting more laughter through the crowd.

Standing behind Mia with his hands resting on her hips, Bode leads the crowd in singing "Happy Birthday." As the song concludes, Bode leans close to Mia's ear and says, "Make a wish." Before leaning away, he places a kiss to her cheek, causing the group to break into whoops and whistles.

Most of the women in the group sigh and swoon, while one shouts out, "A wish? She already has everything she could ever wish for!"

Several guests laugh at the woman's playful comment as the Calders' two teenage children scoot closer to their parents. The family of four is picture perfect, with brown wavy hair in various hues. Kaisley, the couple's eighteen-year-old daughter, leans more toward being considered a redhead, but both mother and daughter have pale ivory skin that would make Snow White seem ordinary. Addison, the couple's oldest at nineteen, is as athletically built and bronzed as his father. Many comments circulate the room on how striking this family is and how blessed one would be to have the privilege of being a Calder.

The women release awes and the men let out rounds of earsplitting whistles as they watch Bode feed Mia her birthday cake. The admiring glimmer in that man's eyes is impossible not to notice. They are most definitely wearing twenty-two years of marriage well and have celebrated their beautiful union with those two lovely children.

Yes, most certainly, the Calder Family is very blessed. They are a family that the neighbors struggle not to envy, but they are so kind, making it impossible not to like them. No evidence can be found of any life struggles, and everything they have encountered along life's journey has been handled with dignity and grace. They are a faithful family so perhaps this is their reward.

With generous slices of cake being divvied out, the couple merges back into the crowd to mingle some more with their guests. Time eases along as the party continues with no rush on concluding.

Mia spots Janice, the long-time receptionist at Sunshine Valley Pediatrics, and eases over to her.

"Happy birthday, sweetheart." Janice wraps her arms around Mia.

"Thank you for celebrating with this here *old* woman," Mia says in a teasing tone.

"Nonsense, young lady." A wide smile causes the corners of her eyes to crinkle. "That Bode sure did a wonderful job." She waves her hand around the room, causing some of the streamers to flutter wildly from her movement.

Both women ease their gazes over to the man in question, catching sight of him leaning his head back in a roar of laughter, rich and hearty in his deep timbre. Neither woman can help but smile. Bode Calder can be one infectious man—there's no denying it.

Mia shakes her head, amazed that after all of these years he still has an effect on her. "That man looks like he should still be a freshman in college instead of raising a college freshman *and* sophomore."

"You've not aged a bit either, young lady." Janice gives Mia a stern look that dares her to disagree. "You are absolutely flawless."

Mia wants more than anything to disagree, for she has proof, but she keeps her manners intact and thanks the older lady instead. Giving Janice one last hug, Mia makes her way through the jovial crowd.

"Tell your mother to pencil me in for a coffee date the next time she's in town. She left before I could tell her," Janice calls out before Mia gets too far away or swallowed up completely by the thick group of partiers.

"I will," Mia answers over her shoulder, then keeps moving on until she finds her favorite neighbor. A smudge of icing on his dark chin catches her attention, so she sits beside him on the couch and uses her thumb to wipe it off. "What are you doing, saving some for later, Maury?"

His face lights up with his wide grin as he looks in her general direction. "Mia, I see you're having a great time this evening."

"I truly am. Thank you for celebrating the day with me."

"I only have eyes for you, sweetheart. It's an honor to celebrate this special occasion with you."

Mia places a kiss on his cheek before moving on through the large crowd. Many women stop her, more to coo over her husband than anything else, but she seems to be a good sport about it all. Bode is one of those guys who had all the girls chasing him in high school. Mia is the lucky one he allowed to catch him—not a small feat considering he led his track team to the state championships all four years of his high school career.

The conversations continue along the same lines…

"That Bode is one good man."

"All those handsome looks and a top computer programmer with that prestigious computer app company…"

"I heard Bode made VP! Y'all are so blessed."

Words begin to whirl and blur together as the compliments rain down on the birthday girl.

You're perfect.
Bode is perfect.
Your careers are perfect.
This house is perfect.
Your family is perfect.

Your life is so perfect.

The picture is perfect…on the outside. The couple's smiles and generous demeanor never falter…on the outside. It's a picture the couple has painstakingly worked to perfect… on the outside.

As with any façade, cracks form over time and start revealing the unappealing truth.

Chapter One

Mia

Shoes have been abandoned and seconds on birthday cake devoured by the time the partygoers trickle peacefully away late into the night. Shaking my head at the festivity's remnants scattered all over the basement, I plop down on the sectional and decide to ignore the mess for the time being.

Neena plops down beside me and places a thick folder on my lap with a simple black bow stuck on top. The questioning look I give her only beckons a wide grin from her in return. *Oh sugar.* Now I'm nervous.

Flipping it open, I regard the contents with apprehension. "Umm... Thanks... I guess?"

Bode has enough gall to laugh. He's just as lean and fit as he was during his track-star running days back in high school and college. His body has held its shape remarkably well for a forty-two-year-old. Mine... Not so much. It's not that I'm overweight at an average size ten—I don't believe in *bony*—but my ladies have seen their glory days and can barely remember that *perky* time before breastfeeding. Other parts of me also seem as tired as I feel.

"Now don't go taking this gift the erroneous way," Neena says, using an odd word. She's in love with unusual words and actually scribbles them on a word-wall at her home. Addison and Kaisley thought this was proper behavior when they were toddlers, each taking crayons to the walls of their rooms. Try explaining the error of their ways to little ones after seeing their grown aunt get away with such behavior.

"What?" Bode grumbles, bringing me back to the present. I look over and find him giving her his confused expression—a look he wears too well and too often.

"It means *wrong*, dork," Neena answers with an exaggerated eye roll.

"You go from a fancy word and then on to name-calling *and* eye rolling." Bode snorts. "You, *Neena*, are such a contradiction." The way he says her name makes it sound like it's a foul word.

"I'm proud you used a word with more than one syllable. Well done, old man."

He throws his hands up in frustration. "Why can't you just use normal words?"

Neena and Bode continue bickering like bratty siblings, but I pull my focus back to the gym membership packet glaring up at me from my lap. That second piece of cake starts to sit heavy with regret in my stomach.

"Back to the point," Neena says. "Mia, you have a gorgeous figure."

I lift my eyes to her and prepare to smart off, but Neena holds her hand up to stop me.

"Yes, you do. The reason for this gift is because you need to put yourself on the list of priorities. Your job is stressful and you balance all of this..." She pauses to motion around the room, but I think she is really talking about Bode and the kids. "You get no 'Mia Time' and it's *time*. You deserve it just as much, if not more than the rest." I follow her eyes and am not surprised when they land on my husband.

The amused smirk from earlier has been slapped off his face by my sister's words, but it's not a look of regret or remorse settling over his features as I expected. Nope. Not even close. It's clearly a look of annoyance.

"I think it's a great gift, Momma," I hear Kaisley say and look up as she passes me a gift bag.

Peeking inside the bag, I find it filled with lots of stretchy colorful workout gear. I pull out a hot-pink tank top and show it off. "Well, I'll look the part at least in these spiffy outfits."

"You'll definitely look the part when you add these." Addison hands me a gift.

I tear the paper off and see a familiar shoe brand on the box. "Happy birthday, Momma." My grown son leans over and presses a sweet kiss to my cheek. Oh, how I wish I could make him shrink from that six foot stature back to the little four-foot kid who I used to chase around.

I flip the lid open and find an outrageously neon pair of Asics cross trainers nestled inside. They look so excited and energetic just sitting in the box—

splattered with greens, oranges, pinks, and blues. It looks like a paint fight broke out on them.

"Very cool, sir," I tell Addison and then look over to my daughter and say, "Thank you, sweetie."

Kaisley wraps me in one of her teddy bear hugs, as we call them. This girl is pure sugar. I run my fingers through her soft hair and pretend she is only a toddler again.

"I love you, Momma," Kaisley whispers, squeezing me closer.

"Love you more," I whisper back.

After a few more moments and another squeeze, she releases me and heads over to help Neena untie the birthday banner.

I shake my head and blink the unexpected tears away. My two children are the greatest gifts I've received in this life, by far.

Last on the gift giving list is my husband. We've celebrated twenty-two years of marriage with a few years of courting added on to the beginning of our life together, so I already know what gift he is about to hand over before he retrieves it from the cabinet.

"Happy birthday, Mia." Bode hands over the card as I suspected he would.

I open it and discover the same thing he has given me every year—a one hundred dollar bill. The same familiar words are scrawled in his sloppy handwriting: *Wish it were a million.*

"Thanks," I say in a dry tone and toss the card onto the end table, producing a bored grunt from my husband.

People have commented over the years that it's sweet he gives me money, so I can get exactly what I want. My complaint is, if he took the time to notice me, Bode would know exactly what I wanted and go get it himself. Instead, he phones it in every year with this impersonal gift. I know what his interests and wants are, and I take the time to seek out and find the perfect gifts each year.

I rub my forehead, trying to push my snarky thoughts away before they spill off of my sharp tongue. Bode seems to sense it too, because he's quick to retreat upstairs where I'm sure he will have no trouble seeking out his remote control in the den. He showed up to the party, after all. With his sentence fulfilled, he'll slide away.

Bode and I have gotten ourselves in some sort of life rut, and we're growing a bit bitter about not being able to find our way out of it. Every now and then, we'll push against it for our children's sake, almost making it over the lip, but seem to plummet back down further with each attempt: me becoming lonelier, and him growing more closed off.

The last year or so, I've realized I married too young at the age my daughter is now. If she were to come home and say she's getting married at all of eighteen years old, I would have a conniption fit. I was too young, too naïve, and beyond crazy in love. None of the wise words of advice my parents delivered about waiting until after college would sway me from saying 'I Do' to Bode Calder. Honestly, I blame it all on hormones—those pesky brats.

Releasing a long pensive sigh, I give the gym information one last perusal before helping my three favorite people remove the happy party façade. Neena and my parents put this shindig together and generously allowed Bode to take all the credit for it, not once correcting anyone's assumption tonight. More irritating was the fact that Bode never corrected them either.

Another, more agitated sigh slips from me as I feel my shoulders tighten in annoyance. Maybe exercise would be a great stress-reducer. A nervous energy tingles the back of my neck. I can only hope this will be a positive change, but a nagging feeling says not to get my hopes up. Either way it's about time something gives around here.

*****

Wiping the sneaky tears away before they can escape my eyes, I watch the taillights of my parents' car wink at the stop sign before disappearing altogether. That car holds precious cargo and is on the path to delivering my babies back to their designated college campuses in Florida.

As soon as Addison was accepted to Florida State, my parents went house hunting. My boy is following in his grandpa's footsteps, majoring in Criminology and Criminal Justice. My dad is a retired professor of that particular subject. He took his vast knowledge of crime and turned it into a lucrative second career, authoring over twenty New York Times Bestselling crime novels. Richard Cameron is our little mountain town's very own celebrity, and we are all quite proud of him.

Kaisley is in Florida as well, but she had to rival her brother and pick the University of Florida instead. My parents are protectively planted in between the colleges. This gives my babies enough freedom, but the security of knowing family is nearby.

Pushing through the mournful morning fog, I escape back into the house for one more cup of coffee before heading to the office. I take the cup upstairs, where I swap my pajamas for a pair of scrubs with fairies flying carelessly over the fabric. After I'm dressed, I shrug into my lime-green lab coat. I've sort of rebelled against the office's protocol. In the beginning, the office manager instructed me to dress in business casual attire, which is the standard dress code for nurse practitioners. I felt the patients' preferences were more important than some silly fashion rule, so I've always stuck with my colorful scrubs and equally vivid lab coats. It took the manager a few years to get over it, but I guess at the ripe ole age of forty, I'm considered set in my ways. No one tries to sway me anymore.

Within an hour, I'm weaving through the already lively halls of Sunshine Valley Pediatrics. My ears perk at a baby crying in one of the exam rooms.

"Good morning, young lady." Dr. Brock acknowledges me with a friendly nod before sliding into the exam room with the fussy baby.

"Good morning," I say just before the door closes and muffles the crying.

There are a total of three pediatricians and all are in the geriatric age range. I'm considered the baby of the group and the wiser doctors have always kept me tucked under their protective wings. We each have our own nurse who keeps us on track. Speaking of which...

The tapping echoes of rushing feet catch my attention. I glance over my shoulder and spot my nurse hustling down the hall. Once Renee reaches me, she quickly scoops my bag and travel coffee mug from my hands.

"Which exam room?" I ask, knowing there's an emergency of some sort.

"Room four. An object lodged in the sinus cavity."

Zooming by the painted jungle animals roaming the wall, I pluck the file from the door tray and scoot inside the room in a flash. I find a little redheaded guy with flushed cheeks and a distraught momma barely hanging onto her composure. I scan over the file before tossing it on the counter.

"Good morning! Mikey, are you trying to build a Lego house in your nose? That's not nearly enough room, if you ask me." I quickly wash my hands and pull on a pair of purple gloves while catching a quick glance at his momma. Some of her tension alleviates with my joke. Good. Calm mommas equal calmer babies. Wielding my handy dandy light, I illuminate the toddler's sinus cavity and see the tiny block peeking at me. I look up at Mikey who is watching me frantically—his bright green eyes wide with panic. "You're building a blue house, I see."

Before I can turn away from him to seek out a pair of long tweezers, Renee is slipping the needed tool into my hand. I smile my thank you and turn back to my patient. "Okay, buddy. Let's you and me get this thing out with my magic wand."

It takes a few tries to extract the tiny block from his even tinier and very uncooperative nose. After washing the block and returning it to its owner, I have Mikey promise to build all projects outside of his body from now on. I'd say from the exuberant head nod he offers, that lesson has most definitely been learned.

Smiling wide, I wave goodbye to them. Mikey is not my first body crevice object inserter and I can guarantee he won't be the last. The fun notion of sharing this silly patient story with my family tonight over dinner flickers through my mind before reality taps on my shoulder. *The kids are at college and Bode is in his own little world.* Loneliness follows this thought. Shrugging it off, I go seek another patient to keep me company.

The morning is much quieter after Mr. Lego, thank goodness. Mostly, I treat ear infections that seem to be ever-present nowadays and some various cases of colds and viruses. My excitement builds after lunch and I'm barely able to contain it. I replace my scrub top with a clean one that is identical to the one I was already wearing, because fairies are a must today. I have the afternoon filled with well care checkups and there is a very special one scheduled. She's first on the list and will be sliding in the back door at any moment to reduce contact with any germs. The cleaning crew took extra care to have the well room ready for my little Sophie.

I'm already perched on my stool in the exam room when my tiny fairy flutters through the door, sporting sparkling pink wings and a lime green tutu with an outrageously bright shirt declaring, *Fairies Are the Fly*. At age eight, this little girl has stolen my heart and has stubbornly refused to give it back. As she launches into my arms, I pull off the oversized hat and plant several silly kisses over her bald head until she's squealing in laughter. Oh, how that's absolute music to my ears.

"Hey, Pipsqueak!"

Those big blue eyes look up at me and sparkle with sweetness. My own eyes try not to linger too long on the dark circles prominent under hers. Sophie's grin widens to reveal an absent front tooth. She's doing it on purpose, hoping I notice her exciting milestone. I have to bite my lip to keep my composure.

Tapping my chin, I lean back and inspect her further with squinted eyes. "There's something different about you, young lady..." I continue to scan over her features, again trying not to linger on her hollowed cheeks. "Did you grow a mustache?" I lean close to check her top lip.

Her giggles are so exuberant, she can barely answer. "No!" When she regains her composure, Sophie grins as wide as she can. Her eyes pinch shut with the effort.

Gasping dramatically, I point to her mouth. "You let a fairy steal your tooth!"

"It's okay. I wanted her to have it. Got five bucks for it!"

"Yay! You can take me out for ice cream!" I bounce her in my lap and cheer.

Yes, we are overly enthusiastic. Fighting a tough fight with leukemia deserves lots of silliness whenever one can plug it in, so I will spend more time celebrating this milestone with my patient than the wellness exam will take.

I've cared for Sophie ever since her mom, Amber, delivered her at the hospital just across the road from this office. My stomach dips as I think back four years ago, when Amber brought our Pipsqueak in with odd symptoms. As she ticked off the list—easy bruising, shortness of breath, loss of appetite, and fatigue—I knew right then and there. After sending her to a specialist for testing, the diagnosis confirmed it. After that, we all rallied around her and set out to go to war. We were victorious for a while. Our brave little girl went into remission for a solid year before leukemia reared its ugly head once again. This time leukemia seems to have brought in the big guns and poor Sophie is having a tough go of it lately.

She doesn't need this appointment today for the wellness checkup. I'm pretty much medically useless to her. Amber trusts me and relies on me to keep the pep in their steps and give some sense of normalcy, so we continue to do the wellness checkups. I gladly do it, too. I have also spent many hours in the ER next door, checking on Sophie when she comes in. Lots of infections and other hiccups are a constant for her.

Standing up with my little fairy in my arms, I walk over and place her on the exam table to begin the routine checkup. Afterwards, Renee has the ice cream waiting for us in my office. It's one of the only foods we can get Sophie to eat, so visits always conclude in this fashion.

The day wears on with me caring for my patients. I love it. I really do. To have such a job is a blessing, yet it comes with a heavy burden. The aches of uncertainty and restlessness prick my heart.

The drive home is unceremonious and somber with dreary skies hanging heavily with clouds. Not quite ready to face what's waiting for me at home, I park by the I Spy house. Our gated community sports pristine landscaping and strict HOA guidelines, and this house has been taunting those rules on the other side of the gates for as long as we've lived here. It's a quaint little house, but the yard is beyond outrageous. The yard decorations are endless and never cease to multiply. My babies and I took to making a game out of the yard way back when they were only in elementary school. Addison had just discovered a unique book that required very little reading, but lots of investigating. I should have realized his destined path of life right then and there.

Sitting in the car, memories show up and keep me company. Sweet voices, filled with silly giggles, cause my throat to constrict as they chime through the car in melodious recollections.

"*Momma, I spy a bumblebee!*"
"*Well, I spy a bear wearing a red hat.*"
"*Momma, I spy six frogs!*"
"*I spy four mismatched rain boots.*"

I blink back the tears and play the game alone. It's not nearly as fun, but then again nothing is anymore. Chores are waiting to be finished, so eventually I abandon the game and happier memories and drive up the block to my oversized brick colonial house. I say house, because just as soon as Kaisley packed up for college a few months back, it stopped feeling like home.

My small sedan squeezes into the garage beside Bode's monster truck. It's a full-sized beast with giant tires, KC lights, and a huge bumper made for dragging things around or pulling other monsters out of unforeseen situations. A truck like this begs to be covered in mud, but glancing over, I notice the black paint shines just as it did the day he drove it off the lot. This was Bode's midlife crisis purchase when he turned forty. I was worried for all of two seconds because whatever idea he had with this purchase faded swiftly like his ideas normally do.

My husband's default setting has always been set on sluggish indifference, and the wish to figure out how to reset that sucker gnaws at me. To be able to at least tweak it a bit would be grand. Too bad humans aren't as easily manipulated as electronics.

Turning my attention away from the truck and Bode's uncontrollable settings, my nose registers a familiar stench of rotting food and neglect.

"Ugh. You've got to be kidding me," I mutter to myself. Walking over to the garbage cans, I know before checking that they are still full and need to be at the curb. Bode puts this one task off until the pungent odor peels the paint and attracts flies. Tossing my keys and bag on the steps, I lug the stinky cans out to the curb and land a few swift kicks to them before heading back into the garage. I know it's not the cans' fault, but it's better them receiving the kick than my procrastinating husband.

I hit the button to power the garage door shut and retrieve my stuff. My blood is already boiling when my hand lands on the loose doorknob that leads to the kitchen. The exact same doorknob my husband has to turn each day when arriving home. The exact same doorknob I've been asking him to fix for the last few weeks. Again, I throw my bag down and head over to his unused workbench to retrieve the screwdriver. Within a few minutes, I have the screws tightened and dare them with a glare to loosen ever again.

Finally, I'm able to make it into the house after ten aggravating minutes of unexpected obstacles. The laundry basket on the counter, full of clothes to be folded, still sits where I left it, a stack of mail sitting by it. Retrieving the mail is the only task my husband seems to follow through on. The reason for that is he also retrieves and delivers the mail to Maury.

Maury is the only neighbor we've gotten to know in this vast gated community. Twenty years with only one acquaintance to show for it. We may only have one, but we certainly picked well. Maury Jackson hung the moon and there's no telling me any differently. A retired school teacher who was robbed of his eyesight, Maury is like family, so we keep an eye on him. He says he keeps an *eye* on us as well.

I toss the bills on top of the laundry and head toward my room. Boisterous voices are recapping the weekend ballgames from the den, so I know my roommate is camped out in front of the TV per the usual. He didn't care to welcome me home, so I return the favor and keep on the path leading upstairs without saying a word. Maybe it's for the best because my tongue has become quite sharp, and I use the weapon frequently to inflict snide wounds on my husband.

In the beginning of this thing we call marriage, neither one of us could wait to see the other after work. Long comforting hugs and deliciously lingering kisses were always the first order of business. Years passed and the hugs and kisses dwindled to just a faint peck and pat and then further plummeted to a tired *hey*. Nowadays, nothing welcomes me but chores and loneliness.

Once the bills are made out and the laundry is folded and put away, I take a shower to try washing off some of this funky mood. Twenty minutes in, I know it's no use. After drying off, I dress in my favorite ratty T-shirt and boxer shorts without bothering to comb out my tangled wet hair, since there's no energy left to tackle it. I glance at the clock and notice it's not quite seven, but the early hour doesn't deter me from climbing into bed.

Snuggling in the cool soft bedding, my body relaxes into its comfort. The dark void of sleep swallows me up fairly quickly, but I'm reawakened shortly after by a strong hand shaking my shoulder. Looking up, I find Bode staring down at me. My eyes drift back shut in hopes of him taking the hint and going away.

"Mia, you sick?"

"No. Just tired," I mutter.

"What about supper?"

I roll over and tuck the cover around my shoulder. "I'm not hungry."

Without pause, he says, "But I am."

Even though my eyes are closed, I see red. Slinging the covers off, I bolt from the bed to square off with his idiocy. He quickly retreats to the door like a scared puppy. Good. He needs to be scared.

"You were home at least an hour before me. What have you been doing in all that time that you couldn't cook?" I don't allow him to answer before plowing on with my rant. "Nothing is what! You didn't fix the flipping doorknob! You certainly did not roll the garbage cans to the curb! And you seemed not to notice the laundry needing to be folded!"

Bode stands his six foot stature as tall as he can, preparing for battle. I think to myself, *bring it on, big boy!*

"I spent eight straight hours staring at a computer monitor. I had a headache by the time I got home." He spits his words through gritted teeth.

"Well, the headache is your own blame fault. If you would wear your glasses—"

"They're broke!" He throws his hands in the air.

"Again. Your own fault!" My fingers rake through my damp, tangled hair. "Why should I have to work all day, and then come home to face your to-do list and my own? I'm too tired to eat and I'm certainly too tired to cook for you, so your best bet is to mosey your lazy butt downstairs and figure supper out yourself." I point to the door.

Without another word and with stooped shoulders, Bode shuffles back out of the room, looking confused of all things. Confused! Are you kidding me? Did I marry this man to be my partner or to take him to raise? Now, An epiphany that's probably twenty years too late, but I have had enough.

A shot of angry adrenaline courses through me and won't let me settle back down. While pacing a lap around the room, my eyes land on the abandoned gym gifts sitting on top of my dresser. I rummage around in the closet until unearthing a tote bag. Tossing the gym gear inside it, I resolve that it's time for some things to change. I'm done being this grown man's caregiver, and I'm done with not being on the list.

Neena is absolutely right. Things *have* to change.

Chapter Two

Bode

Who am I and what happened to the other me? I haven't the earthliest idea, because whoever this is staring at me in the mirror is not Bode Calder. This reflection is of a hollow, confused man. After inspecting the stranger a few more minutes, I give up on figuring him out and head out the door for my early morning run. Three quick miles and I will be able to at least check something off for the day that I can somewhat feel proud about.

The approaching of mile two awakens me and I finally begin to *feel* something with the numbness seeping away. The sluggish haze clears and is replaced by my heartrate climbing along with sweat accumulating on my brow. The slight burning in my muscles as they are pushed is familiar and comforting.

As the warmup jog escalates to a steady run, my thoughts wander to Mia as always. She is the woman of my dreams—gorgeous blue eyes that still hold mystery at forty, silky brown hair with a few stubborn streaks of auburn, and creamy lush skin. She is so feminine, and I have to admit, intimidating. I still haven't gotten over what that strong body accomplished with growing and birthing our children.

My pace quickens as my self-doubts try catching up with me, and I wish I could outrun them. Mia is a force to be reckoned with, no doubt about it. She's accomplished, self-sufficient. Never been one to whine or be needy. In the last few years, I've finally been slapped with the reality I wish I could have stayed oblivious to altogether. My wife doesn't need me. At. All. I know I'm losing her, but I'm just too confused to figure out how to fix it.

These thoughts are ruining this run, so I pick up my pace to a quick sprint and demand my mind to shut off. Three miles end up turning into five and by the time I get back to the house, I've worked up enough courage to go upstairs and boldly stake my claim on my wife.

Pulling my sweaty shirt off, I enter our room and find Mia about to tug on her top with the butterflies all over it. I gently tug it out of her hand and back her sweet little body toward the bed with a grin I can feel all the way up to my eyes. I see the attraction flare in her eyes as she scans my sweaty body, so I know she's game. I wouldn't take this moment if she wasn't. All it would take from her is a head shake or a deep sigh of opposition and I would back off. She doesn't do either, so I don't stop my claim.

No words are exchanged. We've done this marital dance long enough to need none. I'm a man on a carnal mission and she knows it. The adrenaline coursing through my dormant veins has awakened me, and I crave this sliver of power over this intimidating woman. I feel like a real man and want to beat my chest when she lies back on the bed and submits.

*****

During the drive to work, the crash after the high hits and it's all I can do not to cry like a baby. I know I'm just another chore on Mia's list that she can now check off for the day. This should bruise my ego enough to keep my hands to myself, but it doesn't. It's the only time I truly *feel* anymore, and so I selfishly continue to take it. The confusion and angst is always worse afterwards. Watching my wife silently gather her clothes and abandon me in our bed, without so much as a glance back, always cuts deeper than any of her strong-willed words. I know this is not what God intended for a marriage bed, or the marriage. Swallowing the lump in my throat—nearly choking on it—I realize my wife isn't in love with me anymore. And deep down, I think I'm to blame. *How did I mess this up?*

The day wears on with me squinting at the computer screen, deep in coding a new program with all sorts of jacked-up safety encryptions. I've been specifically handpicked to handle this one for a well-known financial firm, so I know I have to get it right. And then some.

"Hey, big guy on campus. How's it going?" Clancy bellows. My colleague always talks like he's still living in a frat house. It's the illusion he chooses to live, so I leave him be. I really don't care enough to call him out on it.

"It's going," is my go-to reply. It's not a lie, but it's also not the truth. Clancy doesn't need to know that. The man really doesn't care, anyway.

"I gotta admit I'm jealous about you getting the security coding project." He makes himself at home in a chair opposite of my desk, but I keep my focus on the computer with hopes he'll wander away sooner rather than later.

Too busy to reply, I grunt out something sounding like *sorry*.

"Looks like you'd give the rest of us a shot at the fun stuff around here."

Jealous of coding? What fun stuff?

I continue on with grunting responses while keying in the code formula. Why is it when I'm focused on my computer screen, working diligently, that's the moment someone will wander in and start rambling about mindless crap? Is it to drive me crazy on purpose?

"So, what do you think?"

My eyes finally take a break from the screen and move to Clancy. I try not to glare at him as he works on straightening out his sissy pink tie. I seriously hope he didn't just ask for my opinion on that.

He keeps looking at me, waiting, so I ask, "What do I think about what?"

"The new receptionist. She's smoking hot. Yeah?"

This married shmuck just said *smoking hot*? Does he not realize he's talking inappropriately about others to his *boss*?

"I'm busy working while I'm here. Not checking out my colleagues. The whole nonsense of checking out the receptionist or any other woman in this place happens to be against company policy *and* my marriage vows." I lean back in my chair, crossing my arms, waiting for him to admit the error of his idiotic ways.

Instead of cowering from my reprimand, the idiot actually laughs like I said something funny. There was nothing remotely funny about it.

"Bode, man, nothing wrong with looking as long as you don't touch." He howls out in laughter, thinking he's so hilarious—he's not. We have a stare-off for a few beats until he breaks eye contact and shakes his head. "You really need to get out from behind that computer screen every once in a while."

The desire to shove him out of my office door is there, but not strong enough to act on it. Instead of entertaining my unwelcomed guest, I go back to coding. It takes several tries to get my eyes to focus back on the numbers and symbols.

Clancy keeps yammering away for a while, but eventually gets the hint, or becomes bored, and wanders out my door. "Catch ya later, Mr. VP," he throws over his shoulder before shutting my door. He's like an irritating mosquito bite that won't leave me alone.

He and a lot of others—both in and out of this company—are under the delusional assumption that my life is a cakewalk since the promotion. That would be a big fat NO. The salary raise and fancy title came with a long list of new responsibilities, none of which I remotely enjoy doing. It's all tedious and boring and too time-consuming.

I stay holed up in my confined office until I've clocked my time and can be released from this stagnant job. Yes, I hate my job. It's not me. So why major in computers? Why pursue this career? Because I had a young wife and a child on the way that needed financial security. Consequently, I chose a career that would pay the bills, but I never thought it would completely overshadow my dreams.

This lack of dreaming is the reason why I sat both of my kids down and had a talk with them before college. I encouraged them to pursue what truly makes them happy and not what they think they should do. This confused useless feeling that plagues me is something I never want my son and daughter to feel. In truth, I want them to go after life like their mother. Mia is a go-getter and doesn't settle. She's passionate about her career and I'm proud to say she's darn good at it, too.

The short drive home is tackled in less than fifteen minutes. Grabbing Maury's mail, I head over to his house. I knock on his door once before letting myself in, which is our routine and has been a constant for as long as I can remember. We both know he can meander to the mailbox himself, but we don't acknowledge it. He may be blind, but he's pretty self-sufficient.

I move through the house and find him sitting on the back patio, looking out at nothing.

"Hey, old man. Looks like you got a fat check in the mail today," I say as I shuffle through nothing but junk mail.

"Then just throw it out," he comments, knowing it's all junk. His retirement checks are electronically deposited and all of his bills are on a bank draft, so this is the normal mail. But boy is it something to see the little guy light up when he receives an unexpected card or letter from family.

"Will do. You need anything before I head home?"

He ignores my question as he normally does and tries to get me to stay longer with conversational questions.

"Looked to me like Mia had a good time at the party. Don't you think?" Maury's face crinkles into a grin at his own joke.

"Yessir. Our ole girl had a blast. Thanks for celebrating with us. All right, old man, I'm gonna do something for you the devil won't do."

"Yeah? What's that?"

"I'm gonna leave you alone. You take care." I push through the door before he has a chance to stop me again.

"You too, boy," I hear him call out in a chuckle.

My eyes are killing me from straining them all day, so I head into the kitchen and retrieve the bottle of Ibuprofen. Mia says age has caught up with my eyes, but I blame the computer. That thing has been relentless on my vision over the years. Letting out a loud sigh, I loosen my tie and allow my feet to lead me to the den. They autopilot me to this spot every day. I plop into my leather recliner and stretch it all the way back. It's new and a gift from Mia for my birthday this past summer. I wasn't too happy to find my old broken-in-just-right recliner gone, but it only took a few sittings to realize she was right. The problem is if I ever sit, I'm done for. Working out and eating relatively healthy have always been a part of my daily routine, but I still feel sluggish all the time.

Slumped in the chair with SportsCenter keeping me company, I listen for Mia to come in from work as I do every day. Like clockwork, she'll bustle through the door around six and I'll stay glued to my chair and silently beg for her to come to me. To show me I'm worthy of her. Each day she proves to me I'm not.

In the beginning, my wife would immediately seek me out, kissing her welcome and wrapping herself around me like I was the only thing that mattered. Man, how that made me feel like a million bucks. Nowadays, I don't feel like my worth is even equivalent to a penny.

"I hate my life!" I yell at the TV, flinching from the pain it causes. I rub my throbbing forehead and watch on as star athletes are highlighted for conquering their worlds. At one point in time, I felt like I could conquer the world. Turns out, it conquered me.

Someone has to be the spectator, right? *Those who can't, watch.* This has become my motto. No, I'm not proud of it either.

Time slips well past six and Mia still hasn't come home. I guess she's still ticked about last night. It's all her blame fault for us going without supper. She's always wanted to run this show—making all the decisions. Whether it is the meal or the paint color for the guest bathroom or the family activities, she's always wanted all the decision-making power. She's never given me the chance to decide. After twenty-two years of marriage, she now makes the decision to drop the ball, and I honestly don't know how to pick it up. *Where would I even start?*

My phone flashes from the end table, catching my attention. I pick it up and squint until the blurriness of the text message comes into focus. *At the gym. Be home later.* Well, this is new and I have Neena to thank for that. Grunting, I maneuver out of the recliner and trudge into the kitchen to whip up a bowl of cereal for supper.

Did I mention I hate my life?

Chapter Three

Mia

Sitting in my car after work, I recount the exhausting day that started with my husband going all alpha male. He showed up after his morning run, shirtless and sexy. I had the urge to punch him in his perfect abs while he stood there and looked hungrily at my soft stomach that's riddled with faded stretchmarks. Bode used to place kisses along those lines and declare them badges of my strength from growing babies. Nowadays, he pays them as much attention as he does the rest of me—very little. This is the reason why I keep going along with his little trysts every now and then. It's the only attention I ever garner from him.

After that, the morning moved along with me being doused down with vomit from a poor kid who had a terrible allergic reaction to something she ate. After administering a shot of antihistamine and setting her up for allergy tests, I had just enough time to change scrubs before my next patient.

I had no appetite once my lunch hour arrived, so I headed straight to the eye doctor's office and picked up not one but two pairs of glasses for my exasperating husband. He won't keep up with his glasses. They are constantly being lost or broken. I know it's his way of trying to rebel against the hands of time, but it's becoming a costly rebellion.

I hurried home for a quick shower and to put my soiled scrubs to soaking before returning to work. I left a note with one pair of the eye glasses on the counter and hid the other pair upstairs. Hopefully, it will be a while before I have to pull them out.

So here I am sitting in my car, exhausted and wanting to go home and relax. My eyes land on the gym bag in the passenger seat. After sending Bode a text, I drive over to the gym just down the street with a good bit of reluctance.

Before I can figure out what I'm doing, I've been given a tour, shown to the locker rooms where I change into my new workout gear, and have been persuaded by the very perky fitness instructor named Andi to join her step class. She's so pleasant, seeing that I have a bottle of water and towel, so I can't bring myself to turn her down. She seems like pure sugar, so I follow right behind her to the aerobics studio.

Forty-five minutes later, I hate Andi the too-perky-drill-sergeant fitness instructor. The little firecracker nearly killed me with moves she shouted out continuously, and in my opinion, way too fast.

Rock on! Elvis! Kick and hustle! Shuffle-turn!

Those crazy moves were at a rapid fire pace, and I felt like that unassuming step and I danced some sort of evil dance until my legs trembled and begged me to stop.

My clothes are drenched and clinging to my worn-out body and my mouth feels like a barren desert by the time I head out. Limping to my car, I call Neena.

"Hey baby!" Neena answers after the first ring.

"Hey yourself. I'm leaving the gym." Holding back a groan, I slide onto the driver's seat and toss my bag behind me.

"Good for you. How'd it go?"

"Great! I joined this dance-step class. I had so much fun! I want you to come with me next Tuesday." I think I'm overdoing my excitement, so I try to tone it down.

"Sounds cool. Can I wear my boots since it's dancing?"

I refrain from laughing. My younger sister wears nothing but a variety of well-worn cowgirl boots on her ever-moving feet.

"You'll need to leave your boots at home, sweetie. Wear sneakers and workout attire and meet me here at six next Tuesday." Jeans, various white shirts, and cowgirl boots make up most of her wardrobe. Don't ask me why, but that's been her uniform for all her adult life.

"'Kay."

"Seriously, put a reminder on your phone. Don't stand me up."

I hear her tapping on the phone screen when she pauses. "Why do you want me to go so bad?" Neena asks suspiciously.

"I want to thank you for my gym gift is all." I grin mischievously at the road as I merge into traffic. After declaring my love for her and her returning the gesture, I hang up.

My sister may be six years my junior, but she seems so much wiser than me. In some ways, Neena has already had to live a lot more life than I have. To look at her all you'd see is a gorgeous, wickedly accomplished woman with a head full of wild light-brown hair that carries wherever the wind blows—right along with the rest of her body. She is a free spirit and takes it very seriously. Neena takes after my dad. She is a genius with words, but has no passion for fiction. She's all about reality and has published critically acclaimed articles from all over the world.

No matter how dynamic my sister is, cancer couldn't care less. At only the age of seventeen, the selfish disease attacked her ovaries. It stole her gift to ever conceive and carry a child. Neena was handed such a profound reality when she wasn't even old enough to properly dream of motherhood. Nevertheless, she's taken it in stride and has claimed my two babies as her own. She may be my little sister, but I look up to her in a big way.

Entering the house, familiar sounds of a ballgame carrying from the den greet me. My gaze lands on the stack of mail and the unacknowledged pair of glasses. Rolling my eyes, I grab the jar of peanut butter from the pantry, a banana, and another bottle of water before heading upstairs in solitude. This empty-nester life is for the birds...

Thursday shows up and my gym bag beckons me to try out the place of torture once more. I skipped last night due to Bible study. Church is about the only thing I can get Bode to do willingly with me anymore. Honestly, I believe both of us have stopped listening lately and are just on autopilot like everything else.

I bustle into the gym after work, still sporting my black scrubs with brightly colored hoot owls. I'm busy digging my keycard out of my bag when I slam into a solid wall of hard muscle. Rubbing the sting out of my offended nose, I look way up and find amused dark-blue eyes taking in my clumsy self.

"Sorry," I mutter.

"No worries, beautiful." His deep voice reverberates over me as his well-formed tatted-up arms reach out to steady my teetering body. He tilts his head to the side and a low groan sounds in the back of his throat. "Hmm... I'm having epic ideas involving hot brunette nurses."

Oh sugar! Is this hot stranger flirting with me? Surely not...

"Sorry, buddy. No ideas with this nurse." I point to myself and try to extract myself out of his embrace. When he doesn't seem inclined to release me, I add, "I'm married." I try to sound stern, but I think it is coming off sounding more flustered than anything.

His eyes flicker to my bare ring finger. "Really?"

He thinks I'm lying, but I never wear my wedding ring during the week. It's a hassle trying to pull on and off gloves with rings. I'm about to explain this, but that seems like too many words for my jumbled brain to extract.

Instead, I simply say, "Yes. Really."

"Is it serious?" Mischief glints through his vibrant blue eyes.

I laugh like he's joking around, even though I'm not so sure. "Yes. As soon as we both said 'I do' it became pretty serious."

With my answer, this big blond guy finally lets me go. Bending forward so he can meet my eyes and invade my personal space, he whispers, "That's too bad."

Big guy saunters off with his big ego, leaving me heated from head to toe. Snapping out of it, I dart into the locker room and have to talk myself out of calling off the whole workout idea. After the blush relents, I decide to buck up and go explore the exercise floor.

The place reminds me of a vast warehouse with endless rows of various exercise equipment. I look for a less populated area and am relieved when I spot such a location. Geared in neon greens and black, I nervously claim a treadmill with no one on either side. Keeping my eyes focused on the controls, I finally figure out how to get the thing moving. After a few minutes, my nerves settle. *No one is looking at you, Mia. Just chill and get a workout in.* This goes well for about ten minutes before a deep voice startles me.

"I don't want to accept you're married."

I look over and find Mr. Blond Bad-boy grinning at me as he sets the treadmill beside me into motion.

"Can you accept I also have two teenage children in college?" I try dousing this guy's flirting. His cockiness is way too overwhelming.

His sexy grin drops and now I can breathe. "Dang." He grumbles out a few more choice words before picking up his pace.

I turn my attention back to my machine, thinking he finally got the hint, but then I hear him speaking again. "What was that?"

"I'm Lee Sutton," he repeats, intimidating me all over again, because I know that name.

My mouth gapes open. "You're the hotshot who builds custom motorcycles for the rich and famous," I blurt.

The man is a celebrity in his own right and I've actually watched his show on the Discovery Channel with Bode and Addison. Well, more like I sat in the den, trying to be civil, while reading a book. Maybe I should have paid more attention. Addison would freak if he knew I've met this guy. I wonder how dorky it would be to ask for an autograph for my son. Lee is also a hot topic in the celebrity gossip world for his bad-boy ways.

"I know who I am. Now, who are you?" He smirks.

"Mia Calder." I avert my eyes from his flirty ones, trying to focus on the treadmill dials.

"You're that sexy yet painfully married nurse."

"I know who I am," I sass back. I'm floored that I just flirted back with him. This feels like playing with a sharp set of knives, knowing it can only end badly, but I have to admit, it's sort of fun.

We talk for twenty minutes with me filling him in on Addison and Kaisley and their college choices. Lee, in return, lets me in on a bike he's building for a country music singer in Nashville. We omit my husband completely from the conversation. Lee eventually demands I pick up my speed on the treadmill until we are both jogging along. I'm in pain but pretend not to be, even though the huffing and puffing is probably giving me away.

"Well, I think we would make great workout buddies," Lee declares as we hit the cool-down buttons.

I ignore his comment and concentrate on mopping the sweat off my face with the complimentary towel. Next thing I know my treadmill stops abruptly. Trying to find my balance before I topple over, my hand lands on firm heated skin. Looking up from the towel, I discover Lee's intimidating form leaning into my space. It seems he definitely lives up to his playboy reputation. He even smells of it in a mix of subtle cologne, sweat, and *metal*.

All sorts of red flags fly up and warn of DANGER, but I find myself agreeing. "Why not?"

Tuesday rolls around, producing no more encounters with the tall, blond, and dangerous guy from the gym. Thank goodness. Well, that may be because I've not been back to the gym since. I'm sort of relieved to be going to class with Neena so there's no worry of running into him today either. I know that man will only cause me trouble. Honestly, it was nice to be paid some attention. The flirting made me feel a flutter I thought was long gone and left back in my teenage years, but I think it's wise to steer clear of Lee Sutton. That became clear as soon as he released me from his flirtatious spell and reality set in on the way home last week. I'm married with children, and not a silly teenage girl turning to mush just because the popular bad-boy pays me some attention.

Hearing a painful huff, I glance over at my sister as we both limp out of the step class. Her cheeks are flushed and her damp hair is plastered around her face. Snickering, I look away.

"That wasn't nice of you," Neena says, almost growling.

Giggling, I wrap my arm around her shoulder. "Come over to the house and we'll order pizza."

Always quick to forgive, Neena nods her head. "You had me at *pizza*."

"I'll text Bode and get him on the order."

"Sounds good. See ya there."

We arrive to the house and hobble into the kitchen where Bode is studying a pizza menu. Surprisingly, his glasses are actually perched on his face. If the man only knew how stunning he looks in those tortoise shell glasses. Hmm...

Neena pulls me out of my ogling when I hear her say, "Hey, nerd!" As soon as she says it, Bode yanks the glasses off forcefully and I can only hope the frames survived it.

"Neena!" I glare over at her and find her eyes twinkling in tease.

"What? The glasses don't make him a nerd. He's always been one." She laughs like she's the funniest thing, oblivious to the tension in the room.

Bode tosses the glasses and menu on the counter and storms into the den to sulk for what I'm sure will be the rest of the evening. Needless to say, I end up ordering the pizza myself as I have to do everything else. All because my sister picked around with him. *Really?* I'm getting fed up with his overly dramatic moods. And I'm even more fed up when I glance around and see the laundry, dirty dishes, and mail are all waiting for me to tackle as usual.

I brush off any sympathy for Bode and enjoy my sister's company. At least this day didn't end like all my norms lately. At least I'm not lonely.

*****

A date night sounded promising enough when I suggested it earlier, but staring at Bode across the table as he sneaks peeks at his phone not so hidden on his lap, it's not as promising anymore. How can I be in a restaurant surrounded by people chattering away and feel utterly alone? After scanning the dining area with envy, I glance back at Bode.

Who is this stranger at my table instead of my husband?

Used to, when we ever managed a date night when the children were younger, we would start volleying conversation back and forth as soon as the car left the driveway until it returned. Bode used to be eager to tell me about some new improved program he coded and even more eager to hear about my little patients. Attentive and compassionate used to be two words to describe this man sitting across from me. Now the words distant and oblivious seem to be a better fit.

I clear my throat, trying to think of something fun and exciting to share with him, but this little noise from me doesn't even draw his attention. Nope. His squinted eyes are glued to his lap.

"You'd be able to steal glimpses of the game scores better if you wore your glasses."

His head snaps up from his phone as he gives me a fleeting look with narrowed eyes. "Please don't momma me tonight."

That sets my blood to boiling, but before a sharp retort spews through my lips the phone in my purse begins singing "Freebird."

"What does she want now?" Bode grumbles as he places his phone on top of the table and openly scrolls through the sports updates. I guess the efforts of the night are over.

Ignoring my grumpy husband, I fish the phone out and answer my sister's call. "Hey, sweetie."

"Hey you. Parker and I just finished up a story and we're starving. You want to grab some supper with us?" Her voice is jovial and hopeful, both traits she seems to constantly carry around with very little effort.

"Actually, Bode and I are at that little Italian bistro down the road from your office. You and Parker should join us," I suggest, earning me a sharp look from Bode. *Just go back to your phone*, I want to sass, but glare back at him instead.

"Excellent. We're on our way." With that, the phone clicks off.

"That guy is pathetic."

I look over and find Bode fiddling with the jar of grated parmesan cheese. "Who?"

"Parker. He follows Neena around like a stupid puppy."

I take a sip of water and shrug. "I think it's awfully sweet how he cares about her. I just wish she would give him the time of day."

Bode shakes his head as our bowls of minestrone soup arrive. After leading us in a quick prayer, he digs in absently as he goes back to scrolling through his phone. The overwhelming desire to snatch the blame phone and drown it in the bowl of soup is short-lived when I spot Neena skipping up to the table.

"Is your team winning?" She swipes Bode's phone out of his hand and begins her own search with Parker looking over her shoulder.

"Tennessee's losing. That sucks." Parker grins over at Bode with Bode returning it with a scowl. Parker is not a Tennessee native, hence he has no commitment to being a Volunteers fan. And he always takes every opportunity to heckle Bode about it. Bode normally returns it, but seems to be in no mood for it tonight.

Parker helps Neena into her seat before taking the other one across from her. He leans over and offers me a quick hug. "Hey, my favorite nurse lady." He produces his boyish grin, already making the night better by his warm friendliness.

"Hey, my favorite photo guy." I grin back.

The waiter is quick to take their orders. As the night progresses, it's clear that Parker notices the waiter noticing Neena with Bode noticing nothing but his food and phone.

Poor Parker. Every time Neena glances his way, he runs his hands through his long dark hair. It's clearer than his gray eyes that he longs for her attention. He's a great guy who seems to be able to take her kookiness in stride. Sadly, my little sister seems unaware of it, or maybe she's just bound and determined to keep hiding from the truth behind those silly walls she constructed around her over the years.

As the empty pasta plates are cleared, Neena and Bode get into one of their word sparring matches.

"You have no decorous rejoinders, really, and you sound more like a petulant child than anything else," Neena sasses after Bode tried to one up her by saying *she needed to eradicate her inhibitions and go on some dates before she ended up a cantankerous old maid.* That was a mouthful, and he somehow managed to deliver it eloquently.

"Me a child? You're the one who still doesn't know how to use a flipping hairbrush," Bode grouches, sounding to have already had enough of her sparring.

"You're so tetchy tonight. Is it the old man's bedtime already?" She studies her nonexistent watch for effect, while absently patting her wild hair down with the other hand.

"Tetchy?" Bode's brows knit together.

"Crabby, grumpy, irritable—"

"I got it." His hands fly up to stop her babbling.

It works for a split second before she goes right back at him, beckoning laughs from our table. Even Bode can't hold on to his grumpiness with my sister around. He drops his grimace and joins in. Laughter sure feels good when it's genuine. That's one thing I can always depend on Neena to provide—comic relief.

"Can't you do anything with her?" I ask Parker as we watch on.

He snorts. "That one is a lost cause."

All I can do is agree and enjoy the show.

We arrive to a dark house, both forgetting to turn any lights on before we left, but I don't want to give up on the night just yet. After changing into a nightshirt, I grab a book and join Bode in the den.

I settle on the couch and notice he's stripped down to his undershirt and boxers with his suit crumpled on the floor beside the recliner. He seems to detest his clothes anymore and just shucks them off wherever the mood strikes him.

I wait for him to acknowledge my existence, but minutes tread on by with not so much as a head nod or grunt in my direction. I wonder, had I walked in here naked, would he have even noticed? Giving up, I crack the book open and try getting lost in a new romance, since clearly none exists here in this den.

Three chapters in, the sweet flirting of the new couple is getting to me.

He caressed her cheek...

She secured her hand in his, reveling in the alluring warmth...

He gave her a flirty smile...

She blushed as he drew near her...

He watched her as though nothing or no one else existed...

I slam the book shut with a sharp thud, actually summoning Bode's attention.

"Is it that bad?" he asks with an eyebrow lifted slightly.

Before I can answer, his eyes are already glued back to the TV screen.

"Worse," I mumble, trying to quell the urge to knock him upside the head with the dumb book clutched in my hand. Instead, I leave him and the fruitless notion of connecting with him and go on to bed as I should have done in the first place.

Crawling under the cool, crisp sheets, I abandon the fictional story and allow a true story lived once upon a time to keep me company. It's been said that memories are the most devoted friend you'll ever have. They may dull over time, fade a bit, but never completely leave you. This memory I don't mind remembering at all. It was one of the happiest days of my life.

The problems of my present life drift away as that happy day of my past settles in the bed with me. The corners of my mouth lift with a smile that only the dark room is privy to as the picture of Bode in his black tux and me in my silky wedding gown hiding in a bathroom flash before me like an old home movie reel.

"I'm not christening our marriage in a bathroom during our wedding reception," I mumble urgently against his young enthusiastic lips.

"Just a little christening," Bode promises before nibbling a path down my neck as his hand gathers the hem of my gown up. Before his hand makes much progress, a harsh knock pounds against the door.

I try untangling myself from my new husband, but he's not having it. "Bode." I push futilely against his shoulder.

"Just ignore it." He reclaims my lips as the pounding begins again.

"I paid good money for this reception. You two best open this door and rejoin the party right now." Dad's voice roars in warning through the locked door as he takes to landing a few more persistent bangs, freezing us both. I feel like a teenager just getting caught making out.

At first I thought Bode must be thinking the same thoughts, but then I watch nervously as his startled features turn smug. He lets go and marches over to the door with a confident swagger and snatches it open to face off with my dad.

"Mr. Cameron, she's mine now. I can make out with her any time I deem fit and you can't do anything about it." Oh he's being so brave—naïve fool.

Dad takes a step closer, being mindful not to look in my direction as I straighten my wedding gown. "Listen real closely, son." Dad points at me. "That woman behind you will always, and I do mean always, be my little girl. She owes me a dance and the both of you owe your guests some of your time." He turns to leave but pauses to add, "Don't you ever forget I am a Criminology Professor specializing in forensics. I know over a dozen ways to kill and dispose of a body without leaving any trace evidence."

Stunned, Bode and I follow him out of the bathroom like two scolded children and are greeted by guests cheering. Embarrassment climbs up my neck and onto my face in a deep blush as everyone claps and whistles. My husband is reacting oppositely from me with fists pumping in the air in a victory he seems to think he's gained. He looks over at me, entwining our hands, with pride gleaming in his rich brown eyes. My embarrassment fades as I revel in Bode's attention. He thinks of me as a prize he just won, but there's no doubt in my mind that I am the true winner.

That beautiful day fades as my wet pillow brings me back to the dark lonely room. My smile disappears somewhere in the shadows. Loneliness is a brutal beast, taunting me, reminding me I'm not winning, but losing.

Chapter Four

Bode

Four o'clock doesn't show up fast enough. *Ever!* My gut starts tightening around two every day as I go to war with the clock, demanding it to hurry up while it stubbornly refuses. There's never any hesitation at a quarter till four when it comes to powering down my laptop and desktop. Today is no different. I have the laptop and other stuff shoved in my leather case when my eyes flicker to the sluggish clock, causing me to groan out loud. Five long minutes are left.

When four finally decides to show up, I bolt out of my office without so much as a glance back. I feel like a caged animal finally being freed. Yanking off my tie, I crank the truck and allow the monster to lead me to the one place I let my dream tease me. I don't even know if it's worth calling it a dream since I don't put any actual effort into it anymore. Well... Maybe that's not completely true.

Honestly, I'm too embarrassed to admit my lifelong dream to Mia. Her career dream was noble with wanting to care for people and heal them when medically possible. Mine sounds stupid and selfish when compared.

I dream of playing outside every day where no electrical cords tether me and no computer monitors are allowed. No matter how pathetic that is, I can't shake wanting it, so I park my truck in the vacant parking lot and stare at the for-sale sign posted on the locked gate. I stare out over the property, pausing on the lodge just behind the gate with a giant stack of abandoned canoes beside it, and release a long sigh. This place is any country boy's fantasy with adventurous mountain trails, water falls to explore, white water rafting, guided river tours. All this, as well as several rustic river cabins available to rent, make up the grandness of Tennessee Valley Outdoor Sports Lodge.

Too many memories of life I've lived on this very land fill my thoughts all at once. Scanning the secluded area, I allow my mind to settle on one memory in particular—wishing time would magically rewind. To be seventeen again...

It's sweltering hot with the sun bearing down on me, making it no fun task to be lugging canoes out to the landing. With summer almost over, my buddies decided we need to make one more trip down the river before the start of senior year, but all I really want to do is dive in. Sweat trickles into my eyes, setting them to stinging, so I give up and drop my end of the canoe. Peeling the damp shirt off, I use it as a mop along my face before tossing it on the bank. Even the mushy ground under my bare feet is uncomfortably warm.

"Marybeth can't keep her eyes off you today, Bode," Darren says. He settles his end of the canoe on the muddy bank when he realizes I have no notion of picking my end back up.

He nods his head in the direction of the dock. My eyes head in that direction and come to a stop on a mighty fine group of bikini clad chicks. Sure enough, the little blonde has her focus on me. Being the polite guy that I am, I nod my head. For some reason, this causes her and the other girls to burst into a fit of giggles. Girls can be so silly about junk.

I shrug their game off with no intentions of playing. I was only being nice. Besides, my eyes have been set on a certain brunette for a while now. Probably since preschool, but only now am I working up enough nerve to do something about it.

"Marybeth is all yours, man," I offer Darren.

"She wasn't looking at me, dude." He snorts.

"Well, I ain't looking at her."

"Take one for the team, Bode," Jason says, dropping the end of his own canoe. Andy is at the other end. He huffs before letting go, too.

"Yeah, man. Take one for the team. It's too darn hot to go canoeing. Let's go join the girls on the dock."

"That Marybeth is hot. I doubt it will cause Bode any pain to spend some time with her," Darren says, making me think he's the one with the hots for her.

Before I can voice a yes or no, Andy starts leading us in the direction of the dock and all those bikinis. By no means is it a bad view, and there's the possibility of a fun time. I find a cooler for a seat and Marybeth quickly joins me. As the day wears on with the crowd hanging out while listening to the radio and sunbathing, she scoots as close as she can to me and keeps finding reasons to grab my arm. I notice Darren stays to the other side of the dock, but his eyes don't leave her much.

"Darren is a great guy," I tell her.

"Is he now? I think you are a great guy," she says in some silly baby voice. I smile at her compliment, but it feels more like a cringe. That voice is raking my nerves.

"I think you should give him a chance." I start to wave him over, but freeze when I hear one of the sweetest voices I've ever heard—always carrying a hint of huskiness like she just woke up. It's a voice filled with a surprising mixture of assurance and vulnerability.

"Hey y'all."

My heart kicks up a few beats just from the sound of her saying two simple words. Even though it's blazing hot, goose bumps rise along my arms. I feel her sidling up next to me. The girl has presence, there's no denying it. Looking over, my chest tightens at what I find—Mia Cameron wearing nothing but a white bikini top and a pair of cutoff jeans, showing off a lot of smooth skin.

"Hey, Mia," Marybeth says. Her body leans more into mine, trying to claim something I have no desire to give her. I scoot as close to the edge of the cooler as I can without toppling over.

No words come to me, so I just openly stare at the prettiest girl on this dock. Mia returns the stare, looking like she's trying to figure something out about me. Sighing heavily, she nods her head, making her mind up. I'm working on unsticking my tongue to ask her what that something is, but my ability to form words leaves me when she forces my legs wider to accommodate her tiny frame.

Watching me with determination, Mia leans close and firmly places her soft lips against my stunned ones. I'm pretty sure I've had a heat stroke, but after blinking a few times to see if she disappears, the catcalls and whistles confirm this is real.

Heck yeah! Brushing off my stunned-stupid response, I start participating in the kiss wholeheartedly. Soon my fingers tangle in all that fine dark hair and pull her even closer. I give this first kiss all I got, totally ignoring the crowd witnessing it.

This little firecracker puts an end to the kiss just as fast as she initiated it. She untangles herself from my grasp and starts prancing away.

"What was that for?" I call out.

She turns and starts walking backwards, wearing a challenging grin. "You were taking too long, and I was tired of waiting."

That's all the initiative I need to get my procrastinating butt off the cooler and quickly start striding in this sassy chick's direction. Turning on her heel, Mia bolts. She knows I'm a runner, so I know she wants me to catch her. And catch her, I do.

The day is spent swimming and kissing the only girl who has made my heart react—it skips beats and squeezes and stops altogether when she's around.

"Thank you for that kiss," I whisper, hugging her goodbye at her car. We've been hugging this goodbye for a long spell now with me not wanting it to end.

"Well, I think it was time one of us stepped up."

I can't help but chuckle at her bold sass. "I agree."

"Plus Marybeth needs to know you're off limits."

My eyebrows arch in challenge. "I'm off limits, am I?"

"You are, and we both know it. Now everybody else knows, too." *The glint in her eyes reveals she's proud of that fact.*

And I couldn't agree with her more now than I did that summer day. I still feel undeserving of her claiming me as her own...

That memory fades, only to be replaced by the disappointing reality. My longtime friend and owner of this property passed away unexpectedly last spring, leaving this place in limbo. Dave and his wife Linda have always felt like family, and it was a punch in the stomach when he died. Now his brokenhearted widow has decided she can't do this without him. Linda contacted me last month wanting to sell, hoping I would express interest in buying. She knows how much this place means to me. And man do I want to, but this dream isn't just about me. Three others count on me to be their provider in the form of a hefty mortgage, college expenses, a dumb truck payment I had no business adding to the list, along with other bills. Yeah. No way can I afford to dream.

I accidently discovered while taking a computer technology class that I had an uncanny knack for programming. After seeing the dollars that went with such a career choice, I was sold, knowing I could comfortably support my family. A family of my own with Mia was the top goal and that job would fit the bill.

Somewhere along the way of conquering the corporate world, I lost myself completely. Just started going through the motions of life, instead of actively participating in it. I haven't paid any attention to the cliff I've been dangling from until Dave passed away and jarred me into realizing I'm close to tumbling over and bringing my life crashing down around me.

Feeling worse than before, I shift the truck into reverse and continue to leave this dream unanswered. My stomach grumbles, reminding me I won't be receiving a home-cooked meal tonight either. Mia has been heading to the gym most nights for the past month and is still on kitchen strike. I just don't know what's gotten into that woman...

After hitting the drive thru, I haul burgers and fries over to Maury's. My old friend and I eat our food while sitting on his back patio. Between bites, I scan the fall scene and paint Maury a picture, describing what I see.

"Your Maple tree looks like it's been set on fire," I garble out around a mouthful of burger.

He sniffs the air dramatically, bobbing his head around, trying to track down the nonexistent fire. "I don't smell any smoke."

We both laugh. "You're such a wisecrack, old man." I sniff the air in response and only detect the musky scent of decaying foliage and the greasy aroma from supper—not a very pleasant combination. Fall is my least favorite of the seasons. Something about everything withering depresses me.

"I see your point," he jokes, bringing me back to our light conversation. We laugh some more.

"The grass is turning brown and is outright boring now. I can't tell the difference between it and the squirrels anymore."

Maury hasn't always been blind, so I know he can see what I'm describing. I close my eyes sometimes and try imagining his world, especially since Mia left that note with my glasses. She sure knows how to leave a sting without even delivering the slap.

This is it. Last pair! I bet Maury wishes all he had to do was pull on a pair of glasses in order to see. Shame on you for taking your eyesight for granted. ~Mia

Yep. I'm still feeling that verbal slap. I'm sitting here stewing about it and her coldness toward me lately when I feel Maury nudge my arm.

"Why'd you go quiet on me?"

"Just thinking." Snapping out of my brooding, I gather all the wrappers and toss them back into the greasy bag. My gut grumbles with disdain over the unhealthy fare I just crammed in it. Luckily, the kids will be home next weekend for fall break, so I'm pretty hopeful Mia will be back in the kitchen. I know my wife will take care of them, so I will gladly reap the benefits, too.

"Well, spill it," Maury says as his hand searches aimlessly around the table for his to-go cup of soda, almost knocking it over.

"You 'bout to be the one spilling it." I catch the cup and place it in his eager hand.

"I can see that." He chuckles before slurping from the straw.

I grab my own cup up and drain it. This salty fast food crap sure does make you thirsty. I toss my empty cup in the bag before glancing over at this man who has become a father figure to me since my own dad lives on the other side of the country. Dad moved after Mom passed away several years back, wanting to be near his siblings. That hurt some, but that's something I've grown used to with him. Besides, we've really never been close.

I watch as Maury scratches the side of his head underneath his tweed newsboy cap. My wife thinks he's the cutest thing. We banter back and forth with me claiming he's the goofiest thing. That's all in good fun, because he is most definitely the wisest man I have ever met. And there's no doubting he won't relent until I answer him either. His face patiently holds that firm look he gets when he's waiting for a response.

"I'm lost," I blurt before I chicken out.

He looks in my general direction while shaking his head. "You may be *wandering*, but you're not lost."

"Leave it to you to say something like that. Lost. Wandering. What's the difference? With either one, you don't know your way." I pull the glasses off my face and place them in my coat pocket, so they won't accidently get squished somehow, and then try to rub the stress away from around my eyes with the palms of my hands. It's not working, though.

"You asked God to find your lost butt many years ago as a teenage boy. He agreed and He hasn't let you go. Now you, on the other hand, have decided to wander off."

I roll my eyes up to the purple sky, noticing night will be here soon, and then glance toward our house, wondering when Mia will make it home. There's no clear way to reply to his comment, so I stand and pick up the trash. "I think I'm gonna *wander* on home. Maybe my wife will decide to grace me with her presence shortly."

As I pass Maury, his grasp manages to find my arm. "You're not lost, Bode, but it's time you find your way back before you start losing more than just your way."

Without comment, I tap him on the shoulder as my goodbye and take the heaviness of this conversation home with me. Now that Mia has decided to go to the gym most evenings, I'm alone more than not.

I shuffle into the house and find my chair in the den. I sit here scowling into the darkness, continuing to hate my life. Same ole crap, day in and day out for me. Not for my wife. Nope. She is ever-changing, never one to sit back and let life leave her behind. Maury is right. I feel it deep in my bones. I'm losing more than my way. I'm losing my wife.

Chapter Five

Mia

Several weeks have rapidly flown by with me settling into my new routine. Work, gym, bed. Rinse and repeat. It keeps my mind busy and too tired to miss my babies too badly or worry over my crumbling relationship with Bode. Since the kids left for college this fall, he has retreated away from me even more. I'm beginning to wonder if our children were all that was keeping our marriage united in the first place. That's a sad realization I've not pondered much, because it inflicts too much pain. I don't want to admit it. Not yet anyway.

The cold November air sends shivers over my sweaty body as Lee walks me out of the gym after a hardcore circuit workout. I'm trying not to limp in front of him even though my legs wobble uncontrollably. Most weeks I only run into him once or twice, and I've learned quickly I can only handle this fire-hot man in small doses.

I steal a sidelong glance in his direction, but quickly avert my eyes when I feel the heat rising in my cheeks. A tight-fitted white T-shirt never looked so brilliant. Oh sugar, is he a fine work of art with the tattoos nicely accentuating his confident swagger. He is so sure of himself that it's quite overwhelming. Does he flirt relentlessly? Yes. Does he take it any further? No. I'm still confused by the fact that he wants to befriend me, of all people.

"Woman!" Lee says with so much repulsion, it snaps me out of my thoughts and causes me to flinch.

After tossing my bag in the car, I turn to find him glaring at my tires of all things.

"You know we're close to snow and ice season and you're driving around with bald tires," he says with a clipped tone and furrowed brows.

"I know. It's on my husband's to-do list." I don't tell Lee I put that on Bode's list way back in June. Shrugging my shoulders, I take the blame. "I'm a grown woman. I should've gotten it done myself by now."

Shaking his head slowly, Lee levels me with a sullen look. "Your *husband* should have it taken care of by now. If you were mine, I would *want* to take care of it for you." He reaches his hand out, palm side up. "Hand me your phone."

"Why?" I ask, confused.

Lee impatiently wiggles his long fingers, so I reluctantly hand it over and watch as he fiddles with it before placing it back in my hand. "Call me tomorrow once you're at work. I'll send one of my guys to pick your car up."

"Why?" I ask dumbly.

"So I can get your tires changed. I have my own garage, remember?" He says this slowly, like he's talking to a child.

"Yeah. But..."

Lee doesn't wait for the rest of my rambling. He turns and stalks off toward his choice of bike today, which is a silver Harley. I've never seen him ride the same bike twice. Moments later, the mean roar of the bike firing to life seems to be in sync with its owner's attitude tonight. He's really ticked off about the tires. *Why?*

The entire ride home, his fervent words whirl around my thoughts. *If you were mine.* Those words make me giddy and nauseous at the same time. I'm not anyone's but Bode's and I don't even feel like he truly wants me anymore.

True to his word, Lee has my car back to me by the end of the work day with not only new tires, but also a way-past-due oil change, new brake pads, and a detailed car cleaning. All of the scratches have magically disappeared from the white body and the small stains have vanished from the interior.

Admiring the nice clean smell of the interior, I ease my shiny car out of the office parking lot. Lee refused to allow me to pay for anything but the parts. We had a heated round or two on the phone until I realized he wouldn't be relenting. He actually growled at me before hanging up. I think he's used to getting his way with women without any lip— probably anyone for that matter. The man is straight up alpha and wants his authority respected. This is probably one of the keys to his tremendous success.

Feeling uneasy by his bold gesture, I ignore my gym bag and decide it's in the best interest of my marriage to go home and let these appreciative feelings die down. Because for the first time in many years, a man has made me feel like I matter. The fact that the man is not my husband scares me.

*****

A break from Lee Sutton has been a good plan. Addison and Kaisley arrived home Wednesday night and it felt so nice to go to our church's Thanksgiving praise service as a united family. It's easier to put up the perfect front that our family and friends expect from the Calders when my children are by our side. I wish I could beg them to stay and never leave, but I know that's selfish and wishful thinking.

On Thursday, my parents came over with Neena and we feasted on a traditional Thanksgiving meal with Bode eating like it had been declared his last meal. He out-ate Addison by a long shot, and that has not happened since our boy hit puberty. I feel guilty for all of a few silly seconds about not cooking for my husband until I think about what he's done for me lately—zilch! That fact helps me get over it real quick like.

Kaisley has talked me and Neena into braving the shopping frenzy today with the rest of the Black Friday fools, fighting the crowds for what I hope to be great bargains. I have my doubts, but Kaisley wants me to go and I would go dig a ditch with my child if that's how she wanted to spend time with me.

I'm glad Bode decided to do something besides watch football with Addison. Those two left Thursday evening for a two-night camping trip.

The sea of bodies fidgeting with excitement in the early morning dusk only adds to my anxiety over the entire situation. This is not my cup of tea by a long shot. Last night, I tried my darnedest to talk Kaisley into a more relaxing activity of manicures and pedicures, but she wouldn't budge.

"I can't believe Kaisley talked you into this mess," I mumble in Neena's direction.

She looks up from her phone and shrugs. "She asked me to go."

"But you hate shopping much worse than I do."

"I miss my niece, so if she wants to spend time with me, I'll suffer for the cause. Besides, I'm sure this will fly by." She motions toward the longest line ever formed in the history of line forming. It wraps around the giant super store with no end in sight. I look forward and then back again, gauging us to be somewhere near the middle of the stupidity.

I turn to face Kaisley and watch her for a moment as she chats up some girls behind her. My daughter's cheeks and the tip of her nose are rosy from the cold, but she's beyond worrying about the temperature.

"Kaisley, tell Aunt Neena what must-have item we are standing in this line for..." I pause to gauge my watch. "Yep, one hour now and most likely another one to go before making it inside."

Kaisley looks down at her sneakers with little confidence.

Neena cuts me a look, scolding me for calling our girl out, before directing her attention back to Kaisley. "Girlie, if you're this committed, surely it means a lot to you. Now don't be worrying about what others think. Never falter with owning up to what you are passionate about."

Oh boy. It's way too early and way too cold for a Neena speech.

"Go on, Kaisley. Tell her what we're *trying* to buy this morning." There's not even a guarantee we'll snag it in this Black Friday Roulette.

Kaisley rolls her beautiful yet sassy blue eyes at me. "Wireless headphones."

Neena's prideful expression stumbles to a confused look. "And?"

"Just the headphones?" My daughter clearly forms it into an uncertain question.

"Are you kidding me? All of this for headphones..." Neena waves her hands in all directions as though directing the orchestrated scene. "You so owe me for this."

"Where did that committed and owning up to it speech go, Aunt Neena?" I snicker, but neither of my shopping partners finds it as amusing as I do.

"These aren't just any headphones, Aunt Neena. State of the art sound that's guaranteed to block out all outside noises. And don't forget they're wireless.

These babies aren't even out yet and this is the only store in town to have only twenty advanced pairs, and at a much discounted price." Kaisley is selling it hard, but from the firm set of Neena's mouth, my sister isn't buying it.

"How about we call this off and I'll order you a pair online?" Neena bargains.

Kaisley buries her gloved hands into her coat pockets and shakes her head adamantly. Now that Neena is in the know, this may be one very long morning. My eyes clamp shut as I silently pray for patience.

Big mistake!

Another irritating hour later, I've decided God misunderstood my request and accidently put my patience on a marathon of endurance. Neena went downhill fast after the one hour mark of waiting in line, whining about her feet hurting. I tried warning her to dress properly for shopping combat, aka comfortable sneakers with lots of heel support. Cowgirl boots have done the poor girl in.

"You're going to be dirty," I mumble, nudging her leg with my sneaker-clad foot.

She adjusts the hood of her coat and lies back down on the sidewalk, burrowing deep in the recesses of her coat. "I'm over this. So over this," she grouches.

The sun is up and the view of the door is just in sight now. The store is trying to prevent a repeat of the stampede that took place last year, so they are only allowing small groups in at a time. "Not much longer."

"Mia, come here," Neena mutters.

"I am here."

"Closer." She waves me to join her.

I squat down beside the only body sprawled on the sidewalk. "What?"

"Those old geezers are schooling your daughter."

"What are you talking about?" I glance over my shoulder and watch Kaisley giggle as the gray-headed lady says something obviously amusing. That child hasn't had one complaint about waiting all this time. She is her father's child for sure. They both seem to have been divvied out a small country's worth of patience. Not me. I'm completely over this as much as my little sister.

"They've been slowly skipping in line for the last little bit. It's quite brazen."

"How do you know this from your sidewalk bed?"

She tsks. "I pay attention for a living." She rolls to a seated position and stands as another group is let in the doors, drawing us closer to the headphone prize. "Don't let them talk her into letting them ahead of us."

"Kaisley, come on. The line has moved." I wave her over and notice the older couple hobbling right on her heels with a hopeful look shining from their wrinkly faces.

"Momma, this is Mrs. Harriet and Mr. Clay. Can we let them ahead of us? Mr. Clay has arthritis and this icy wind is too much on him." My sweet girl looks at me expectantly.

Neena mumbles close to my ear, "Don't."

Ignoring Neena's warning, I wave them to pass us. "Sure. Why not?" Might as well do a good deed for the day.

"Thank you, sweetie," Mrs. Harriet says in a willowy voice as they hobble by us.

Well, I get the 'I told you so' speech as soon as the doors open and we follow the older couple right up to the electronics department counter and find they are on a mission for the headphones as well. Bet you can't guess how many pairs are left.

One.

Just one.

And the old couple snags them without so much as a thank you to Kaisley. I worry my poor girl is going to deflate in a heap of despair for not getting the one thing she really wanted, but she's a trooper about it and heads back out of the door emptyhanded as though we didn't just completely waste two hours of our lives.

"That's so not fair. Those headphones were yours and those geezers stole them!" Neena, on the other hand, is not handling the situation gracefully at all.

Back in the comforts of my car with the heater cranked to full force, I peep at Kaisley in the rearview mirror. "I didn't know you were a headphone kind of girl anyway?" She does not like for her hair to be askew. Ever.

She shrugs while focusing out the window. "They weren't for me."

Neena and I cut each other a sharp glance, both of us probably on the same page. *Were they for a boy?*

"Then who were they for?" Neena asks, trying to sound nonchalant, but her nosy side is evident in her insistent tone.

Kaisley surprises us when she says, "Addison. He's been complaining about his roommates being so loud and disruptive. With finals coming up, I thought the headphones would help him out."

And there my girl goes, perfectly reflecting her daddy again. Bode has always been a person looking to put others before himself. I'm proud to know our daughter has learned well from him.

The day isn't a complete bust. We all snag new boots, because they were on a killer sale and Neena said every mountain girl should have a proper pair— she probably has hundreds. The shopping shenanigans concluded with a much needed trip to Starbucks to indulge in oversized and overpriced cups of pumpkin spice lattes and thick slices of pumpkin bread. Black Friday wasn't so grim after all.

Saturday, the guys arrive home looking like scruffy mountain men. I watch from the kitchen window as they unload their gear in the back shed, both wearing their hats on backwards and sporting wide grins. Outdoor adventures have always seemed to rejuvenate my husband, like that's where he truly needs to be to thrive.

They come bustling in, talking animatedly as they zero in on the fridge. Bode offers me a hug as he passes by, and I can't help but sink into his warm embrace. I inhale deeply, enjoying the earthiness he wears perfectly after weekends such as the one he just went on. It's an attractive scent he wears incredibly well.

"I miss you," I mumble into the collar of his coat.

"You did?" he asks, rubbing my back.

"I do," I clarify, but already know he understood me the first time.

He nuzzles my neck and bites playfully, completely pushing off my declaration to join Addison in raiding the fridge of Thanksgiving leftovers.

Later in the day, Addison begs me for homemade lasagna. I'm no fool, and when I spot Bode hovering near the door, it's clear he's the reason behind my son's request. Of course I won't refuse, even though between the homemade marinara sauce and the whole assembly process, I will spend most of my day in the kitchen.

Kaisley offers to help and we are halfway through the lasagna assembly process when her phone pings with an incoming text. She stops ladling sauce over the noodles to read it and starts jumping up and down hysterically.

"What is it?" I ask, wiping my hands on my apron.

She hands over the phone, showing a message from Neena.

The headphones have been ordered and will arrive to our boy by Wednesday with you being noted as the giver.

That's our Neena. Always a persistent go-getter. There's no telling how much time she had to log in to unearth them before they are officially released in two weeks.

Kaisley swipes the phone back and replies. *You so rock!*

Neena responds. *Nope. You so rock!*

After this, the cooking goes by in a more jubilant manner, and I gladly serve my family this supper. We settle around the table with the warm aroma of Italian spices and garlic whirling around our conversation. Both children have talked nonstop about college happenings and I try absorbing as much of it as I can. These two awesome humans are a vitamin supplement for my soul. I glance over at Bode and see that the only thing he's trying to absorb is sauce with his piece of garlic bread. I shrug off my frustration with him and focus on this family time instead.

"So, what's the plan for tonight?" I ask.

Addison shrugs his shoulders. "The youth group wants to hit up a movie, if that's okay?"

"Of course." My boy knows I covet as much of their time when they're home as possible, but I'm not selfish either. I know they miss their friends.

"Can we take your car? It looks killer with the new tires and the cleanup."

"Sure." I glance over at Bode and find him wearing that confused look he seems to favor as fondly as the thread-bare Tennessee shirt he's splattered with marinara. I wait for him to comment, but instead he tucks back into eating. *Yeah, buddy. You better live it up. Kitchen closes as soon as my babies head back to Florida.*

Addison and Kaisley take my answer as their cue to claim their night's freedom and start scrambling away from the table.

"Drop off a plate of lasagna to Maury and be home by eleven please," I say before they get away.

I receive a *yes ma'am* from both as well as a kiss on the cheek.

After they bustle out the door with a generously portioned plate in hand, I push away from the table to begin the unappealing task of cleaning the messy kitchen. Of course, Bode has already retreated to his den, with the big screen keeping him company, while dirty dishes offer to be my night's date.

Eventually, he shuffles back in, but not to help me. Oh no. I cut my eyes in his direction as he helps himself to leftover sweet potato pie. He leans his hip on the counter while digging in to his dessert. I sense a question wanting to escape him and wonder if he'll care enough to ask. I keep sliding plates into the dishwasher and wait him out.

Two bites in, he must decide he cares enough to ask. "When did you get new tires?"

Anger rolls over me as I grab up the remainder of the pie and shove it in his face!

No. Not really.

But my fingers tingle with wanting to live out that flash of a daydream. Instead, I continue slinging dishes, keeping my hands busy for his sake.

"This week," I mutter.

What ticks me off is the fact that he didn't care enough to take care of this for me, but actually seems offended that I took care of it myself.

"Where'd you get them?"

I look up from my task and shoot daggers at him with my scowl. "A friend of mine offered to take the car to his shop and do it. Got brake pads and an oil change, too. So if you can ever find that elusive to-do list of yours, you can mark those tasks off."

Bode completely ignores my snide remark. "Friend? What friend of yours?" His confused expression is accompanied by a strong edge of anger now. Wow. A new emotion. I'm impressed.

"Lee Sutton." I slam the dishwasher shut and set it on the cleaning cycle. "Didn't even have to ask him. He *volunteered*." I mouth off, wanting to rub it in a little.

That name seems to get Bode's attention enough for him to set the pie down. "Lee Sutton? *The* Lee Sutton?"

"Yes. *The* Lee Sutton. We work out together every now and then at the gym."

"That man's a womanizer. He's not got any business with my wife!" Bode threads his fingers through his curly locks, causing them to stand on end.

"The only business he's done is be nice to your wife! And I'm appreciative for his help with the tires.

I'm sick of having to take care of everything around here! I had to find a repairman for the roof last week since you keep forgetting. I had to get a plumber here yesterday to fix the broken toilet you've been ignoring." I could keep ticking off a longer list. Instead, I sling the washrag into the sink and kick the cabinet in front of me for good measure. Again, for his own good—better the cabinet and not my husband's shin. Bode looks to be trying to cut in on my rant, but I plow on without giving him a chance. "You keep ignoring all the small issues and eventually the entire mess is going to fall down on itself!"

Anger flushes Bode's cheeks as he spits out, "You talking about the house or us?"

He knows it's both just by acknowledging it in that question, but why doesn't he care enough to do anything about it?

Before I can continue, Kaisley barrels back through the door and closes it with a sharp thud, starling both of us. The quarrel is forgotten as soon as I see her face and realize she heard us arguing.

"What's the matter, sweetheart?" I ask as she rushes over to me and my arms instinctively pull her close.

"I just miss you so much. I'd rather stay home with you and Daddy." I hear her sniff against my chest.

"You sure? Has someone or something upset you?" I ask this knowing full well Bode and I are the cause. I'm pretty sure the yelling could probably be heard from the street. I can't believe how much resentment seems to be bubbling out of the both of us lately. This surely can't be good. We've never been an arguing type couple. Snarky and snappy sometimes, but never voices raised with tempers uncontrolled.

"No," she mumbles out. "I just want to maybe watch a movie with y'all here. Is that okay?"

All I want to do is retreat to my room and hide from whatever this is that's starting to smother my husband and me. Again, I push that aside with hopes of it disappearing altogether and muster a smile for my daughter's benefit. "Whatever you want."

And so we spend the evening watching a family comedy, but I can't bring myself to laugh at any of the cheesy jokes. My eyes keep glancing in Bode's direction, but I can't read him with the glasses and the glare of the TV concealing his eyes. He's quiet and his posture is ramrod, so I know we have a silent storm brewing. Maybe it's time to let it out. I'm fairly certain as soon as the children are tucked back in their college dorms, something will finally give under the pressure.

Chapter Six

Bode

Lee Sutton... Lee Sutton... I can't get that jerk's name out of my head. The past hour on the sluggish clock has been dedicated to Googling my wife's new *friend*. Each search finds him with a different woman, some celebrities and some not—all beautiful. Sure, he's some famous motorcycle design genius, but that doesn't give him a pass to befriend my wife, who happens to be just as beautiful as all those other women he's used and discarded. *What is Mia thinking?*

Exiting the search window, I plop my head onto the cluttered desk. What feels like a paperclip is pressing uncomfortably into my forehead. I fling it away with a quick swipe and lay my head back down.

My mind won't let this mess with Mia go. *Did I do this?* I should have told Neena to leave well enough alone when she clued me in on her gift idea for Mia. I should have told her a spa gift certificate or some crap like that would have been better, but now it's too late. Obviously my wife has gone out and found herself a new life that happens to include a friend—a dang celebrity hotshot to boot!

Sure, Mia and I have minor struggles like any other couple. However, I had no clue we were this far gone.

How'd this happen?
When did this happen?
Why is this happening?

One minute we are coasting along, and then the next, from out of nowhere, we're sinking. Fast. So fast, I didn't even notice.

Pushing away from the desk, I wander down the hall to the breakroom for a change of scenery and hopefully away from the tension I've built in my office.

"What's up, Bode?" Don asks while rummaging around in the fridge. He is a software developer I've gotten sort of familiar with since he joined the company a few years back. He's younger than me by about a decade and could probably do my job better than me. I wish I could hand it over to him and make a run for it.

I hate my job...

"Nothing, man. You?" I reply absently. I plop one of those single serve coffee things in the Keurig and push a cup underneath it.

"Same ole same ole. Good Thanksgiving?" he asks before popping a cracker in his mouth.

Lee Sutton's cocky face pops into my head. I shake it away. "Pretty good," I mumble. "Say, you ever heard of Lee Sutton?"

Don snorts. "Who hasn't heard of the man? He can create Harley art! And I can't help but call him hero with how he snags up all the hotties in a hundred mile radius."

The first sip of my coffee is too bitter and I almost spit it back into the cup. Somehow my wife has landed on his *hottie* radar...

"Hey boys," Natalia coos as she joins us. She's one of those women who cannot just talk normal. It's always exaggerated and full of flirt.

I mutter a quick hey without making eye contact. The woman is too friendly for her own good. She's my age acting like she's younger than Don.

"Hey, gorgeous. When are you going to stop breaking my heart and let me take you out?" Don asks, puffing out his chest. Here goes the frat house episode. *Where's Clancy when you need him?*

The folder she's carrying just so happens to slip out of her hands right in front of me and Don. Turning to bend over, Natalia offers a view of her voluptuous backside in one tightly fitted skirt. I glance away and catch Don tilting his head for a better view.

I want to pull Natalia to the side one of these days and inform her that men would rather have to work a little for it. That's the fun part—the chase—right? Where's the adventure and mystery of it, if a woman just offers herself up with no effort on the man's part? What do I know? I've not been on the chase in over twenty years, but still...

Pushing off my concern, I dump my coffee in the sink and leave Don to make a fool of himself. This little breakroom visit did nothing but make me feel worse.

Next up on this day of *fun* is a longwinded board meeting that I zombie through. My focus is scattered due to Lee Sutton and the mess with Mia, and there's no collecting it. Those Internet searches keep flashing through my mind—cheating scandals, late night rendezvouses ending in arrests, and this famous chump being painted as a rebellious hero for all of it. Nothing I read this morning sits right with me. Does Mia even know what kind of wolf she's hanging out with?

"Bode, can you give us the latest on the Carmichael Project?" someone asks me, but I wasn't paying enough attention to notice who.

Oh crap...

"Umm... That will be ready by the next meeting," I say with as much assurance as I can muster, hoping they buy it. I knew there was something I was supposed to do this morning.

Soon we are dismissed, but not before Marx, my boss, encourages me to get to work on that project. I head to the office with that task on my list, but it slips as soon as I pull up the search screen and see that devil's name taunting me from where I didn't clear it out.

Plopping back in my chair, I scrub my hands over my face—wishing I could find an off switch in my brain.

The last few weeks play on a continuous reel with a mix of shame and anger. I just about lost my cool this weekend. Luckily, Kaisley came back home and that helped defuse the situation, but it hasn't stopped me from stewing on it. I've spent hours going over how Mia responded. There's no guilt to be found, so I don't think she's cheated...

Cheated...

Just thinking the word sends a nasty dread shooting to the pit of my gut. Old insecurities from my youth start plaguing me again.

Mia and I are not my parents. This is the pep talk I give myself while staring blankly at the computer screen. Hoping if I say this enough times I'll believe it.

Working today is a lost cause. Shoving my belongings in my satchel, I decide my wife has some explaining to do tonight. No way am I allowing this to happen.

Chapter Seven

Mia

My children have ridden back off into their future sunsets once more and have left me longing for them to return to being obnoxious preteens again. What I would give to have those younger, pimply, hormonal brats back under my care fulltime. I would even welcome the moody eye rolls with open arms. The crisp mountain air and I bid them goodbye only minutes ago, yet I'm still standing in the driveway like some lovelorn girl beckoning her love to return. A few more minutes pass unproductively before I give up on anyone returning.

Sophie. I need to focus on my little companion, who I'm about to visit for a while this morning before heading into the office. I'll soon find her tucked into the children's chemo wing of the cancer center in one of those plush recliners, her IV connected to her port. I double check my bag for the proper supplies— brand new princess coloring books, crayons, stickers, nail polish, and Lemonhead candies. Yep. I'm ready.

Weaving through the pediatric chemotherapy center, I find her exactly how I pictured, except she's standing by her plush chair so she can reach her mom's nails better.

"I hope I'm next. I'm in dire need of a manicure," I grumble and claim her chair.

"Thop that whining and I'll thee what I can do." She lisps her words due to the absent teeth up front. She lost the second one just last week, officially making her a full-fledged snaggletooth and the cutest darn thing I've ever seen.

I can't help but giggle. "Yes, little bossy breeches."

Her upbeat demeanor indicates she's feeling well, so it's going to be a good day. I take a few moments just to admire my little friend as she finishes up painting the fingernail she's working on. She keeps shifting on her hot-pink high top Converses. The lime-green and neon purple stripped leggings are paired with a bright orange blouse. My eyes have to actively work on focusing on all of the busyness that makes up Pipsqueak's outfit of the day. She's forgone her normal hat and in its place is a headband with a giant teal daisy decorating one side.

"What did you bring me?" Sophie's bright eyes twinkle with hope as she turns her full attention toward me, pausing the progress of her mom's manicure. She knows I never show up empty-handed.

I start rummaging around in my bag. "Let's see... Umm... Here's my checkbook. Thought you could help me balance it." Waving my wallet in the air, I look up and find her glaring.

"Fine. I'll do that myself." I toss it back in and keep digging around while looking at the goodies in question just to draw out the suspense. "Ah ha! Here it is. All the usual stuff just for my Pip."

"Yay! Can we color before I do your nails?"

"Of course." There's no holding the smile back, as I watch her hand over the bright yellow nail polish to Amber, completely abandoning her mom with only a half-done manicure.

"I'm always chopped liver when you're around." Amber sticks her tongue out at me with me returning the gesture full of tease.

"That's right. Now go get lost. Pip and I have important business to take care of." Sophie climbs in the chair beside me, careful not to disturb her IV. This little fairy is a pro at something no child should have to experience. She deserves health, not tubes delivering an attack against a ruthless disease wreaking havoc on her poor little body. We set up our coloring supplies as Amber watches on, reluctant to leave. I push a Starbucks gift card in her hand and shoo her away.

The tired mom finally shuffles off for a much-needed break while I enjoy some quality time with my Pipsqueak. And that's number one on my priority list today. I place a kiss on the side of her fuzzy little head and pick up a crayon.

*****

"How was our Pipsqueak this morning?" Renee asks.

I look up and find her sticking her head into my office. Her raven ponytail is high and still fluffy with the newness of the day. I offer her a smile and wave her in as I finish making notes in a few patient files.

After she perches in a chair across from my desk, I answer, "Better than I've seen in a long time. This round of chemo seems to be less harsh than that last round."

"That's great. Poor baby has been through so much."

I eye Renee closely as an incredible idea strikes me all of a sudden. "Didn't you say you're a member at the gym down the block?" She's tall and youthful, with an enviable athletic physique.

"Yep. I figured we would have run into each other by now."

Knowing my first patient is due soon, I push up from the desk. "I'm heading there after work. I'd love for you to work out with me." I debate telling her I need to use her gorgeous body as a buffer from any wayward bad-boys, but decide to keep that to myself. Lee won't be able to look in my direction if Renee is around.

"Sure. I'll grab my gym gear during our lunch break today."

"Sounds good." A sigh of relief escapes me as I pick up the patient's chart waiting outside the exam room. Scanning the file, my eyes land on symptoms of sore throat and fever. "Will you prepare a strep test for Justin while I get started with his examination?"

"I'm on it," she replies, scurrying down the hall to the medical supply room.

My lunch hour was spent *washing* some stubborn gray out of my hair at the salon with Neena keeping me company. The only thing she had washed out of her hair was too many travel miles from her recent trip to Guatemala where she spent a week following a medical missionary team around for an article she's writing. We both indulged with a blowout too. It feels amazing to not have it bound on top of my head, and so I can't bring myself to pull the silky locks back into my normal ponytail style. This seems like an okay idea until the afternoon is spent with sticky hands playing in my new do while I perform well exams.

I hurry into the gym after work, looking around for Renee when I find Lee sauntering in my direction. The man never just walks. It's always a form of swagger. I just don't think those lean hips know any other way.

As soon as he's in front of me, he tilts his head and studies my hair. "Nice."

Never have I heard the word nice sound so sinful.

"Thanks," I stutter out. "Salon visit today." I know that's not even a complete sentence, but the way the guy is admiring me, my brain won't form anything more than that.

His hand slowly reaches out and gathers a section of my hair. *Oh sugar!* My neck tingles from the contact, and I'm about to tell him this is very inappropriate, when a mean tug causes me to yelp.

"Ouch!" I rub the stinging spot behind my ear where his hand just left, along with some of my hair.

Smirking, he pulls his hand back to show me a piece of candy that I guess was lodged in my new and improved hair. Wow. Talk about a quick confidence deflator.

"Red Jolly Rancher. A favorite of a few of my sticky patients." I try to joke my embarrassment away.

Lee barks in laughter as he tosses the hairy piece of candy in a nearby trashcan. Thankfully, Renee bustles through at this exact moment. I grab her up and do exactly what I planned earlier. Planting her beautiful self firmly in front of me, I offer her up as bait to Lee.

"Renee, this is Lee. Lee, Renee," I introduce and all but shove her closer.

She giggles quietly at my forwardness before shaking his hand. He croons some reply, causing her to giggle some more before she sidesteps him and mad-dashes to the locker room.

"Renee?" I call to her, but she's already disappeared behind the door. Looking back to Lee, I offer, "An *available* hot nurse." I widen my eyes and nod my head suggestively.

I declare this doesn't go down as I had hoped, because this bad-boy leans precariously in my personal space and refuses to move until I meet his gaze. "I prefer brunettes." He gently tugs the end of my hair before walking away. I'm sure his stride is of a sauntering gait, but I'm too stunned to check.

After a quick change into my workout gear, I head out to the floor to find Renee and am not surprised when I see Lee has taken a treadmill beside her. Good. *Please be interested in her,* I silently beg Lee. This man needs to find someone else to toy with besides me. Hopefully he will soon realize he prefers Renee. As I'm nearing the line of treadmills, a woman hops on the one beside Renee, leaving me no option but to claim the one on the other side of Lee. Great.

"Renee was just telling me you two work together."

Glancing over, I find Lee eying me suspiciously. "Yep." I set the machine in motion, hoping he directs his conversation back in my friend's direction.

"She told me you are one of the most sought-out pediatric Nurse Practitioners in this area." He sounds quite impressed.

I lean up to cut a glance at Miss Mouth. "Well, Renee is an amazing nurse herself. She's also single." This earns me a sharp look from my friend. Serves her right. I don't need her trying to win any points in my favor with this guy. He's off-limits for me and he needs to get that and not be encouraged in any other direction.

Lee chuckles quietly instead of commenting. Oh well. I shrug this unsuccessful match-making off and accelerate my speed into a steady jog.

"So, you got a manicure today, too?"

Lee's focus is on my electric-blue nails with lime green polka dots. "Oh yes. From an eight-year-old fairy." This earns me a confused stare from Lee, and I wonder how he doesn't fall off that treadmill from not focusing forward. But there he is in all of his tattooed-up hard muscle glory, running with a perfect balance while steadily watching me.

For the next thirty or so minutes I tell him all about my Pipsqueak. Well, I do the best I can between huffing and puffing. Renee chimes into the conversation as well, and it feels so good to have an adult conversation for a change. Lee is a great listener. He's attentive and asks questions that make him seem genuinely interested in what I'm saying. He's been doing this for several weeks now, always asking how my day went and how my patients are doing.

By the time I snap out of my Lee Sutton spell, I'm almost home and the idea of having to push through the door is not appealing at all.

I've not had to survive any tragedy thus far in my life—both parents and both sets of grandparents are still living; no major illness has taken anyone away from me, no major accidents... I'm beyond blessed. I know this, but I'm miserable just the same. And I know I'm not the only one. Bode is just as miserable.

This discontentment has wedged a bitterness between us and has repelled us from each other. It's been festering for quite a while now and happened slowly. We got wrapped up in raising our children—loving and nurturing them, educating them, and providing for them. Somehow, we forgot about each other along the way.

This barrier pushed me to pursue goals with stubborn drive—trying to prove to myself that I still mattered—that I was still somebody significant—a defined individual.

But the barrier has had an opposite effect on Bode. He seemed to throw his hands up in defeat, exiling himself into a comatose state of work and SportsCenter.

We're heading in different directions—away from each other, and I'm not sure how to get us back on track. Nor do I know if either one of us cares to do so, for that matter.

With all of these thoughts pressing on me, I know it's time I get Maury's opinion on this mess I'm getting into. He always sees things clearer than the rest. His words, not mine, but I believe in them just the same. After parking and lugging the garbage cans to the curb, I let myself in Maury's house.

I find him sitting at the dining room table like he's expecting me. I take the seat beside my dear old friend, but stay silent. His weathered hand starts patting the table, seeking mine and so I offer it to him.

"Tell me why my sweet girl is so down?" He offers a kind smile with his question.

I shrug my shoulders even though he cannot see it, and struggle with finding the words for how I feel. After a few moments of hesitation, I mumble, "I'm worried about me and Bode."

The warm smile slips from Maury's face and a somber look takes over. He nods his head in understanding and that makes me wonder if Bode has already confided in him. I want to know, but decide not to ask.

Maury offers no words so eventually I press forward. "We're heading in different directions." I know it's a bit cliché and sounds too casual for how I'm feeling.

"Then turn around and head back to one another." Maury's words sound simple enough as well.

"It's more complicated than that." I focus on the long hem of my bright blue tank top and start worrying it nervously between my fingers.

"You know Bode is a good guy."

"I do... I do know."

"And he's the same boy you fell in love with." Maury makes this problem sound so easy to fix, but I'm not so sure.

Shaking my head, I mumble, "That's the thing, Maury. Neither one of us is the same person we were over twenty years ago. We've changed. A lot." Quietness takes over again until I can't take it anymore. "I've met someone," I blurt. I need to relieve the guilt of Lee Sutton.

"Mia?" Maury groans out disapprovingly.

"No! Not like that. I didn't mean I've had an affair!" *Oh sugar.* My cheeks go up in flames. Maybe I need to take care to form my thoughts more clearly. I stutter on, trying to fix my tongue misstep. "I meant to say I've met a new friend. Nothing physical has happened. It's just..." I trail off, trying to figure out what in the Sam Hill I'm trying to say.

"Mia," Maury whispers, getting my attention back.

"I'm lonely, Maury. So lonely. I've not wanted anything physical with this guy, but I have been leaning on him emotionally. And he doesn't mind. He's such a good friend. He pays me attention—"

Maury squeezes my hand to hush me up. I button my lips and beg the tears to stay away. "Then this guy really isn't a good friend to you, Mia. If he knows you're married, he knows he has no business taking care of you the way your husband is supposed to be doing."

"That's the problem. Bode isn't doing anything he's supposed to be doing! I feel like I'm living with a stranger anymore." I sniff the angry tears back.

"You need to talk to him about it. You two need to stop looking away from each other and remember what you have. I think Bode needs you to help him find his way."

That doesn't sit well with me either. "All I do is take care of Bode, but he's a grown man and I'm sick of it." *Why is Maury taking up for Bode?*

"I'm just calling it like I see it, Mia. Bode needs you to reassure him he matters."

Standing up in frustration, I say, "That's exactly what I need from him."

Maury pats my hand before releasing it. "Then go tell him. I don't know why either one of you thinks the other is a mind reader."

Stomping out of Maury's house, I storm over to my own to do battle. That's it! I've had enough. Everything Maury just said has rubbed me something wrong! Slamming the kitchen door, I immediately come to a halt when I find Bode standing in front of me. I cautiously take a step back. The man looks menacing, leering over me with a deep scowl. I guess I'm not the only one ready to do battle. Gone are his tie and coat. I'm surprised he's not taken the time to rid himself of the rest of his dress clothes he seems to loathe.

"We need to have a talk. Now." His words are low and clipped and sting just as hard as if he were yelling at me.

I prepare my ammunition and open my mouth with my target in sight. "I'm not happy!" I blurt this out, but it comes off as whiny and not very threatening. I blame it on the tears burning the back of my throat. Watching Bode cross his arms, I swallow the emotions as best as I can.

"Well, that makes two of us." Taking a deep breath, Bode continues, "I won't be sitting back letting some other man stake claim on my wife. He has no right!"

What? "What are you talking about?" Anger boils back to the surface as I regard him in confusion.

"Lee Sutton, Mia. I feel like a fool." Shoving his hands through his hair, Bode finally moves so I can push past him.

"You should feel foolish. Nothing is happening between Lee and me. He's a friend. That's it." Taking a deep breath, I try calming my racing pulse. I know I'm going to say something I'll regret, so I quickly take the path toward the stairs. Bode is on my heels, so I guess this discussion isn't over quite yet.

"I won't stand for you being *friends* with that womanizer!" Bode is so close, I feel his words brush harshly across my neck.

"Lee is a great friend. He pays me attention. Makes me feel like I matter. Always asks me how my day was." I turn back toward him when we reach the hall, so I can witness the infliction of my words. *He asked for it.* "It's nice to talk to someone besides a grunting wall!" I gesture toward him and can all but see the rage coursing through him—fists coiled tight by his side and nostrils flaring.

He laughs bitterly, causing me to flinch. "Give the guy a while. He'll get sick of hearing about kids either puking or snotting on you." Bode knows he cut me deep on that one, as is evident when he uncoils his fists and backs away some.

I also take a step back to encourage myself not to punch him. Instead, I sling my bag against the wall, listening to the contents inside it bang in protest. I'm too angry to care if anything is broken. My marriage is broken and that's all I can focus on at the moment.

We've never hit each other, and it blows my mind how violent I feel in this moment.

"You do nothing for me. Nothing! Physically, emotionally, supportively. Nothing! Who are you and what the heck did you do with that man I married, who seemed totally sold out to me?" My shoulders sag. "I'm so lonely! You've forgotten about me. You pay me no attention!"

Something seems to snap in Bode at my words, and he is suddenly stalking in my direction. The tension between us has finally reached a limit and explodes. I can't even react, just stay rooted in my spot.

"If it's attention you need, I can give you attention he best not!" His words release in a growl.

In a blink, I'm pinned against the wall with my legs wrapped around my husband's waist. Teeth collide as our hands claw at each other's clothes. I hear buttons scatter as I yank Bode's dress shirt off and a faint rip registers as he rids me of my tank top. His fingers dig into the soft flesh of my hips. I welcome the pain of it as I tug his thick hair and relish the sharp hiss escaping his lips.

This angry passion is abrupt and visceral—almost an out of body experience. Yelling escalated to growling. Growling to groaning in two point zero seconds flat...

I must have lost consciousness somewhere in this wild romp, because the next thing I know I'm being tossed on my bed and left breathless and overheated. I lay nearly paralyzed as my lethargic eyes appreciate my husband's naked form retreating out the door, thinking he's gone to retrieve our abandoned and now slightly tattered clothes.

Minutes ease by with my mind wrapping around what just happened. That's the most passion Bode has displayed in a very long time. I should be mad about what evoked it, probably will be tomorrow, but right now all I'm thinking about is asking him for another round when he comes back into the bedroom...

I doze off waiting for him to join me, but keep rousing back awake with hopes of finding him snuggled next to me, but that never happens...

I wake up this morning alone with the right side of the bed untouched. My hand skims over his cool pillow, wishing he was here. Wishing we could get back to where we once were—affectionate and attentive to each other.

After a long shower and pot of coffee, I give up on the unattainable notion of going back in time. Life moves forward and change comes along with it whether one wants it to or not. Back to autopilot, I don't let it worry me—just go on with my day as usual.

The worry is kept successfully at bay until I pass the guestroom after work and notice my husband has moved a good amount of his belongings in there. With a sharp sting of dread, I realize we are still broken. Last night's passion did nothing to mend it.

Maybe it broke us even more...

Chapter Eight

Bode

Angry. I'm so angry. Ashamed. I'm so ashamed. I feel like I should be writing this confession on paper, repeatedly. What has happened to me? To us?

Never have I mistreated my wife. *Never.* However, something came over me, and I just had to stake my claim. She's mine. I'm hers. But we're unraveling, and I'm not sure how to prevent it. I'm falling into a deeper depression and can't shake it no matter what.

The drive to work is just too dreadful. There's no making this truck go another mile in that direction. My mind is a jumbled mess, so the truck has its own plans. Parked on the side of the road, I email my secretary and explain I won't be in today. The SEND button is hit before I think it through.

Am I having a mental breakdown?

This must be it, because I'm not aware of anything for a spell. Next thing I know, the truck has somehow found its way to the Lodge and has parked at the locked gate. Blinking at the scene several times, I try to get a grip. The mixed urge to yell and cry burns my throat as the cab of the truck starts closing in on me. The stupid tie that is ever-present around my neck starts choking me, so I snatch it off and abandon it in the truck as I climb out and study the gate.

I yank on the lock, sending a ping to echo around the ghost town. No give there. Humph. A lot like the challenge of my life as of late. The gate isn't that tall, so scaling it shouldn't be much of a problem. I leverage my hands on the cold top rail and hoist my body up and over the gate, but my shirt gets hung up. Giving it a good tug, the sound of fabric ripping causes me to cringe before it comes free.

After hopping down, I pause long enough to inspect my mangled shirt. A good-sized hole is now added to the side of it. Yep. It's ruined.

"Shoot!" My foot lands a swift kick on the gate, causing it to wrench out more clanking moans. "Dang it!"

That's two tailored dress shirts in less than twenty-four hours. The worry of it ebbs away as I finish untucking the tails and head over to the cabins. *It's just a stupid shirt.*

The reason for what I'm doing won't reveal itself, but my body is still directing this show, landing me on the porch of my favorite cabin. It only takes two stomps before finding the loose plank. I squat down and pry it back. Sure enough, the hidden key lies in wait.

The door swings open, and a musty smell from being closed up too long greets me. I ignore it and shuffle into the one-room cabin. With the thin veil of dust and the draft coming from an unrepaired window, this place appears as abandoned as I feel.

I plop down on the small couch, sending a plume of dust floating up around me. I ignore it as well and settle onto the worn cushions. It's really a crime for this place not to be used.

"A pure shame," I tell the dark wood walls that are holding a few spider webs.

Tears start burning my eyes with the wish my mom were still here. She would have some advice for me. I pull the cellphone out of my pocket with the contemplation of calling my dad, but how could he possibly help with this problem?

My last few years of high school were plagued by my parents' failing marriage. I don't know all the details—never wanted to know—but my dad cheated. It sent my mom into a debilitating depression. My dad hurt her so bad, and in turn, hurt me as well. My mom was the queen of our family and I couldn't stomach seeing her in pain.

I clung to Mia for strength and distraction to keep me away from the storm at my house during those years. She never wavered.

The idea that my dad, a deacon at our church, could commit adultery just confused me. He begged us to forgive him, saying all sin and fall short. Mom eventually forgave him and they remained together until her death.

His contact information is pulled up on my phone with one swipe of the screen. I'm too much of a coward to talk to him, so I send a text instead. Feeling like I'm that confused teenage boy again, I text—*Why did you cheat on Mom?*

I toss the phone on the cushion beside me, figuring he'll be too chicken to answer. Minutes pass before the phone pings, startling me out of my stupor.

Dad—*Not a text conversation.*

Me—*Only way I can have it. Please answer.*

The text bubble indicates he's answering. The answer must be long or tough, because I stare at it until my eyes cloud over.

Dad—*Stupid, selfish mistake. Was lonely. Dumb reason, but it's the truth.*

Me—*You were a deacon!*

Dad—*No one is perfect! I regret it every day. Worst mistake of my life and I've paid dearly for it.*

Me—*How'd she find out?*

Dad—*I think her heart told her long before I confessed. I ended it and came clean.*

Before I can stop myself I send—*You didn't deserve her.*

Dad—*I know.*

I feel stupid now. I'm one to talk. I may not have cheated on my wife, but I am guilty of neglecting her. What business do I have casting stones at my dad?

Me—*Having a bad day. Sorry. I had no right to say that to you. Didn't mean it. Love you.*

Before he can reply or I send something else that is stupid and inappropriate, I power the phone down.

I know Mia and I are not my parents. I feel in my heart she's telling the truth, but it's still clear she's got a friendship with the man and that's got warning bells ringing all kinds of crazy-loud. If I'm going to be honest, I'm giving her plenty of reason to seek attention elsewhere.

The day wears on and the temptation to just hide here forever is pretty strong, but I know it's not realistic. Sometime in there, I actually manage to doze off for a while. No dreaming. No restlessness. Just flat out sleep. It's so nice that I'm disappointed at reawakening from it. I stay put until the sun dims for the day. No matter how painful reality is, it's time to go face it…or at least edge closer to it. After going back and forth with myself on not cowering, I push to my feet, slap the dust off my pants and head home.

*****

The last several years, my wife and I have allowed a thin wall to build between us, but now, with a few weeks since we literally attacked each other in the hall, that wall somehow got hyped up on steroids and grew miles thick. We go days without seeing each other and we've not talked since. I want to apologize, but the words refuse to unstick from my mouth.

So instead, I sort of sleepwalk through my days—work with little interaction with my colleagues, short visits with Maury, and then I sequester myself in the dark den until I work up enough energy to go hide in the guestroom only to get up and repeat my pathetic routine the next day. I'm embarrassed for how I reacted that night to Mia, so I felt it best to give us both some space and stay in another room for a while.

I keep to my morning runs, but my heart just isn't into it.

Something has to give, because the kids are due home for Christmas break—either today or tomorrow. And we've still not done one thing to acknowledge the holiday—no wreaths, no gifts, and certainly no home baked treats.

After work, I hit up yet another drive thru before heading home. Leaving my tie and jacket in the truck, I go straight over to Maury's.

"Taco night, old man," I announce, placing the bag on the kitchen table where he sits waiting.

"Mia made tacos?" I hear the hope lift his voice.

Looking at the greasy white bag, I contemplate lying to him, but think better of it. He would know after one bite anyway.

"We can pretend," I offer this along with the tacos—two for him and three for me. I sure wish they were home cooked. "Say, Maury, have you ever thought about checking into maybe taking some cooking classes?"

I watch as he dumps most of the taco filling into his lap. Without pause, I clean him up before pushing his chair closer to the table. Here's hoping that'll help with the mess. I join him at the table and tuck into my greasy dinner.

"I think we both can see what a disaster that would be," he answers before crunching into the taco, raining a confetti of shell and diced tomatoes all over the place.

I'm thinking maybe this wasn't the best supper choice, but I'm sick of burgers and pizza. "Yeah, I suppose you're right."

We both finish off a taco before he speaks again, and I wish the old man would have just kept eating.

"How are things with Mia?"

"Good. Fine. We're fine," I say a little too fast. Not wanting to elaborate, I chomp down on my last taco. The crunching echoes through the kitchen, but I realize I'm the only one smacking. I look up and see Maury giving me a stern look, albeit slightly off to my right. "Don't look at me that way."

"Then don't lie to me."

I notice he tries to direct his scowl closer to where my voice just sounded. I give him a good looking over and snort. "You missed a spot shaving, you know." His dark face is smooth but for a small strip of gray stubble on his left cheek.

"Don't change the subject," he says as he runs his hands along both sides of his face until he hits the overlooked spot. "Huh."

"I'm still in the guestroom and we still aren't talking. Things are the same as last time you and I discussed it. Maybe a little worse..." I swallow the lump in my throat and toss the half-eaten taco into the bag, appetite gone.

"When are the young'uns getting in?" Maury hands over his taco wrappers, leaving a trail of shredded lettuce and cheese across the table.

I pick up the mess and cram everything in the bag before tossing it in the trash. "Tomorrow, I think."

"Good. Having them home will maybe help you and Mia put things in perspective. You know your marriage is more than just the sum of the two of you."

"Yessir," I mumble, knowing he's right.

"My little girl is picking me up tomorrow evening and keeping me in Richmond with her until New Years. Have Addison and Kaisley stop by early, so I can give them their Christmas gifts."

Maury's little girl is well past fifty, but I totally get it. Kaisley will always be my little girl, too. Thinking about this fact reminds me of how close I am to failing my children this Christmas. I head out after agreeing to send them over tomorrow as soon as they arrive home, with my mind already searching for where the wreaths and decorations might be.

Darkness of night is seeping all around when I step back over to my yard. I'm instantly struck dumb at what I find. I even pull my glasses out of my shirt pocket and slide them on to be sure I'm seeing right. Yep. There's no mistaking the transformation. What once was devoid of life is now lit up in holiday spirit. The brick exterior of the house is twinkling in clear lights, and thick evergreen garland is laced over each window. I guess I don't have to worry about finding those wreaths after all. They have somehow found their rightful spots on the front double doors already. Scratching my head, I try to figure out just how my wife pulled this gigantic feat off. Was it decorated this morning? How did I not see it when I parked earlier? I've really got to start paying attention.

Feeling like a failure, I load back up in my truck and go try righting some wrongs for the sake of my family.

Chapter Nine

Mia

Today has been productive to say the least. My to-do list was long and challenging, but I managed to knock most of it out. I had the handyman, who Dr. Rogers recommended, at the house by eight this morning. He tackled the outdoor decorations while I knocked out the inside. I've been so weighed down that I almost dropped the ball, but I've somehow managed to shove the despair off and buried it way down so that I can focus on the holiday. I pulled my big girl pants up and set out to preparing for my children's homecoming. I miss them so much it overwhelms me. Those babies are my security blanket—the only thing right in my world.

I shake off the gloomy feelings building up before they bubble out in the form of tears and focus on starting the car after work. I rummage around in my purse until finally unearthing the grocery list. The war wages between skipping out on my workout and heading straight to the grocery store. I've got a lot of baking to catch up on. I can't let Addison and Kaisley arrive home tomorrow without my cranberry cookies waiting on them. Yet the tension is clawing at the back of my neck. I look over at my gym bag and resolve to go ahead and get a quick workout in. Neena was so right about the exercise. The stress relief of it has made whatever mess my husband and I are going through a little more bearable.

Bode flashes in my mind, so I try glaring him away. If he were here in real life, the look alone would have him scurrying away to the den. That man hurt me deep when he moved out of our bedroom. It's like I did something so repulsive that he had to flee from me. I've done nothing wrong, yet I feel guilty just the same. My insecurities flare and taunt me.

Did that wild hallway romp with me disgust him? Is he not attracted to me anymore? Has he had enough of me?

I wheel into the gym parking lot and try locking my angst in the car quickly before sprinting inside the building. I really want to learn how to live in denial. Maybe that should be my New Year's resolution.

After changing in a flash, I summon a treadmill into motion with familiarity and take off with hopes of clocking a few quick miles, so I can check it off and head on to the store.

"Hey, hey, beautiful." A warm voice calls out.

I glance over and see that I'm trapped in the dreamy blue snare of none other than Lee Sutton. I've not seen him since before Thanksgiving and am struck dumb instantly by his overwhelming presence. I hate that this is my reaction to him.

After staring too long, I demand myself to snap out it. "Hi, stranger. Where've you been hiding?"

"Just got back from a Denver bike show." He smoothly picks up the speed of his treadmill.

"Wow. How'd it go?" I huff out, realizing I'm going a bit too fast. Either that or seeing him after a few weeks' absence has me flustered like some silly girl with a crush.

"Good. Arrived with ten bikes and came home empty-handed. Also got a dozen new orders for custom builds. Enough about me. How's my favorite nurse been?"

"Fine," I mutter, looking away. The fight with Bode flashes in my mind.

"Pipsqueak?" He asks this and I can't help but melt some in appreciation. He gets how much she means to me.

"Hanging in there. Make-A-Wish is sending her family to Disney for Christmas."

"That's tight. When's your crowd getting in from Florida?"

A smile blossoms across my face. "Tomorrow and it can't get here fast enough." I glance over and find Lee returning a smile. "What are the famous Lee Sutton's Christmas plans?"

"A friend and I are heading to Cabo."

The way he says friend leaves no doubt he's speaking of a woman. Jealousy surprisingly taps me on the shoulder. I shrug it off, because it has no business there. I'm about to halt this machine and escape with my pathetic self, when Lee speaks up.

"Say, Mia. Will you answer me something?"

"Sure," I say, apprehensively, not so sure I want to answer anything.

"So, I'm perfectly happy with my bachelor lifestyle for the time being. But one day, if I'm lucky enough to run across an amazing woman such as yourself and even luckier to snag her, tell me how to keep her?" He hits the cool down on both treadmills without permission, but I'm glad he did, or I would have probably flown off the back of mine in shock.

I say the first thing that pops in my mind. "Don't forget about her." It's evident he wants me to elaborate, but I focus on mopping the sweat off my face instead.

"That's it?" He huffs, obviously not satisfied with my answer.

"Yep."

"That's all the advice I get?" He tilts his head, trying to meet my distracted eyes.

"That's all the advice you need." I don't meet his gaze as I start ticking off a long list. "Don't forget about her. Don't forget she's a human with needs. Don't forget she's special. Don't forget to surprise her. Don't forget to steal kisses from her. Don't forget why you fell in love with her. Don't forget to simply flirt with her." I pause on that point, because there's plenty of proof Lee needs no help in the flirting department.

"I think I can handle that last one." He quietly chuckles.

Suddenly those blame feelings of loneliness decide to wash over me in this moment and my eyes prick. I swallow it down the best I can, but my voice still sounds hoarse when I say, "Just don't forget she needs you."

Lee drops the smile and grows serious. "Mia..."

Embarrassed, I stop my machine and take off to the locker room. Before I reach the door Lee's warm hand grasps mine and pulls me to a sudden stop, but I don't turn to acknowledge him. I hate that I've allowed him of all people to see my vulnerability. And I hate even more how nice my hand feels in his rough massive one.

I miss holding hands...

"If you were mine, there's no way I would ever forget you." His words are raspy and hot against my ear and hold a dangerous promise of what could only lead to more hurt.

Stunned and scared all at once, I pull away and keep walking. He just pushed it to the uncomfortable and unacceptable zone, and I'm not this kind of woman.

"You want me to knock some sense into him?" I hear Lee say from behind me, breaking the growing tension. We both sputter a laugh, but it's forced and fake.

I play along half-heartedly. "Nah, but I'll keep it in mind." With that, I flee, wishing I had never stumbled upon the temptation of Lee Sutton.

Regret follows me all the way to the store. I'm so mad with myself that I barely register the shopping trip. Well, that is until I make it to the check-out counter. The grocery store visit cost me a small fortune and my purchases take up all of the available space in my car. This is what I get for not going since Thanksgiving.

The car is about to zoom by the I Spy house, but my foot finds the brake first as though the millions of lights are a beacon. The Griswolds have nothing on this place. It's nearly blinding. A multitude of Santa Clause figurines, every color of icicle lights imaginable, and more snowmen than are found at the North Pole litter the tiny yard right along with the normal garden gnomes, wind chimes, and some other random yard decorations. It's really just too much for any set of eyes to take in, which makes it perfect for an impromptu game of I Spy. The sudden need to connect with my children has me fishing my phone out of my purse and taking a picture of it. I send a group text to Kaisley and Addison with the picture.

Me – *I spy ten snowmen.*

Moments later Kaisley texts back – *Found them. I spy a broken icicle light.*

I glance back up to search for the broken light, but Addison beats me to it.

Addison – *Found it on the left side of the porch. I spy an upside down Christmas tree.*

These kids are too sharp for this game. I'm the one who took the picture without catching any of this.

Me – *Found it on top of the mailbox. I spy Elvis wearing a Santa hat.*

We keep on with the game for a good ten minutes before I remember the obscene amount of groceries I still have to get into the house. I text them my goodnight sentiments, feeling more grounded, and head on to the house.

It takes four trips back and forth to unload it all, and not once does Bode make an appearance to help. His truck is home, so I know he's hiding out somewhere in this giant house. Surprisingly enough, the den is deserted, so I guess he is holed up in his newly claimed room upstairs. I take a calming breath, loosening my grip a little in order to try not to take my frustrations out on the innocent groceries as I put them away.

After leaving the cookie ingredients out for the morning, I head upstairs for a much needed shower. I step into my room and come to a halt.

"What are you doing in my room?" I ask sharply. After my conversation with Lee and the emotions that followed, I'm in the wrong frame of mind to deal with Bode tonight.

"*Our* room. And what does it look like?" He shifts on the floor where he sits, his shirt sleeves rolled up to his elbows and the front mostly unbuttoned. I look away from the smooth expanse of his chest and focus on the wrapping paper, bows, and tape littered around him, which happen to be all of *my* supplies for gift wrapping.

I ignore that but lay into what's really been eating at me. "You made the choice of this not being *our* room any longer when you moved out." I toss my purse on the bed and firmly plant my hands on my hips, trying to produce my best glower.

"Can we not do this right now?" Bode mumbles as he places a piece of tape to secure the snowflake designed paper over what looks like a new Xbox game I'm assuming is for Addison.

"Sure. No problem." I point to the door. "Get out of my room."

Bode makes no move to leave and that's rubbing me really wrong. "The kids... They'll be home tomorrow... Shouldn't we... shouldn't I be back in here?"

"You're the one that moved out. Now you'll just have to explain to them why, because I don't even know the answer to that myself." I sniff back the tears, because I can't cry and hold on to my anger, and right now I need it like a lifeline.

He keeps working on wrapping the gift, easily ignoring me, so I try again with hopes of provoking him into answering. "You mind filling me in on why you practically attacked me one night and then moved out the next day?"

Nothing. He says nothing. I should have known better.

He holds tight to his silence like a protective shield. The anxiety has me trembling as I watch him finally push off the floor, abandoning everything right where it is and storming out of the room.

"Way to handle this like an adult, Bode!" I yell at his retreating back. "Great answer. I'm sure the kids will totally understand beings that it is so crystal clear to me now!" My sarcasm lashes out in a near scream.

"I'm not happy!" he yells back, exasperated.

"That makes two of us!"

Didn't we already establish this a few weeks back? What's the cause of our misery? Neither one of us seem to want to voice that part. It's as if once we go there, we won't be able to return from it.

One way or the other, Bode is going to have to man up.

Chapter Ten

Bode

I'm dreaming a heavenly dream that smells so tantalizingly sweet, my mouth waters. Before consciousness fully catches up to me, my pillow dampens along my cheek. I ease my head back and find a puddle of drool. Rolling over to swipe Mia's pillow, I realize I'm still in the guestroom. I shove my face in a dry spot on the pillow and let out a groan. This room... The room she decided to paint a frosty-pine green. The room I moved into when I wanted to rebel and show her who's boss. Lying here, missing the sweet scent of my wife that's absent from this guest bed, the reality of just how lame I really am clarifies.

Heaving myself to the edge of the bed, I inhale deeply and suddenly notice I wasn't dreaming that heavenly scent. Ah yeah! There's no mistaking it. Mia is downstairs in the kitchen where I know she is *baking*. My mouth waters more, just thinking about it. Brushing off our frustrating marital problems, I pretend all is right with the world and go on a hunt in order to find what might be cooling on racks in the kitchen. Here's hoping they are those oatmeal cranberry cookies. A half dozen of those sure would go good with a cup of coffee...

Walking into the kitchen, I'm surrounded by all things tradition. Countertops littered with treats. The oven glowing with more to come. Coffee percolating. But more than that. Way beyond that is the laughter from those two kids sitting on the barstools, as they watch their mom sassing on about something. She's so animated in her red, ruffled apron with flour smeared on one of her flushed cheeks.

I rub my eyes and look again to be sure I'm not dreaming, because it's too perfect to not be a dream. The picture is absolutely magnificent in my sight. *Please don't be dreaming...*

Kaisley squeals out, "Daddy!" causing Mia to glance in my direction, and there's no denying the coolness in her eyes that is all directed at me. Nope. Not dreaming. Reality. Broken marriage is still broken reality. My daughter slings her arms around me and loves me enough that I can shove the marriage mess successfully away for now.

"When did y'all sneak in?" I ask around a face full of dark-red curls. She eventually lets go so Addison can grab a quick hug and manly slap on the back.

"About an hour ago, sleepyhead," Kaisley answers. I glance at the clock and see it's a little after nine.

"What time did your grandparents make you get up?" I laugh, shaking my head. They had to have hit the road around midnight in order to be here this early. That thought has me glancing around at all of the baked goods, wondering if Mia even went to bed last night. There's no way she did.

"Blame it on Kaisley. She whined and whined until Nana and Pop agreed to it. She's been really homesick." Addison rolls his eyes.

"I can't help it." She pouts up, so I reach an arm around and pull her into my side.

"I'm glad you're here. I missed you, too." Placing a kiss on my daughter's forehead, I release her and grab a cookie or ten. Mia might have growled in my direction, but I'm too busy chomping down to know for certain. I give her plenty of space just in case.

"Can we bring our stuff upstairs now, Momma?" Addison asks as I pour a cup of coffee.

I toss a questioning glance in my kids' direction.

"Momma didn't want us to wake you," Kaisley answers my unspoken query.

I cut my gaze over to Mia, but she won't look at me. "That's mighty considerate of your mom."

There's nothing considerate about her intentions. I know the real reason, and it's most certainly not for my benefit. She didn't want me to miss having to explain our new sleeping arrangements. I watch helplessly as both kids dart up the stairs with their bags in tow. I'm pretty sure I didn't close the door and both will have to pass it on the way to their own rooms.

A few minutes later, they shuffle back down the stairs wearing frowns, confirming that yes, I did leave the door open.

"Why's your stuff in the guestroom, Dad?" Kaisley quietly asks.

I glance again for help from Mia, but she's not in the giving mood. Taking a deep breath, I dramatically say, "To be honest with you guys, your mom snores louder than a lumberjack and I can't sleep!"

"Mom?" Addison asks skeptically.

She shrugs her shoulders, not turning away from dipping what I'm hoping are peanut butter balls into the melted vat of white chocolate. "I don't know if he's telling the truth or not. How am I supposed to know if I'm snoring when I'm asleep?" She's rambling, and I have a feeling the kids aren't buying it. She turns around, grabbing a good-sized cookie tin and thrusting it in Addison's direction. "Here. You two take this over to Maury, please."

"He's got Christmas gifts for you, too," I add, hoping to distract them more from the subject.

They both go, but from the look on their long faces, my kids' minds are in the same place as my own. The door shuts and I deflate onto a stool, scrubbing my hands over my face. "Humph. What a mess."

"Yep. You should be so proud of yourself. Openly lying to your children. Way to go." Mia's voice is ice and it freezes me in place. Looking up, I find her glare is just as cold.

"What do you want me to say? Your mom has a guy friend she hangs out with, and she and I aren't talking because of it." I throw my hands up in frustration.

"That's just pathetic, Bode. Really pathetic. If you think we are in this sorry place all because a guy befriended me, then you are one delusional man." She pauses to wash her hands before turning back toward me. "I went out to lunch with Dr. Rogers last week, just so you know. He's a *man*. Oh, and I spent the morning with the handyman yesterday, decorating the house for Christmas—something I should have been doing with my husband. And Parker stopped by yesterday with Neena and he *hugged* me before they left. Now that is some pretty inappropriate stuff... Maybe all that merits you moving into the garage." Her sarcasm is thick and administered with enough bitterness that I have to abandon my cookie feast from feeling sick. Shoulders slumped, I go hide in the den, the only place I seem to belong anymore.

*****

The next several days stretch on in what can only be described as a well-orchestrated act. Well, at least I hope Mia and I are pulling it off. The kids keep giving us these odd looks with narrowed eyes and mouths set in a firm line, so I have my doubts. Everyone mimes through the motions of the holiday season, ticking off the long list of parties, carol sings, church programs, and other Christmas events along the way. There's been no more mention of me sleeping in the guestroom. Seems we have silently pledged to pretend what's happening isn't really happening...

My fingertips firmly rub my temples as I realize that thought just confused me as much as the whole situation has. Maybe I did overreact to Mia's friendship with Lee Sutton, but my gut tells me another story. Even if Mia sees him only as a friend, I seriously doubt that schmuck's intentions are innocent. I'm getting mad all over again. Tamping it down as best I can, I refocus on placing Santa-gifts around the tree. I guess we are pros at this pretending stuff...

I make the mistake of glancing over at Mia and have to stifle a moan by biting my lip. The fact that my wife is bent over in nothing but a nightshirt, showing off perfect lacy pink panties, is not helping my cause. It's been four *long* weeks since I've *been* with my wife. Sighing loudly, I angle away from the temptation, knowing I won't be allowed to unwrap that particular gift. The tease peeking out from under the wrapping is killing me. A grumble slips out before I can hold it back, but she keeps right on ignoring me.

We work in silence—me shoving handfuls of candy in the stockings and Mia adding iTunes cards, Chapstick... She leans over again to grab something, and my eyes zero in on those smooth legs on display... My fingers flex, begging to test the feel...

Another groan rumbles up my throat, causing Mia to abruptly stand back up. Her narrowed eyes dart around, looking for the animal wailing, I suppose.

"What's wrong with you?" Her words sound as annoyed as I feel.

"Nothing," I grouch, stalking out of the den before I do something stupid like attack my wife again.

This is the first time since I was nineteen years old that this woman has been off-limits to me. I feel like a hot-blooded teenage boy struggling with abstinence all over again. I wonder if I apologize, we could have some make-up—

"Can't you at least finish the stockings?"

I turn around and come face to face with the little spitfire who's glaring up at me. Yeah. No. There will be no making-up possibility from the looks of it. I stand here like a salivating wolf licking my lips.

"Stop looking at me like that!" Mia hisses.

I play dumb. "Like what?" I ask, pulling on my confused look—cue scratching the side of the head and drawn eyebrows with pouty lips. Yeah. I'm good at it.

"Ugh." She points in the direction of the den. "They'll be up soon, and I have to get breakfast started."

I brush past her, back to the den and away from those tempting legs. By the time I'm done with the stockings, the sky is turning light and the house smells of yeasty cinnamon goodness. I amble into the kitchen, but movement outside the window catches my attention before I can swipe a cinnamon roll. The first flurry of snow for the season. The ground isn't even covered white yet, but from the size of the fat flakes, there's lots of potential for some epic outdoor fun.

Bolting up the stairs, I holler, "It's snowing! Merry Christmas! It's snowing!" I pound on Addison's door and then Kaisley's. Addison opens his door and meets me wide-eyed in excitement. My boy knows what we will be up to later today.

"Boogie board," Addison blurts out in a voice too deep to be from my son. Man, I just can't get over these kids growing up so fast. It's like it happened overnight and without my permission.

"In the back shed." Turning to go find it, I nearly plow Mia down. I didn't realize she followed me up.

"Breakfast and gifts first. Y'all need to give the snow long enough to accumulate." Mia's trying to be stern with us *kids*, but I catch her lips twitching and it makes me want to eliminate the few inches and kiss them. But I know there's more than that between us so I keep away.

"Did you say snow?" Kaisley mumbles in a nasally voice as her door creaks open.

"Yep! But breakfast and gifts first," I say in a mock-authoritative tone while waggling a finger, earning me a pop on my back from my wife. Giving in, I turn around and place a kiss on her cheek before dashing to the bedroom to retrieve my Bible.

Halfway down the stairs, I backtrack to grab my glasses. Maybe that'll earn me a point or two with Mia. Everyone is sitting around the small breakfast table by the time I get to the kitchen. Reading the birth of our Savior, Jesus Christ, from the book of

Luke is the tradition we started the very first year of our marriage and the sentiment of it is making it hard for me to swallow. I sure hope it's not our last.

After pulling myself together and the reading is concluded with a prayer of thanks, we tuck into the bounty of breakfast Mia has prepared. Two pots of coffee later, we are all camped out around the Christmas tree in the den. A quick peek out the window confirms an epic afternoon will ensue with at least five thick inches of snow blanketing the yard already.

I pass the gifts out, and we all sit cross-legged beside small mountains of wrapped surprises. I'm itching to see what the children have received. The mountains include mine as well as Mia's, Santa's, and gifts from my dad. Mia's crowd will be over for a late dinner so more gifts are to come.

Patience runs out and I can't wait any longer, so I motion toward my kids' mountains. "Go ahead, already." Mia and I chuckle at my eagerness, but it dies out when we realize neither Addison nor Kaisley are joining in.

I catch my kids having one of those private conversations conveyed only through looks and head nods. Addison glances in my direction without making eye contact before nodding again toward Kaisley. She clears her throat to begin, but seems to lose her nerve and exchanges another look with her brother instead. I'm wondering if they paper, rock, scissored to see who has to deliver whatever this is. Obviously my poor girl lost.

The tension grows past uncomfortable in the room, and I'm thinking maybe I should be having one of those silent conversations with Mia. Because clearly something is going down. Looking over at her, I raise one eyebrow and try my best to let her know we should probably be worried. She raises her brows slightly as to say, *you're probably right*. Wow. She's admitting I'm right. In this instance, I wish I was actually wrong. Way too many scenarios race through my head, causing my pulse to pound in my ears.

My stomach dips when one frightful scenario flashes. I start silently chanting, *please don't be pregnant, please don't be pregnant...*

"No, Dad! No!" Kaisley shouts, hands raised as stop signs and eyes rounded.

I didn't even realize I was saying that out loud. Mia lets out a shuddered sigh of relief from beside me. The overwhelming urge to run out in the snow and take a dip in the icy fluff to cool off this heated tension from my body has me shifting uncomfortably.

"No. Nothing like that." Addison fans a hand around.

With this, they both slide their gifts away, confusing me even more. I notice Mia has said nothing and I'm not comfortable with that. She normally takes lead in these situations, but here she's left me flailing around like a dopey idiot. Does she understand what's going on? If so, why hasn't she clued me in?

"We don't want any gifts this year," Kaisley mumbles.

"Why not, sweetheart?" I ask.

She lifts her eyes to meet mine. "Why are you in the guestroom?"

Well... This wasn't where I saw this going. At. All. "I..." My mouth hinges shut when my mind goes blank.

Mia clears her throat. "What does that have to do with your Christmas gifts?"

"Everything," Addison answers. "You and Dad aren't acting like yourselves. I know Kaisley and I are young, but we're not that naïve. These gifts don't matter at all if our family isn't right."

"All that truly matters to us is our family." Kaisley gestures around to each of us. "All we want for Christmas is for you and Momma to fix whatever you broke." Kaisley starts sniffling as she stands, abandoning her Christmas. A Christmas I am responsible for ruining...

Chapter Eleven

Mia

Stunned and embarrassed. That's all I feel as I sit motionless in this spot on the floor, surrounded by festively wrapped presents and a tree winking happily along as if our world isn't falling apart. I want to yell at it to stop being so merry. There's nothing merry about this situation. Bode and I have failed our children—something I've worked diligently on never doing. I thought we had succeeded. Wrong. I've been very wrong.

Everyone has grown uncomfortably silent, except for Kaisley's sniffles sounding from the hallway. She's not gone far, so I know she just needs a minute to collect herself. She's never handled any type of animosity very well. She's non-confrontational and it's obvious my tenderhearted daughter has reached her limit.

I try to come up with a solution to fix this, but I'm coming up blank. It's Christmas, for goodness sake! This cannot be how this goes down. Panicked, questions start flooding my mind.

What about our family coming over to spend the holiday with us?

What about the big meal planned?
What about the other gifts to come?
What will they think?

"We're just...just going through...a rough patch. No big deal. Nothing the two of you should worry about." A nervous cough escapes me. "No need to not enjoy your holiday."

"We're serious, Momma." Addison pins me with a stern look.

My breath catches at noticing just how much he resembles his dad. How can I feel such hostility toward the very man who helped to create this fine young man before me?

I wave toward their gifts again once Kaisley shuffles back in. "How about your daddy and I promise to work on us, and you two promise to enjoy Christmas?"

Any shred of hope for salvaging this moment is lost as both children shake their stubborn heads in unison. Their minds are definitely made up.

"We already told you what we want for Christmas, and we won't be finding it in any of this stuff wrapped up," Kaisley whispers.

Deflated, I ease off the floor and give them a hug. I even include Bode, which feels awkward at best. "Well, the crowd will be here shortly, so I'm going to go shower and get to cooking." I regard the snow still dropping heavily outside the window. "And you three have some snow to go boss around."

Bode, who has fallen mute now that I regained my voice, joins me in an uncomfortable laugh. I don't wait for their reply. Instead, I dash upstairs and come undone.

As the shower whirls to life, the dam inside me breaks. After months of holding it in and not allowing myself to slip, my composure spills down the drain. My legs give out and send me to the floor of the shower. I can only hope the kids have gone outside and are unaware of the sobs echoing around me—sobs so violent my entire body convulses from them.

The façade is slipping and I don't know how to resurrect it. The world around us is becoming privy to the flaws the Calders have been keeping neatly tucked away. Kaisley and Addison showed me clearly that we weren't concealing those cracks in our armor too well after all. The perfect front is disintegrating and starting to show the tarnished truth.

Eventually, I manage to pull myself back together with the help of eye drops and a magical eye cream for puffiness. I give my appearance one final scan in the mirror before reemerging for what will probably be a very long and painfully awkward day. My reflection emulates sadness and a little bit of the cry still lingers in my features, but I brush it off and head out of hiding to seek out some semblance of normalcy in the kitchen.

Although the gifts were ushered into our rooms before my family's arrival, the first thing Dad wants to know is what Santa brought the kids.

"Momma and Daddy haven't been acting right. We've decided all we want for Christmas is for the two of them to make up," Kaisley tattles with Addison agreeing.

An uncomfortable silence stretches on for a painful spell with all eyes on me and Bode. Thankfully, Neena swoops in and saves the day by ushering the kids outside on the challenge of her being able to build a better snowman than them. For that, I'm thankful. That's Neena. She's a pro at defusing an explosive situation. That character trait is probably one of the main reasons she kicks butt as a journalist. To be sure, situations can get a bit sticky for her at times with the investigative side of her career.

As I work in the kitchen I keep catching glimpses of Neena streak by the window as she starts a snowball war with the three other stooges. Her infectious energy has to be vital enough to rebirth a zombie. For that I'm thankful, because if anyone can pull my kids out of their funk, it's Aunt Neena. Bode's boisterous laugh reaches through the windowpanes, so I'm glad her magic is working on him as well. Even though I'm spitting mad at that man, I never want him to be unhappy.

Dad has taken Bode's normal spot in the den, and Mom is bustling around the kitchen with me. There's no denying she's watching me, though. It's making me nervous.

Mom takes it upon herself to crank up some Christmas carols to add ambiance while we cook. It's on the tip of my tongue to point out that there's no hope in conjuring the Christmas spirit, but I keep that to myself and try pretending—even though it's painfully clear I suck at it. I look up from the mixer after adding a few eggs to the batter, and catch Mom staring at me.

"You want to talk about it?" She tucks a silver lock of hair behind her ear and offers a weak smile.

"I'm not sure what to say." I shrug.

"Well, the children have had a lot to say about it in the last few months."

I switch the mixer off to pay better attention. It's becoming clear that Bode and I are the worst actors ever. A snowball collides with the windowpane, starling me. Addison runs by it, screaming like a girl with Bode on his heels. The picture outside still looks perfect...

Mom pats my arm to get my attention. "Mia, can I be completely honest with you?"

"By all means." I gesture for her to continue. She's going to whether I want her to or not.

"You and Bode are not that original. Your situation is no more unique than any other marriage hiccup."

"Gee, thanks." I already feel foolish about it all. Hearing enough of this, I go to turn the mixer back on, but Mom stops me.

"But what will make you unique is how you handle it." She pauses to pin me with her blue stare, being sure I'm listening. "Every marriage faces valleys. It's never a continuous mountaintop experience. But you can choose a different route back to the top. Please consider how to get back up there *together*."

Sniffing back tears, I shrug my shoulders. "I don't know exactly how we got on this path in the first place. How can we figure out the right route?"

"Oh, honey. You need to start by putting God back first in your marriage. And don't forget how *good* the good has been. You two deserve to honor the beauty of your commitment together. That man loves you. He's just going through something. He needs you to be there for him."

Now she sounds like Maury. "But what about me?" And now I sound like a selfish child, even to my own ears. I avert my gaze to the yellow batter in the bowl.

"Focus on loving Bode and supporting him, and I guarantee he will reciprocate it. There's no room for selfishness in a relationship."

My mom must be done dishing out her advice, because she turns her attention back to peeling the potatoes. So I do the same, finishing off the cornbread mix and popping it in the oven. I've had enough of her honesty, anyway. I only feel more foolish now.

The rest of Christmas day eases by in a haze of forced family chatter and ill-placed Christmas carols with my mind stuck on the mess Bode and I have made.

I'm just not confident of it being fixable.

*****

Kaisley didn't get a big enough dose of holiday shopping madness, so as soon as the after-Christmas sales paper arrived this morning she was all about it. Not me. The memory of a sea of rabid shoppers with the eyes flickering in every direction, prepared to pounce on anyone who got in their way, reminds me to never go there again. I sent her off with a group of her friends instead.

Neena invited me over to her townhouse, and that sounds ideal. My car slowly drives through the quaint gated community where she resides. It's very hip and family friendly with a youthful vibe—much like my sister, so it's a perfect fit for her, even though she's adamant on keeping her bachelorette status firmly intact.

As soon as I park the car, she appears on her porch, barefooted while wearing an oversized knit cap. Her breaths hover in thick clouds in front of her, so there's no doubting the freezing temperature has registered to my silly sister.

"You're head cold, but not your feet?" I ask, eyeing her weird ensemble, completed with a white tank top and orange fleece sweatpants embroidered with a T. Bode would dig the pants for sure.

"Something like that," she answers, embracing me tightly. "You okay?"

"Sure," I answer halfheartedly, but she already knows better than to believe that. I look over my shoulder to the right at the vacant townhouse attached to Neena's. "You think it'll ever sell?"

"Now that you're empty nesters, you and Bode should downsize and buy it."

My eyes dart back in her direction. "The two of you would kill each other if you lived this close. Besides, I may need a place of my own if things don't change." I head inside and stumble upon a calamity in Neena's living room. Several cases of M&Ms, various hard candies, snack cakes, and apple turnovers are stacked haphazardly. I nose around in a few of the unmarked boxes and discover several copies each of Dad's novels and a thick stack of Popular Mechanics Magazines. "Are you preparing for a blizzard in true Neena style?" I ask while plundering.

"No, silly. I'm shipping this stuff to some soldiers stationed overseas."

"I didn't know you had soldier friends," I comment while pulling open another box and finding it filled with dreamcatchers of all things. I pluck one out and hold it up while arching an eyebrow in her direction.

Neena takes the dreamcatcher from my hand and places it back with the others. "'Greater love hath no man than this, that a man lay down his life for his friends,'" she quotes. "I don't need to know them to thank them for their sacrifice for this and other countries." She flips the lid shut and crosses her arms. "Now how about explaining that little comment you dropped out there on the porch."

As soon as that slipped out of my mouth, I knew she wouldn't let it go. So much for my efforts of sidetracking her.

"Bode and I are living parallel lives that seem to never intercept anymore." My throat goes dry, making it impossible to swallow.

"Oh, Mia." She pulls me in for another much-needed hug.

We settle on the couch, surrounded by a fort of boxes, as I fill her in on the latest. Neena is sharper than any tack, so she already knows most of what's going on with Bode growing distant. Taking a fortifying breath, I also tell her about Lee Sutton and watch the disappointment register on her face as I do.

"He's just a friend," I say defensively.

"Not from what you've just told me." She secures my hand in hers. "Mia, that man is up to no good."

"It hasn't felt that way, except for when he grabbed my hand... Neena, it felt good. So good it scared me."

"Good. That means you know better. Stay away from him, please."

"I'm just so lonely." I rub my forehead and slump.

"We've just got to figure out what's going on with Bode and then maybe the two of you can get back on track."

Before we get very far on that mystery, someone knocks on Neena's door.

"Are you expecting company?"

"Oh shoot! I forgot Parker is stopping by. We've got a little work to do on next week's article." She skips over to the door. This girl never just walks. It's always some entertaining dance, skip, hop, or sashay, and it never fails to pull a smile from my lips.

"Neena, when are you going to let that poor guy catch you?"

"Now what would be the fun in that?" She shoots me a wink over her shoulder with her hand resting on the doorknob. "Ooh. Let's get Parker's take on your man troubles."

"No!" I say sharply as she opens the door.

"Too late. I heard her through the door." Parker gives me a knowing look before sliding his focus back to Neena. "Darling, you'll never know just how fun it can be, if you don't allow me the chance to catch you."

"Oh... You heard that, too?" Her cheeks actually pink up. Such a rarity to be able to embarrass that one. It tickles me that Parker calls her out like he does.

"Yep." He runs his hand through his shaggy hair as the winter wind ruffles it. He eyes her head to toe. "Nice outfit. Did you forget to do the laundry again?"

"Something like that. Get your fine self in here." She grabs the lapels of his navy pea coat and yanks him through the door before shutting it firmly.

Parker walks right over to me, drops his black messenger bag, pulls me to standing, and offers a hug. "You want me to beat him up?"

This guy has been a part of my life as long as he has been in Neena's, which I'm guessing to be at least a decade now. It's like he deemed my sister and me a package deal, claiming both of us as friends.

I plop back down on the couch. "I'll keep that in mind if he doesn't straighten up. For now, how about you give me your guy opinion on how to get the old Bode back."

"He sure wasn't himself last time we all went out to eat. He seemed miserable, but I really doubt it has anything to do with you." Parker shrugs out of his coat and joins me on the couch.

"I just wish he would tell me." I twirl my wedding ring in a circle.

"Mia, us guys aren't into talking about our *feelings*." Parker wrinkles his nose and makes a face.

Neena jumps up from her chair, startling us both. "This calls for a few emergency pints." She scurries into her kitchen and comes back with cartons of ice cream and spoons.

Digging into the indulgent chocolate ice cream, Parker spends a little while telling me how guys don't like to talk and I should do some investigation as to what seems to be making him so miserable. Neena agrees with him. With both being in journalism, their advice doesn't surprise me.

After the cartons are empty, I hang out with them as Neena helps Parker select photos to accompany her article. Those two make a pretty solid team. Too bad I can't talk her into giving the guy a go at being on a relationship team with her.

Neena walks me out, and I can't help asking her one more time why she's dressed the way she is.

"You remember Van, my neighbor?"

"The cute redhead who begs you daily for a date?"

She snorts, leaning on the porch rail. "That's the one. Anyway, I hid his skateboard, telling him he needs to establish himself as a more serious guy. All on a tease, of course." She swats at the air as if to rid her own silliness. "So in retaliation, Van snuck in my house and stole a part off of my washer. He's holding it hostage until I give over the skateboard."

"If you'd learn to lock your door, things like that could be prevented. So you're not able to do laundry? Is that it?" I motion toward her odd ensemble.

"Heck no. Who do you take me for? All of my laundry is done. Had a new part the next day, but he doesn't know it. So when I'm home, I parade around like this."

"You are so weird." I laugh, rolling my eyes.

"It's fun to be weird."

"Let me guess, Van isn't going to get his skateboard back any time soon. Nor will he be securing a date with you."

"Yes on the skateboard. And a big NO on the date. He's barely legal." She shakes her head vigorously, causing the fuzzy ball on her knit cap to flop around.

"But he's a med student. That's promising."

"Let me reiterate the NO. Too young. Not interested." She pops me playfully on the backside. "Now get out of here and go play pretty with my favorite brother-in-law."

"He's your only brother-in-law."

"Exactly!"

"Get inside before you catch a cold in your contradiction of an outfit." I point toward the door as I head down the steps.

"Yes, ma'am," she calls out, but stays put until my car pulls out of her driveway. I guess she hopes Van will catch a glimpse of her bizarreness.

Chapter Twelve

Bode

New Year's Eve shows up and we gather at an old apple orchard owned by a family in our church to celebrate it, but all I want to do is go hide in my den back at the house—where it's warm with the big screen. Instead, I'm standing in the middle of a freezing field. I pull my knit cap farther over my ears, which are close to forming icicles. Midnight can't get here fast enough.

Three bonfires reach high into the night sky and are circled with large groups trying to keep warm while the band from our church rocks out on the front porch of the old barn, the space lit up with a copious amount of twinkling lights. Everything is festive and cheery—opposite of what I'm feeling. I breathe in a deep icy breath, catching the scents of smoke mingled with the sweet treats set up along the space.

Scanning the crowd, I spot Mia at a long table giving out cups of cocoa while her mom and sister give out cookies and bags of popcorn. She's talking up some kids, looking lively as always while sporting a bright red nose. I want to go over and offer her my cap, but some sort of wall continues to keep us apart.

And that wall has a type of tense force field that wards me off.

The tradition around here on New Year's Eve is for each family to set up a table and give out treats for the party. I'm cold and thirsty and would really like a cup of Mia's homemade cocoa, but I'm too much of a coward to approach the three of them. That's just asking for it and I'm somewhat smarter than that. I wander over to another family's table and gladly accept the cup of hot apple cider a little old lady offers me.

"Hello there, young man." A tap on the shoulder summons my attention.

I turn and find Linda standing beside me, buried in a thick red coat and huge fluffy white hat. She could be Mrs. Claus.

"Nothing young about this old man anymore," I comment with a weak smile.

She clucks her tongue. "Nonsense. There's plenty youth still left in you."

"Yeah, yeah." I sure don't feel it.

She gives me a hug that I cannot refuse. Linda and Dave have always felt like my favorite aunt and uncle—you know, the ones that spoil you and let you by with everything when your parents aren't looking. Yeah, that's them. I release Linda and step back before I cry like a baby and ask her to hide me away for a while. It wouldn't be the first time. That's how the hidden key under that cabin porch came to be. Dave took me out there the day after the news of the affair leaked out.

As Dave showed me the key location, he said, "You're welcome here anytime you need a break." And I took him up on that offer—sometimes days at a time.

The crap had hit the fan with my dad's cheating scandal, rocking our church as well as this small town—prominent figure in the community caught cheating with the church secretary. Yep, it was nasty. The scorned secretary aired it all out for everyone to judge after dad ended it. That's why I don't go to Linda's church anymore. Dad sort of put a bad taste in the congregation's mouth with being a philandering deacon, so we ended up finding another church home eventually. It was for the best. People can forgive, but they sure as heck don't forget.

I do have to give it to my old man on that. He could have easily cowered away from society as well as his faith in God. Eventually, Dad got back on track and was forthcoming on giving God praise for his restored relationship with my mom.

Letting that thought fade, I refocus on this New Year's Eve night. Linda grabs herself a cup of cider, laces her free hand through the crook of my arm, and directs us closer to one of the bonfires.

"And just what are you doing mingling with us nondenominational folks tonight?"

She nudges me with her gloved hand. "We Baptist folks might as well get used to hanging out with y'all. We are going to all be in heaven together one day."

"I agree." Leaning closer, I say, "It's really good to see you."

"So much so, you want to take the Lodge off my hands? I really think tonight is the perfect night to put that resolution in effect." She gives me that determined look she used to give Dave all the time. The sucker always gave in to her, and every bone in my body wants to give in, too.

I stare into the fire and mumble, "I wish it were that easy."

"It is. You're the one making it complicated by overthinking it. Mia would support you in taking it on."

I give Linda a noncommittal shrug, doubting Mia feels up to supporting me on anything anymore.

"Just promise you'll think about it, okay?"

"Yes, ma'am." I give her a quick hug and move along. This special lady reminds me of too many happier times. Odd how that is making me hurt all over.

While sipping the last of the cider, I catch sight of Addison talking with a cute blonde from their youth group. No wonder the kid has wanted to invest so much time with the youth group as of late. Smirking, I toss the empty cup in a bin and head closer to the porch and listen to the band play. The group of twenty-somethings is singing a cover of Need to Breathe's song "Multiplied" and is doing a fairly decent job.

As I take in the lively scene, the rich aroma of chocolate drifts through the air. It reminds me of a resolution Mia made to give up chocolate after Addison was born to help her lose the baby weight. I thought she wore it well, but evidently my opinion didn't matter. She started out strong on the first of the year and gave it a good go until Valentine's Day showed up with me being emptyhanded of the heart-shaped box of Turtles chocolates. She almost went postal on me that day, so I hauled tail to the nearest store and bought every box they had left. Before I gave them over, Mia had to make the *resolution* to never try the resolution of giving up chocolate ever again.

"Hey Bode!" a friend from church shouts out with a raised hand as he scoots past me, holding his bundled-up toddler close.

I wave back before drifting off to another fond resolution. It's my favorite by far, and most of that memory I'll keep to myself. A smile cracks my frozen lips just thinking about it. I made the resolution to make a baby girl with my wife by year's end. Mia wasn't too much on board with this since she was holding our baby boy on her hip at the time I declared it. The celebration of me beating my chest in the ultrasound room when it was confirmed a baby girl was growing perfectly inside my wife's rounding belly within my year timeframe is something I'll never get over and still makes me proud.

A few songs later, midnight starts creeping considerably close. The band stays in position, but motions our pastor Chase to join them on the porch stage. Shoving my hands deep in my wool coat pockets, I settle a shoulder on a tree trunk and wait for what message he's going to share.

The lead singer offers Chase the mic and his gloved hand accepts it.

"Good evening!" he shouts a little too forceful into the mic. The crowd chuckles out their good evening responses back to him. "What an amazing year we've just been blessed with." He pauses for people to agree with shouts of amen. "If you've been blessed to spend this night celebrating with family, I want you to gather round them now." Again he pauses so that people can shuffle to their designated group.

I've been avoiding mine, but push off the tree and seek them out as he has requested. I spot everyone gathering near the other edge of the porch with Addison waving me over. I sidle up close to Kaisley and keep a slight distance from Mia. She seems on the same page and bundles up to Addison's side.

After everyone seems to be in place, Chase continues.

"Wow. I see no one is alone. What a blessing. Oh how we take that for granted. God created us to lift one another up. To support one another. To love one another." More amens ring out. "Have you taken your blessings for granted this past year?"

Even though I'm freezing, I feel my cheeks begin to burn with shame. Taking a look around this mix of Calder and Cameron family, the answer is a resounding yes. I want to ask for forgiveness from each one and beg them to help me, but my pride keeps my jaw hinged tightly shut at not wanting to admit I'm fighting depression. I'm a blessed man with a healthy loving family and a successful career, so to admit I'm depressed sounds selfish and weak. Shoot, I've only just admitted it to myself.

"A new year is the perfect time to lift up your burdens to God and to ask Him to guide your path for the upcoming year. The only resolution I suggest you make tonight is put your focus back on where it rightfully belongs. Put God first and lead your family in a close second behind Him."

The cute blonde Addison was hanging out with earlier joins Chase on stage.

"Miss Ashley is going to sing us a song. While she sings, take this time to thank God and your family." Chase hands over the mic to Ashley.

"This song has become my theme song and I'd like to encourage you to let it be yours as well for this year. It's entitled 'First' by Lauren Daigle. The words inspire us to seek God first and to keep Him first." Ashley gives the band and nod and they begin to play.

As she sings, I notice some of the groups dropping to their knees while others huddle close and wrap their arms around one another. My family is doing the huddling thing, so I close in and wrap my arms around my children. They are in the center of our huddle, and my prayer automatically goes to thanking God for them. Before I know it, tears have worked out the corners of my eyes and my prayer changes to silently begging God to help me.

Midnight arrives as Ashley sings and we pray. It's how a new year should begin—praising God and asking for His guidance. Even though I'm begging, I don't know what I want or how to proceed after we say amen. I'm still confused and still hurt. With Mia not making eye contact with me, I'd say she's feeling the same.

Please, God, please help us. Please help me be a better man.

Chapter Thirteen

Mia

Entering through the back door of Valley Church, we are met by a heavy silence. So quiet that the hum of the heating system seems to be the only presence in the building. I glance over to Bode, but he won't look at me. It's clear neither of us is here of our own free will, but we made a promise to our children and those two are stubbornly holding us to it. The unwrapped gifts in their bedrooms are proof of it. They left for school yesterday without so much as taking a single piece of candy from their stockings.

"Go ahead in my office. I'll be there shortly." Pastor Chase's voice sounds from around the corner. Looking in that direction, I notice he has a phone to his ear. Without comment, we shuffle into his office and have a seat in the leather chairs set before his cluttered desk.

"Feels like being sent to the principal's office," Bode mutters as he studies his shoes.

I've only had one such visit in all of my youth, and it was actually this guy sitting beside me now who was to blame for that lone visit my junior year of high school. I almost say this out loud, but I'm not in the mood to point fingers.

By midway through my junior year and Bode's senior, Bode was my steady boyfriend and we were inseparable. I was totally in love with him. He was fun and adventurous, always dragging me along for his shenanigans. A sure hand was always planted protectively on my back or grasping firmly to my hand, and I knew he would always protect me.

Just past a thick line of ancient trees behind our alma mater is the coolest stream that rushes from the tops of the mountains. It was the meeting place for students most days on their lunch break or sometimes when they ditched class altogether.

An unmeasurable amount of hours were spent at the back of those woods, goofing around the old wooden bridge stretched across a wider part of the stream. A few hot and heavy make-out sessions highlight those memories with Bode.

I thought that my boyfriend was the most romantic creature God had ever created when he led me to that bridge one early evening before the light left the day completely. He placed his portable CD player on the rail before pulling me in his arms to dance us to the twangy melody of our song. Trisha Yearwood serenaded us to "She's In Love with the Boy" while Bode held me close, and I couldn't have agreed with her more. I was absolutely in love. Wrapped in Bode's young yet steadfast arms, I knew we were meant to have all of our dreams come true. I'd make sure of it.

Such determination back then...

After dancing for a long stretch, I'll never forget Bode leading me to the bank of the stream as he shined a flashlight to illuminate the graffiti freshly sprayed along the side of the bridge.

Mia Should Marry Bode.

I remember him nudging me in the arm mischievously with a full can of spray paint. Without hesitation, I swiped the can and painted my own reply.

Mia Agrees With Bode.

And that was what landed us both in the principal's office the following day.

The principal asked, "Well, what do you have to say for yourself?"

Bode sat straighter in his chair and said, "I think the bridge says it all, sir."

The giggles nearly choked me as I had tried swallowing them unsuccessfully. The principal didn't find it funny one bit that we vandalized school property with our declarations of love. He threatened to prevent us from attending the prom even though we were a shoo-in for prom king and queen. I remember looking down at the half-carat engagement ring with an unstoppable grin, knowing I didn't need a crown.

An uneven sniff sounds from beside me. A sidelong glance causes my breath to falter. Bode's face is slightly flushed and twisted in agony and his glistening eyes won't meet my own. I know he's reliving the same memory as me. It's impossible for him not to be.

Shaking my head, I direct my attention back to the messy desk. How odd to have such a profound moment of our life stir us while our marriage is teetering on such a fragile precipice. My nose begins to sting as I try to blink the tears away, but it's useless. I bat them away as quick as they can escape.

My blurry eyes stray back over to Bode. A small shake of his head indicates his own bafflement about our predicament.

How did we get here? How?

The door lets out a somber creak as it opens, producing an apprehensive Chase. Oddly enough, he seems more uncomfortable than Bode and I do. As he slides in the chair behind his desk, he forces a smile that goes nowhere near his eyes.

"I'm not going to lie to y'all. You're my friends and this... Well..." He runs his hand through his thinning blond hair that's more on the gray side these days.

We nod our understanding because it is painfully uncomfortable. Chase was only a junior pastor, fresh out of seminary, when he officiated our wedding. We were his first and proud of it. He and his wife Rebecca have always been our go-to double date couple over the years—except for recently that is. Now he's the senior pastor, only proving that time flies by way too quickly.

"If this is about infidelity—"

"No!" we both say adamantly at once.

Bode decides to look at me pointedly afterwards. I huff out another, "No!" How could he think I would ever do that to him? But then I think back over how lonely I've been and a flicker of a *maybe* sparks, causing me to cringe. *No!* I reinforce this to myself. No. Never. I made vows...

Chase releases a sigh. "I love you both and don't want to risk our friendship by getting into the middle of this. But as your pastor, I would like to give you some advice."

"Okay," we both mutter.

"Just so I'm clear, there's no major event or problem that has caused the rip in your marriage, correct?"

I think about what Chase may be implying—infidelity, drug abuse, Internet porn, various forms of abuse...

"Nothing like that," I say quietly, noticing Bode shifting uncomfortably in his chair.

Again, Chase seems relieved. "Good. Good. Most every couple goes through a rough patch. It's perfectly normal, so don't beat yourselves up over it. A lot of the time, it only takes focusing on priorities to get back on the right track." He pulls out his Bible. "I don't know how your relationship with God is going lately beings that the two of you have been laying considerably low, but you need to have Him first and foremost."

Bode grunts a response and I keep to a head nod. I dab the back of my hand along my hairline and am relieved when the heating system finally takes a break.

Chase flips through his Bible. "I'd like to read a few verses to you from Ephesians. 'Wives, submit to your husbands as to the Lord. For the husband is the head of the wife as Christ is the head of the church, his body, of which he is the Savior.'"

Bode lets out an obnoxious snort, and I have to firmly press my foot in the carpet to fight the urge to kick the fool out of him. He's the one too lazy to take the lead of anything nowadays, which forces me to lead.

Chase ignores us and continues on. "Ephesians also says, 'Husbands, love your wives, just as Christ loved the church and gave himself up for her.' Marriage is a sacrifice that you committed to when you pledged your vows before God." He produces a piece of paper and hands it to Bode. "These are the very same vows you pledged that day to one another. Each part is significant and I want you to reexamine how you fulfill your promise... Or lack thereof."

"Can I get a copy, too?" I ask.

Chase smiles weakly. "That one copy is for the two of you to share. You have to do this together if it's going to make a difference."

Bode angles the paper so I can also read it.

I, (name), take you (name), to be my (wife/husband), to have and to hold from this day forward, for better or for worse, for richer, for poorer, in sickness and in health, to love and to cherish; from this day forward until death do us part.

The top of the paper just simply states it. Then underneath, each part is broken down separately.

To have and to hold from this day forward,
For better or for worse,
For richer, for poorer,
In sickness and in health,
To love and to cherish;
From this day forward until death do us part.

Chase says something else, but I don't catch it because I'm already stuck on the first vow. What does *to have and to hold* even mean? The realization that I've pledged things to this man I call husband that I don't even understand strikes me in a peculiar way. I mean, most of it makes sense, but maybe we really didn't fully grasp it enough. We were only dumb teenagers, thinking love would be enough. It's shameful to admit, but I haven't given those vows another thought since the day I said them.

We both rise, but Chase hold his hands up to keep us from leaving. "You two think this is doable?"

We both shrug our shoulders like sullen children.

"What choice do we have?" Bode mutters in a tone that doesn't sit well with me.

One thing about that death do us part bit rings true, because if we don't figure this mess out, we're liable to end up killing each other...

"You actually do have a choice." Chase motions toward us. "You can choose to go at this as a burdening chore... Or you can remember the blessing you two have been granted with this marriage, and seek God to restore it. You owe it to Him and your family to open your eyes back to the love He's blessed you with and stop taking it for granted."

I catch Bode giving me a sidelong glance. I'm sure he's feeling like a kid being scolded by the principal just as much as I do. Ashamed, we both nod our heads and mumble a thank-you and goodbye before finally shuffling out of the door and away from the tension we dumped on Chase.

*****

Pushing through the door back at home, I don't feel any better about our situation than I did when we left earlier. Bode grabs himself a glass of tea as I stand looking over the puzzle of these darn vows.

"Do you even know what *to have and to hold* means?"

"Yeah. It means you are to let me *have* my way with you." He waggles his eyebrows, but I'm not in the mood for his goofiness. It's odd how the old Bode keeps popping up every now and then, but seems to disappear just as bizarrely.

Rolling my eyes, I hold up the paper. "I seriously doubt there's anything sexual about these vows."

Bode pulls on his confused mask—head tilted with softly pinched eyebrows. "No? Well, I think it's implied."

Before I can mouth off, Bode drops to his knees, wraps his arms around my waist, and rests his cheek against my belly.

"There. I have a hold on you," he says. Yes, the old Bode is visiting and it's nearly my undoing. The old him is so easy to love and it's tempting to pretend for a while.

I try blinking it away, but the memory is steadfastly playing in a mimic of what my husband is doing before me now. It was another day he held me this way, and a very significant day it was.

The day Addison was born, Bode freaked out completely. We endured the thirty hours of labor, then childbirth, and he handled cutting the umbilical cord like a champ before everything hit him. As the nurse placed our baby on the little lit bed to clean him up, Bode turned to me and flipped a switch. Gone was the strong confident man and in his place was a terrified little boy.

"Mia!" His voice was all squeaky and high pitched, eyes crazy-wide. "Your body..." He pointed from me to the eight-pounds-two-ounces of perfection several times in a double-take manner. "You grew that!" Bode lightly touched my then squishy abdomen in what could only be described as reverent awe. "We made him and you grew him and your body..." He pointed to the baby exit on my body, gasping. At that moment the afterbirth decided to make its exit, completely freaking him out. I've never witnessed flushed cheeks pale so fast in all my life. He screamed out for help, thinking something was really wrong with me.

"She's fine, and you're fine. Don't pass out on us now, young man." The doctor spoke to my twenty-year-old husband sternly while he and the nurse fought a smile. They probably thought us two idiots were in over our heads with starting a family so young.

After they had me cleaned up, Bode draped himself over my stomach, resting his cheek near my protruding belly button.

"I'm a blessed man," he murmured, his tone sincere, melting my heart.

"Promise you'll never let go," I requested while running my fingers through his soft brown hair.

He held me a little tighter. "Promise."

The memory washes away as the traitorous tears pour once more. Pulling out of Bode's grasp, I flee to the bedroom to get away from the pain as fast as possible. I hear him call from behind me, but ignore him and the rest of the situation. I just don't have the strength to try to figure out how we messed up something so beautiful.

Chapter Fourteen

Mia

After our meeting with Chase, not much sleep found me that night to offer comfort. Misery and shame had no problem sticking by me though. Sometime before the sun rose the next morning, I began to pray. Well, it was more like begging. I've always been diligent in my prayer life. Always thanking God for my salvation and blessings. Steadfast in asking His protection and blessings for my children, but for some reason, I've started leaving out my marriage. Why? Have I finally thrown my figurative hands in the air and admitted defeat with Bode? In the last few years, he's gradually slipped away from me, and I don't know how to get him back.

With all of that whirling around my head, the prayer shifted from begging God to help me to begging Him to help Bode through whatever he's wrestling with. That's been a few frosty weeks ago now and sadly we've made no progress. Bode is right back to lethargically shuffling through his day until it lands him in his den. And I'm back to trying to find myself a life, which includes dodging Lee Sutton as best as I can. I've taken on more of the little devil's aerobics classes to avoid any uncomfortable situations with the man. I'm lonely and being near him spells trouble.

Every time I move today, I think of that little aerobic devil. Two nights ago, Andi sprung a surprise boot camp workout on us—hundreds of push-ups and a gazillion squats. Well, it felt like that many. Either way, it's all I can do to *squat* when nature calls and my chest feels like someone used it as a punching bag. It hurts to write in my little patient's chart right now. Even my jaw aches when I speak. If Andi ever mutters the words boot camp again, I will flee without any glances back.

"Okay, Miss Kallie, I need you to remind your momma to put this ointment on the rash twice a day and you'll be good as new in no time." Slowly limping back to this cutie pie, I hand the prescription to her momma and a sticker to Kallie before heading out to the nurses' station to wrap up the chart.

"Sophie's at the ER and they are asking for you," Renee says as she walks up to the counter. We exchange concerned looks.

Signing off on the chart, I hand it over and slide my cellphone in my pocket. "Okay. Let them know I'm on my way." I look down at the princess scrubs I'm donning today, knowing my little friend will love them.

The icy wind hits me with a jolt as I stiffly jog across the street, dodging traffic on the way. Shoving my hands into my pockets, I try to keep them warm so I don't send the poor baby into shock with my touch. I let myself in through the administration entrance and book it to the ER where I'm sure Sophie is already settled in the pediatric exam room this hospital offers, for which I'm grateful. She has to visit too often and I'm glad she has the comfort of a kid-friendly room.

"Where's my Pipsqueak?" I sing out while sliding the curtain open in a quick swoosh.

Confusion freezes me more than the cold outside, because I could almost swear to you someone has just sucker-punched me in the stomach. Pain ricochets through my body and vomit assaults my throat before I can manage to blink or breathe. I fight to swallow the vomit along with the acute agony as I take in Sophie's still body. Without examining her closer, I know. All color and movement from her little form has been completely wiped away. *No...*

I take all of my hurt along with all of my grief and shrug it off as I would a coat. I have no other choice because in this moment I have to focus on Amber and Dean. Two stunned statues, suspended in what can only be described as shocked disbelief, sitting on each side of their lifeless daughter's body. I worry they are no longer breathing themselves. A nurse and doctor stand back in helplessness, watching on, making it obvious Sophie just passed. Maybe I missed the very moment by mere seconds.

As I touch Amber's shoulder, she releases the most awful gut-wrenching scream I've ever heard in all my life, reality finally hitting her with vicious force. I take a seat by her, and this poor momma collapses into my side while the entire bed vibrates from her trembling. I demand my lungs to function as I hold her. *Breathe... In... Out...*

Reaching around her, I grasp Dean's hand in mine. He's still not moved, not even to hold my hand back, but I don't let go. He needs to be grounded some way, too.

The sounds of hospital life moving on around us are mere distant echoes, as I pray silently to God to give me strength for Amber and Dean's sake as they sit here trying to wrap their minds around the fact they just lost their only child.

I begin praying out loud. "Dear God, please take care of our little Pipsqueak. Please give her precious parents strength until they see her again. Please help us..."

My prayers continue in repetitions for longer than I can comprehend as the day moves on without our consent. My scrub top is soaked through at the shoulders from Amber's heartache and eventually Dean's too when he finally collapses. People move in and fill the small room, but I couldn't recall any of them if my life depended on it.

Time draws near to say goodbye, and so I allow myself some time with Sophie. Placing my fingers along the edge of her purple knit cap, I look over to Amber for permission. She nods her head. Choking back a sob, I gently free the cap and am not surprised it is still desperately clinging to this precious girl's warmth. Passing it to Amber, I watch as she clutches the cap tightly to her face. Another tremor breaks free, presenting a new round of heart-wrenching cries that echo painfully around the small exam room.

Turning away from Amber, I refocus on my farewell with Pipsqueak and shake my head in disbelief. It's just not right for her tiny body to be so still and quiet. What I would give to be able to indulge in the tinkering melody of her giggles one last time. I place several kisses along the peach fuzz on her head, greedily gathering as much of her remaining warmth on my lips as I can before it's lost forever. A deep inhale fills me with her sweet scent. This little fairy has always carried a sugary fragrance that reminds me of cotton candy.

I steal another whiff before whispering, "I love you, little Pip." I sniff the tears back as the hole in my chest cracks further open. "I'll miss you."

I realize this is not my moment to grieve, so I demand myself to stay strong for her parents. Reining in all the shock, heartache, and grief, I force myself to release her for the last time and focus back on Amber and Dean. I don't leave them for a second until little Sophie is collected, and Dean's parents take the grieving couple home.

Afterwards, I stumble back across the street to finish out the workday. I'm no use to patients, so what remains of the day is spent in my office with colleagues filtering in to check on me and to release their own tears of heartache. I'm not sure if I speak a word in that time. I vaguely notice Mrs. Janice bringing me some form of food and drink and then collecting it later when it goes untouched.

Later, I make it home but go straight over to Maury's and fall to pieces. I'm not sure how much later after that, I stumble home, ears pounding and eyes burning. Entering the kitchen, the familiar laundry basket and stack of mail greet me. My hands reach out in robotic movement with picking up the mail and basket while my brain registers none of it. Luckily, my feet know the way to my bedroom and head that way on their own accord. The sense of being suspended out of my body makes me dizzy. Everything feels so peculiar and nothing is right in my world.

Chapter Fifteen

Bode

The ballgame is scheduled to start in thirty minutes. Man, is it going to be epic. I've looked forward to this all week. I'm trading my stuffy suit for flannel pajama bottoms and my Tennessee hoodie when I hear the kitchen door close. Good. Mia's home early. Maybe she'll be in the mood to cook us something. I'm starving. I noticed she laid out some chicken, so the odds are looking to be in my favor. Since meeting with Chase, I've received a few hot meals, so that's progress.

I kick my suit over to the laundry pile and head out of my room just in time to see Mia disappearing in her room.

"Hey, you," I call out.

She says nothing, so maybe she didn't hear me. I shrug it off and head to the den to catch the pregame show.

The first quarter of the game comes and goes with Tennessee only scoring a field goal. I glance at the clock, wondering if Mia is going to come down and cook. Man, I'm hungry. I'm about to go ask her when my phone goes off.

Grabbing it from the end table, I see it's Maury. "Yo."

"Hey, boy. Your wife left her purse over here earlier and I just tripped over it."

"Ah. Hate that. Sorry."

"It's okay. She's not answering her phone. You want to come get it for her?"

"Sure thing. On my way."

I leave my phone in the kitchen as I pass through on my way out. I knock once before letting myself in. Maury is sitting in his dark living room, so I flip a light on. "It's me."

"So I see. Is Mia doing okay?" Maury asks, his voice sounding a little off.

"Sure. Sure. She's great." I scan the room and spot her purse spilled over by his couch.

"Really?"

"Yep."

Maury lets out a huff. "Come here," he says as he reaches out a hand.

Eyeing the door, I contemplate grabbing Mia's bag and making a run for it. I'm missing some of the game, but I reluctantly obey. Standing in front of the old man, I watch as he takes to tapping along my torso until his hands land on the strings of my hoodie. He uses them to pull me into a kneeling position in front of him. I'm a bit confused at what he's doing, but decide to placate him for a spell. He runs his fingers curiously over my face. I can feel my day's worth of stubble meet his palm. Out of nowhere, he lands a fiery blow to my blame face.

"Dang, Maury. What the heck?" I can't believe this old man just punched the daylights out of me. I scramble out of his reach, not sure if he'll try to land another one.

"Wake up, you fool, and see that woman!" The harsh tone and the scowl severely etching his face confuse me. Never has this man looked or acted this way toward me. More than my jaw is hurt.

Rubbing my scalding cheek, I mutter out, "What?"

"She lost a patient today... Little Sophie..."

My stomach drops like I just took a plunge with a steep rollercoaster. "No..." My legs give out, causing me to sit back on my butt in shock.

"Yes. Poor girl was over here crying her broken heart out. She spent most of her day at the hospital, trying to console Pipsqueak's parents. Afterwards, she came here instead of home to mourn. Now what does that tell you?" Anger sharpens his words as he spits them out.

And I don't blame him one bit, for that's exactly what I feel in the moment. Ashamed for not being the man my wife could lean on, I say nothing. I can't. I hate myself. I grab the purse, rush back home, and head straight to Mia.

Easing into the bedroom, I find her passed out on top of the covers still wearing her scrubs. My chest burns when I notice the princess crowns on her top. Sophie would have loved it. I lightly brush my fingers over her puffy closed eyes. Red swollen blotches along her face still shine with tears. I notice the

Ambien bottle resting on the nightstand and know it's bad. Really bad. Mia only takes them in dire situations. Her phone, silently flashing beside the bottle, draws my attention. I pick it up and almost throw it against the wall when I see who the message is from.

Lee – *Renee told me about Pipsqueak. Call me if you need me.*

Pure fury slams into me as I text him back. *I'm good. Got my husband. Thanks.*

I don't stop until I've deleted the text feed, blocked the jerk's number, and erased his contact from her phone.

I've failed my wife and some guy she barely knows, who has no right to know her for that matter, comes to her comfort rescue before me. My chest begins to burn in the same manner as my throbbing cheek. Well, I'm not having it. Mia is mine to take care of. I pledged to have and to hold her.

I pull the covers back, settle them over her, and climb in the bed beside my wife and do the only thing I can do—I hold her. The game forgotten. Supper forgotten. Only the fact that I need to remember my wife matters. Undeserved comfort settles me as I feel her body relax into mine. I bury my face in her soft hair and breathe in her scent as I beg God to forgive me.

*****

A few days have passed with Mia stumbling through her day on autopilot. I'm very familiar with that mode. She took Friday off and now it's Sunday and she's not doing much better. I try talking to her, but she just mutters that she's fine and retreats away from me. She's allowing me back in our room where I hold her each night, so I feel good about that. Like I'm doing my part as a husband.

I'm loading the few cups in the dishwasher when Neena barges in as always.

"Hey, twerp."

She squints at me. "What happened to your face?"

I rub my palm over the fat bruise marking my cheek. It's still pretty tender. That little man has one heck of a right hook. "Maury punched me."

"Good. Someone needs to knock some sense into you."

"What are you talking about?" My brows pinch together and I try kneading them back apart. I'm not in the mood for her sass.

"Don't give me your stupid confused look." Neena braces her hands on her hips, and that's when I notice she's dressed oddly. Never does my sister-in-law wear anything but worn denim and white cotton with beat-up cowgirl boots, but today she is sporting a long black dress with her boots. "Where's your wife?"

"I don't know. I went for a run, and she was gone when I got back." I scratch the side of my neck and look around like she might suddenly appear.

"She and I have been at Sophie's funeral. She's now with the family back at their house." Neena crosses her arms and levels me with a glare. "You want to explain to me why you were not there for your wife?"

"I... I didn't know the funeral was today. I—"

Neena picks up the newspaper and slaps it against my chest before I can continue stuttering. The same paper I noticed Mia reading with her coffee this morning. I unfold it and see the entire front page is dedicated to Sophie.

"There's no excuse. You're not the guy who stole my sister's heart. What did you do with him? Is he buried in the backyard? If so, go dig him up or so help me, I'm going to dig a six-foot-deep hole for this excuse of a man you've become." Neena storms out as fast as she entered, leaving me with my stomach churning. That one doesn't mince words.

I glance over the article with the byline N.L. Cameron. Of course, Neena wrote it. And she's written a piece that captures the free-spirited soul of that little girl and how she impacted people around her. Mia is mentioned in a quote by the family. *Mia Calder was more than Sophie's pediatrician. She was our little fairy's angel.* A picture of Mia with Sophie perched on her back is included along with several other photos. Both are laughing while holding dripping ice cream cones in the shot.

I'm rereading the article for the third time when a shadow of my wife drifts through the door. Her black dress hangs loosely on her frame, showing off her recent weight loss. Uneasiness clamps ahold of my throat for not noticing until now. She doesn't look like the healthy vibrant woman who normally bounces around this place. Instead, she's a puny washed-out version of herself and it scares me. I offer her my arms, but she bypasses me.

Before she gets completely away from me, I reach out and smooth my fingertips down her back. She still doesn't stop or even react in any way to my touch, just keeps drifting away. "I wanted to go with you, Mia. All you had to do was let me know when."

She pauses at the base of the stairs, looking drained with swollen red eyes. "Why? They're just snot-nosed brats that puke on me."

My insensitive words from weeks ago repeat from her lips, causing me to flinch. I can only imagine how much hurt I inflicted on her when I delivered them in anger. My poor Mia. Her heart of gold is bruised and battered, and I'm just now realizing I've been the one swinging the bat when I should be the one protecting her.

Ashamed, I follow her cold path upstairs to apologize only to find the door locked. My legs give out, planting me against the locked door. I'm losing my wife. I've not realized the severity of it until this very moment.

We made vows to love each other. More vows to stay. She vowed to always be mine, but how can I expect that of her when I'm not giving myself to her? I've taken so much for granted. Neena's right. I don't know what happened to the man Mia married. I've lost him. And honestly, I can't say I'll ever find him in the exact shape I left him in, but I do know it's time to be the man I promised Mia I would be.

Chapter Sixteen

Mia

Time has moved forward somberly and I wish I could say things are better, but they're not. My body aches all the time. It feels like I'm coming down with a cold, but I know the aches are from losing a special part of me. I pep talk myself each day with *she's not hurting anymore, she's with God now, I'll see her again one day.* No matter, the pain won't alleviate. I know only time will be able to do that and a mere few weeks are nowhere near enough.

No one says anything to me at work. Really, what can they say? I see it all over the faces of the wiser, older doctors. The 'I told you so' looks mingle with pity. They are always schooling me about maintaining a safe distance from my patients, but that's not me. Even though I'm devastated, I would do nothing differently. I love Sophie as well as my other patients, and so I keep doing my job with my whole heart.

Earlier this morning, my eyes landed on the abandoned marriage vows paper that was halfway hidden under a stack of shirts on our dresser. Addison and Kaisley will be home for spring break before we know it, and we haven't even gotten past the first part. Well, to be honest, I think we can place a check by *to have and to hold*. Bode has done nothing but that since Sophie's passing. It felt awkward at first, like an old sweater that didn't fit just right anymore, but it didn't take long for me to settle back into his embrace.

I moved to the next part on the list, *for better or for worse*. I feel like we've already lived out the beauty of *better*. The first decade or so of our marriage was the definition of beauty. Bode and I were a team, and we reaped the benefits of a loving marriage with the birth of our children. Now it seems we've headed down a slippery slope of *worse* in the past several months.

As I stood in the bedroom this morning, Chase's words revisited me. He was relieved when we assured him no major crime had been committed against our marriage vows, but the nagging question plagued me as I stood there regarding the significant piece of paper—why was our relationship treading through such rocky terrain of *for worse*? No answer came to me, so I gave up and left the paper on Bode's nightstand, hoping he would take the initiative to figure it out.

I'm dragging by the time I park the car in the garage and it's all my tired body can do to make it inside the house. The day was buzzing with too many flu cases. The crud season has hit hard this year. With my mind elsewhere while opening the door, I nearly trip over Bode's dress shoes. Before I can get too aggravated, curiosity overtakes me. A trail of abandoned dress clothes—a tie, shirt, coat, pants, and socks—lead a path straight to a dark den. My first thoughts are someone is hoping to get lucky and that someone is going to be disappointed. I flip a lamp on at the entrance to the silent den and am surprised to find Bode sitting in his chair in only boxers and an undershirt, cradling his head in his hands.

I move over and stand in front of him. "Bode, are you okay?"

"Forgot my glasses at home... Paying the price," he whispers in a gravelly voice. It must be hurting pretty bad, because the TV is still off.

"Have you taken anything?"

"No."

I hurry into the kitchen to grab extra-strength headache medicine and a can of soda from the fridge, hoping the caffeine will help kickstart the medicine. "Here," I say, handing over the goods.

He slowly lifts his head and squints at the pills in his palm before downing them with most of the soda before setting the can down. He looks so miserable that I have an overwhelming need to comfort him as he has done for me lately. Kicking off my shoes and shrugging off my lab coat, I work the scrub top over my head and toss it to the floor. Down to the thermal shirt I was wearing underneath and my pants, I step closer, still unsure. Why am I even struggling with the need to comfort him? He is my husband, for crying out loud.

Those marriage vows go both ways, so I settle on his lap, tangle my fingers in his hair, and slowly massage along his scalp. He releases a low moan as I work along in circles. His curls are so soft as they glide through my fingers and the subtle scent of his cologne draws me closer, feeling like I'm visiting a cozy spot I've stayed away from for far too long.

We keep quiet with me doing this for a good long while before I speak. "Why is there a trail of clothing leading to the den?"

"It led you to me," he whispers, letting me know he's still hurting, but not enough to stop him from teasing a little bit. Even though it's a tease, his words form a lump in my throat.

"Seriously," I squeak out.

He releases a pensive sigh. "It felt like they were choking me. *Everything* is choking me anymore," he whispers harshly.

My fingers still. I try to stand up, not wanting to crowd him, but he tightens his grip on me and reclines his chair all the way back. His actions make it clear I'm to stay put, and also calm my fear that I am a part of what is choking him. I snuggle close and smile against the side of his neck. This I've missed. The holding each other. The simple closeness. I settle more into his lap and go back to massaging his scalp for another long stretch of time while I think over what he said.

Eventually, I whisper, "Bode, whatever is choking you, I'll support you in getting rid of it." And I'm serious about it too. Whatever he needs, but at the moment it seems all he needs is for me to hold him as he begins to lightly snore.

*****

My gym bag is packed for the first time since losing Sophie, and so after I wrap up with a patient who swallowed a handful of change, my intention is to go work out. Two nickels, a dime, and three pennies to be exact. I told his grandma, who has custody of him, that our little Stephen will be great in the money saving department one day. I sent them in care of Dr. Rogers over to the emergency room for x-rays. He gladly took the case from me since I'm not quite ready to step a foot in the ER yet. It's too soon.

I'm relieved not to run into Lee at the gym. Distance from him has made me examine the crush I was forming. Perspective firmly in place, I won't be allowing him in arms-reach again. Having the man befriend me was flattering and dangerous, so I will keep away. My phone alerts me of a new text message as I finish up. It's Dr. Rogers letting me know Stephen is fine and is being sent home to wait on his *deposit* to clear.

Tired and sweaty, I arrive home and am surprised to find Bode sitting at the kitchen island with Italian take-out waiting for me. My mouth waters at the heavenly scent of garlic and tomato sauce. I've not had an appetite as of late, but I think the exercise has sent it back with a vengeance.

Bode pulls the stool out and brushes my cheek with a soft kiss. "Hey, you."

"Hi."

"Chicken parmesan for my lady."

"Thanks." I can't help but give him a looking over to be sure this is my husband and not some stranger. I regard the loose tie and untucked dress shirt. The man should be on a GQ cover with his messy curls and the dark stubble on his angular jawline. My mouth waters more for something else entirely now. He pulls his glasses off and I almost beg him to put them back on. Bode Calder can so pull off sexy in those frames.

He speaks, snapping me out of my ogling. "I've already dropped Maury off a plate, too." He didn't have to tell me this for me to know. If there's one thing Bode doesn't drop the ball on that's taking care of Maury.

"Thanks," I say again, knowing I don't give my husband nearly enough credit. Probably because I'm too focused on the scarce flaws to appreciate all the good this man is.

Bode entwines our hands and leads us in prayer. This is something else he always does and I don't appreciate enough. I do pick up on a faint nervousness in his voice and wonder why it's there. Instead of spending time deciphering it, I dig into the first meal that's registered on my radar in weeks and enjoy the savory goodness of the chicken and creamy garlic potatoes.

As we eat, I notice Bode stealing glances of me. He seems to be gauging my mood and this makes me uneasy. I'm sure something is up when he scarfs down his food and patiently waits for me to finish mine. Odd. Very odd. He should be bee-lining it to the den by now. My appetite disappears as he slides the paper with our marriage vows printed on it beside my plate.

Bode taps the paper, summoning my attention. "Can we talk about this?"

I look down and see he has bypassed *for better or for worse* and is pointing at *for richer or poorer*. I put the fork down, trying to brace for whatever he's about to deliver. "Sure. I guess."

He shifts on his stool beside me and clears his throat. "Mia..." His voice pinches off.

Oh sugar! The food I managed to eat starts churning in my stomach as I try to figure out what type of bomb he's about to drop. I can feel it. This is where my husband reveals a dark secret I had no clue was coming. A million scenarios race through my head, knowing we will be refocusing on the *for worse*.

I spent our entire life's savings on a get rich quick scheme. And it went belly-up.

I have a gambling problem with a large debt. Now loan sharks are after me to pay up.

I'm addicted to online shopping. The shed out back holds our life savings in the form of useless junk.

Clearly, I've been watching way too much TV lately.

Shaking those absurd notions away, I brace myself for whatever blow he's about to deliver. "Just spit it out already," I say through gritted teeth.

Tense seconds pass with only the sluggish tick of the old-fashioned grandfather clock making a peep down the hall. Pinching the bridge of my nose, I whisper a silent prayer, asking God to help us get on the other side of this life rut once and for all before it kills us.

Taking a deep breath, Bode admits, "I hate my job." He scrubs his hands over his face.

I have to refrain from laughing in relief. I know from the looks of him, Bode wouldn't take too kindly to that right now. He's being completely serious.

"I have to admit, I had no clue," I confess, reaching over and rubbing his shoulder. Boy is he tense.

Bode was always such an outdoorsy guy, and I was surprised when he chose a career in computers. He did so well at it that everyone decided it must have been his true calling. From his expression, I'm guessing we were all wrong.

Bode drops his hands and looks over at me in pure misery. "I want to make a career change."

"Go for it. Do whatever will make you happy." He's been telling me every so often lately how unhappy he is. Truly, I want him happy. If a career change fixes whatever is broke in my husband, I'm all for it.

Skepticism flickers across his face as he purses those full lips together. My eyes drift and hold on that plump bottom lip, thicker than his top, complementing his mouth in a delicious heart shape. Good grief. Now I sound like I've been reading one too many romance novels...

"You're really okay with this?" His apprehensive tone draws my eyes back to his own velvety chocolate ones.

With great effort, I blink my lusty haze away and refocus on the seriousness of our conversation. "Yes, but, Bode, you are going to have to do it without me. I'll support you, but I can't take on the task of figuring this out for you."

His brows pinch. "What are you talking—"

"I have to handle everything. Work, bills, car maintenance, housework, children, family... I could go on and on. You name it and I have to do it in this marriage."

"I didn't ask you to do it for me. I'm not a child, Mia!" He jerks to his feet, sending the stool toppling over with a loud bang.

I mimic him, only my stool stays upright. "Then stop acting like one. I have to tend to you like a child and I'm sick of it!" I motion around the room like it holds the entire fault of our troubled relationship. "This has to change. I don't want to endure the weight of everything all on my own anymore. It's exhausting. If things don't change, then I can't see how this is going to work."

"What do you mean?" He towers over me, waiting for me to say it.

I don't know why I even went there. Maybe I'm hoping to rile him up enough he'll get off his figurative butt and figure out what he really wants. I can't fix his happiness. It shouldn't be my weight to bear.

I mutter, "Divorce," but wish I could suck it back in.

"Maybe that's what we should do!" he yells, face flushed and hands thrown in the air.

"What?" I yell back. His words sucker punch me, causing me legs to almost buckle. I threw those words at him carelessly, not meaning them one bit. I can only hope he didn't either.

He stalks forward, backing me up until I'm pinned between him and the refrigerator. "What's with you anymore? You infuriate me." He growls close to my ear, the throaty sound sending a zing through me.

Heart pounding, breath panting, my body presses against his to suggest another way to spend the evening. Even though Bode sounds livid, his body is responding to mine in a downright friendly manner. This has been the longest dry spell our marriage has ever endured. I have the overwhelming desire to slap him and then make out like lovesick teens.

Bode's body presses into me as he takes a deep breath, but he's still not close enough, so I wrap my arms around his neck to bring him closer. He pulls back and gazes down at me, eyes blazing, but after a few beats they cool to stone.

"What is wrong with us?" Bode sounds desperate, so I'm about to suggest we go work the wrongs out in the bedroom, but he shakes his head as if sensing my thoughts. On a hoarse grumble, he disentangles our bodies and storms off.

What just happened?

Shaken and confused, I slide to the floor and take several stuttered breaths until they begin to smooth out.

One minute, we're making progress in reconciliation, and then the next, it feels we've taken not just a step backwards, but an entire leap. Hopeful to defeated. This back and forth... I just don't know if this trouble is worth it.

Chapter Seventeen

Bode

All I wanted was for my wife to say she had my back. That she'll support my decision to quit my job. I don't expect her to type my flipping letter of resignation. Nor do I expect her to search out a new job for me. All I wanted was her blessing, and I was relieved she gave it until she just had to go there—slicing me with her sharp tongue.

She's always clear on how worthless I am. I want to scream to the top of my lungs that I know! I feel trapped by life lately. I wanted to tell her that the career change is me trying to push the boulder off before I suffocate. It's either that or I'm ready to give up.

Mia nearly killed me on the spot when she muttered the word *divorce* two weeks ago. I guess I was stupid thinking we were getting our marriage on track. What an idiot I am. I don't want to live without her, but I don't know how to keep her. We're back to the silent game, and it's looking like no end in sight. I've stayed in our bed, but keep to my side while having to fight every second to refrain from touching her. What a mess...

All I do know is I have to work on myself some and I guess I have to do it alone. And that's exactly what I'm doing after work today. I finally made a monumental phone call last week. Never did I imagine it would set so many things in motion so rapidly. I'm the kind of guy who likes to ease into things, but I guess it's time to turn a new leaf. I might as well or it looks like that stubborn leaf is gonna do it without me.

With a combination of excitement and trepidation, I park in front of the gate that no longer holds the sign that said my dream was for sale. Out the corner of my eye, I catch Linda's sedan pulling up beside me. Nerves roll through me like a pile of tumbling rocks. Mia told me to handle it and so I am, but I'm pretty sure she didn't mean for me to handle it in such an extreme way.

Well... Serves her right...
My wife is going to kill me...
Tough... Too late...

Two days ago I sat down with the board and requested an early retirement, cashing out my stock in the company as well. At forty-two years old, I went from a man with a fat retirement to being close to penniless.

Mia is absolutely going to kill me...

Trying not to totally freak out, I climb out of the confines of the truck cab. The crisp breeze does very little to help calm me as it brushes against my sweaty face. My entire body feels clammy all of a sudden. Beckoning my unsteady legs to move forward to greet

Linda, I know it's too late to turn back now. Nope. No hightailing it from this decision. The papers were already signed yesterday, making me the rightful owner of Tennessee Valley Outdoor Sports Lodge, or just the Lodge for short.

What in the heck was I thinking?

Mia is either going to divorce me or kill me...

My crazy thoughts are about to get the best of me, so I'm hoping for the latter. I'm scared stupid all of a sudden. What over-forty-year-old-man does this?

"Bode!" Linda's cheerful voice helps to silence my freak-out momentarily.

I offer Linda a hug once we reach the gate while her lawyer unlocks it. I take a step back to appreciate this epic moment in my crazy life. It feels beyond just a padlock being freed. That act brings my freedom along with it.

"Bode," Linda says again, sounding more like a question this time.

Swallowing hard, I mutter, "I can't believe I've done it." Blinking a few times until my eyes focus, I scan the property. "I think I'm gonna be sick."

Linda and her lawyer laugh, but I'm being serious. My throat burns with the acid clawing up it.

My wife is going to kill me...

Or divorce me...

Or maybe both...

Linda shoves some papers and a hefty key ring in my shaking hands. "Here's all the keys you'll need. Lodge, cabins, buildings, maintenance truck, transport bus..."

She names a few more keys, but the rush of the river gliding by steals my attention. I focus on the adventure and try wiping away the business of the weighty decision I just made on a frantic whim without my wife's input.

She told me to...

Her fault...

She's still going to kill me...

"Fred is meeting you here tomorrow. He knows this place like the back of his hand."

I nod with a slight portion of relief. "Okay. I look forward to seeing him again. It's been too long."

Fred is the Lodge superintendent and longtime river rat extraordinaire. I've been on a few adventures with the guy over the years. He can't be more than ten or fifteen years my senior, but he brings lots of inside knowledge along with the support staff already in place. They all seem pleased to be back in a job. Linda asked me to keep them on as a favor, but it's clearly the other way around. They are doing *me* a great favor.

Studying the six keys marked as cabins, I'm relieved a little in knowing I have a place to live if Mia kicks me out.

"Come on. Let's go have a seat on the porch for a bit." Linda weaves her arm through mine, leading me to the rocking chairs with the muted lawyer following. I guess his word count was met yesterday with him guiding me through the paperwork.

"You remember about five years ago, Dave almost had you talked into taking over this place?" She motions in front of her.

"Yeah. Me and Addison were practically living out here every chance we could get." Chuckling, I nod my head toward the dark body of water easing along in front of us. "Dave dared us to jump in the river. It was the dead of winter with several inches of snow on the ground. Told us he'd sign the place over for half its value if we'd do it."

"Sounds like Dave," the muted lawyer finally speaks. I don't remember his name and don't care enough to ask.

"Yeah, well, Addison was all gung-ho. Before I realized it, my boy was running off to take the plunge. I had to tackle him and put him in a fireman's hold across my shoulder to stop him. Mia would have whipped us both." We all share a laugh. "Dave and his dares." I shake my head.

"Well, Dave had faith that you'd someday get around to taking him up on his dare." Linda hands me an envelope.

Unfolding the piece of paper from inside, I silently read the handwritten note.

Bode,

It's about darn time you came to your senses. This place is as much a part of you as it is me. I knew it the moment I met your adventurous be:*ind at no more than ten years of age. You showed up here most weekends with your old man, acting like you owned that river or whatever trail you took to at the time.*

I bought this lodge from some old geezer who was probably around the age I am now. Well, I guess I just called myself old... I was fresh out of my teenage years and just couldn't pass this place... no, this <u>adventure</u> up. And do you know what that owner made me do before he'd sign it over? Made me take a swim in the river as bare as the day I was born. And in January no less!

So here's hoping for your sake, you decide to finally buy this place from me in a warm month. Tradition is tradition and I can't give you my blessing until you take the plunge! So go dip your skinny in the river.

There's no way around it, so stop trying to think of one. Get on with it, so you can finally get on with your rightful calling. I know you can do it!

Dave

Refolding the letter, I have to clear my throat several times, but my voice still comes out all hoarse. "You know about this?" I lift the letter.

"Yep." Linda rises from her chair. "You're a real cutie and I sure do hate to miss the show, but I think it's best we give you some privacy."

"Today? I have to do it today?" The tingle of goose bumps creep up my neck from a mix of the cold and outright fear. I flip up the collar of my dress coat to ward it off.

"Yes. Today."

"How are you going to know I completed the dare?" I challenge.

Linda pauses at the car door. "I have faith in you. And so did Dave. He was adamant that this place needed to be yours one day."

"The extremely reduced price for which you acquired this business is proof." The lawyer says this like it may taste a little unpleasant on his tongue. It must have lessened his commission.

Shrugging off his comment, I focus back on Linda. "You sure about this?"

"Absolutely. I have no desire to be here without my Dave, and we both knew one day you'd finally come around. I sure am glad you finally did." She pats my cheek before climbing in her car and deserting me.

After dropping off the contents of my pockets and the other stuff Linda handed over in the truck, I hesitantly move over to the riverbank. My breaths billow out in faint clouds and I can feel the tip of my nose ice over. Crouching down, I test the water with my fingers and gauge the temperature at being in the glacial range. *Man...*

I glance around to be sure I'm completely abandoned. Not even a bird can be found out in this frigid weather. Common sense taps me on the shoulder. *No one will know if you bail on the dare...*

It's tempting and I almost listen, but I'll be darned if I don't feel obligated to Dave to do this ridiculous dare. I got this place for a steal all because he and his wife had enough faith that I could handle it. I walk the bank for a stretch, hunting down a better spot. Not liking what I find, I retrace my steps back to the original spot. Observing the current, I know it's less strong here with the slight bend and more than likely I can make it back out before turning completely into a popsicle.

"Enough hem hawing around. I'm man enough!" I shout to myself and it echoes off the mountains on the other side of the river.

Some frantic need takes over and adrenaline starts courses through me as I wrench off my tie. The binding thing dangles in my hand as I study it. It near about became my noose. With a great deal of satisfaction, I chunk it into the water and watch the current carry it away.

"I'm free..." The tie disappears and makes me realize I no longer am trapped in a career I hate, in a designer uniform that was choking the life out of me. A wild man takes over as I toe off my shiny leather shoes. One by one, they send out a satisfying *kerplunk* before the splash. Then the dress coat and pants get hurled in. This maddening fight for freedom keeps on until the river claims every piece of clothing and I'm completely naked.

Sucking in a deep breath, I take the leap and allow the icy depths to claim me as well. The water hits me like shards of razor-sharp ice, prickling all over my exposed skin. As quick as I can climb my frozen body back out, I meet the dry bank. It only takes seconds, but it feels like years wash away with the frigid current.

"WOOHOO!" I shout at the top of my lungs, dancing around. "YEAH!" My voice roars in victory as I fist pump. *I did it! I really did it!*

Mid-dance, reality slams into me along with an arctic blast of wind. My body convulses in shivers as I look around for my clothes.

"You idiot!" I can't believe I did that with my clothes. "Stupid! Stupid! Stupid!" I chant all the way back to the truck, hopping in and cranking the heat to full blast before icicles can form on my manhood. My newly-turned leaf is now shaking uncontrollably. Everything stings and tingles from the bite of the cold and icy river water. Looking around, I realize today was a bad day to forget my wool coat at home. "What was I thinking?" I stammer out through chattering teeth. I have obviously lost my flipping mind. I hope like mad I don't get pulled over or get in a wreck or something on the way home.

I procrastinate on leaving until the combination of my adrenaline overworking and the truck heater on blazing hot causes me to start sweating. This can't be good for my body in general...

Pulling out of the lot, I silently pray that Mia decided to go to the gym today.

Please don't be home. Please don't be home...

Chapter Eighteen

Mia

Bode and I do something we very rarely do—we arrive home at the exact same time. He pulls into his right side of the garage before I claim my side on the left. Oddly, it's the same arrangement we have in bed as well. By the time I've gathered my purse along with a couple of bags of groceries from the trunk, I realize Bode still hasn't gotten out of the truck. I stand by the car, peering in his direction. He must notice, because he powers down the darkly tinted window just enough to show me his cellphone and shoos me with his other hand before powering the window back up. His silhouette looks all scrunched down... Odd...

"Okay..." I mumble to myself, heading to the door. My nose catches a pungent whiff of the garbage, which does nothing but tick me off even more. I'm about to lower my stuff on the steps to take care of it when I hear Bode shout.

"Just leave it. I'll get it."

I look over and find his window sliding back up again. Shrugging his weirdness off, I leave the stink where it is and mutter, "Whatever." I hear the whirl of the garage door lowering as I head inside. I decide not to try to figure out exactly how the garbage is going to get on the other side of it.

After stowing the few groceries away, I realize I've left my cellphone out in the car, so I head back out to retrieve it. Opening the door, I'm greeted by a sight that leaves me stunned in my tracks. Blinking several times, I take another look to be sure I'm seeing right. Yep. There's no mistaking it.

"Have you lost your ever-loving mind?" I screech.

My *very naked* husband freezes for a split second before slamming his truck door shut and scoots in the house in a mad dash. Cellphone forgotten, I follow in his naked wake and notice his hair is wet.

"Where are your clothes? Have you gone mad? Why's your hair wet?" The questions spill out of me in a rapid-fire procession.

He's heading out of Dodge, but backtracks to where I'm stunned into stone by the kitchen island.

"I've got a new job," he blurts out a bit frantically, only confusing me more.

"What? As a stripper?" I motion toward his naked bronzed form, wondering how that rich skin tone never fades from him. He would probably make a killing in that profession, but that's beside the point.

He throws his hands in the air. "No!"

"Then please say something that makes some sense! I'm about to completely freak out!"

Bode is practically panting, and I can't help but admire the movement it causes along his broad chest.

He sits at the kitchen table and motions for me to do the same, acting like it's completely normal for him to be buck naked. The man is driving me to distraction. With great effort, my eyes ease up to try focusing on his, but that sucker won't meet my gaze. Crossing my arms, I wait. Yet he still says nothing.

"Why are you naked, Bode?" My words are slow with me refraining from losing my cool.

"I'm getting to that, okay?" He rubs the back of his neck. His nervousness is making me nervous.

I motion my hand out in a flick to encourage him to get on with it. The suspense is killing me.

"Before you get mad, just remember you're the one who told me to handle this all on my own." He has enough nerve to jab his finger in my direction along with a challenging glare. He's the one who arrived home naked of all things and has the audacity to be placing the blame on *me*? Before I can unstick my mouth to point this out, he plows on.

"I resigned..." This is how he begins and continues on for the next hour until everything is explained—leaving behind his career, cashing out his retirement, buying the Tennessee Valley Outdoor Sports Lodge. At one point, he streaked back out to his truck to grab the paperwork confirming his actions as well as the letter from Dave that explained why my husband came home naked. Well, it sort of explained it.

We sit in silence as he awaits my reaction to all of this unexpected news. The only noticeable sound for a long stretch is produced by his fingers tapping a nervous tune on the tabletop.

After a while, I say the only thing stuck in my head. "Dave didn't say anything in that letter about you drowning your suit." I'm having a hard time keeping the amusement out of my voice. I mean, really. Now that the shock has worn off, it's pretty hilarious. Never in my wildest could I have thought up this bizarre episode—Bode arriving home naked. Completely naked. Nope. No part of my imagination is that gifted.

Bode releases a weak chuckle. "Yeah. That stupidity is all on me. I just… It just felt so freeing."

"Oh, I bet." My eyes scan over his body that is still *freely* on display.

He scoots his chair back from the table boldly to allow me a full view. *Well…*

The smoldering stare retreats away after a few heated moments. "Mia… There's something else."

His words brush the lust away. I brace myself. "What?"

"We need to sell the house and downsize."

"Oh…" I'm actually impressed that he has put this much thought into it.

"It's too much house anyway, and the accountant said we'd be able to make ends meet with a smaller mortgage."

"Oh…"

"I won't be making the money I used to make at the company."

"Okay."

His signature confused look arrives as he leans back in the chair. "Is that it? You're okay with this?"

I shrug my shoulder. "Yes."

"You're not mad?"

I shake my head.

He doesn't seem to buy it as his brows knit together. "You don't want to kill me?"

I shake my head again. There are other more productive things I'd like to do to him, but I don't voice them.

A long sigh escapes him and his brows retreat back to their normal positions.

Glancing at the clock, I notice we only have an hour before church. "How about you go find yourself some clothes while I cook up a quick supper?"

"Yeah? Okay…" He stands up and turns to leave the kitchen.

"Bode," I say while admiring the ample roundness of his firm backside.

"Yeah?" He glances over his shoulder.

"I'm proud of you."

A thankful smile stretches grandly across his handsome face. With a quick head nod, his naked form disappears from the kitchen. I mourn this loss of the lovely sight for a few beats before getting to work on supper. To be honest, I'm surprised at how calm I'm handling these changes. I'm wondering if the shock of his nakedness helped…

*****

After a quick meal of sautéed chicken and vegetables, Bode and I head to church as we do most every Wednesday night. We are in the midst of a Bible study on John the Baptist, my bookmark holding the spot for the continuance tonight.

Entering the sanctuary that's dressed in rich royal-blue carpeting and oak pews, I try to leave all the day's stresses at the door. Settling in a pew near the middle, I catch my mind wandering even before the class begins. I glance at Bode, who is now dressed in dark-washed jeans, a T-shirt with a thermal shirt on top, a scarf, wool coat, and thick-soled boots. He now looks very *warm*. And *cozy*. And *inviting*. Even with all those layers, the man is still distracting.

Neena scoots in beside me and launches into telling me about a writing assignment our dad is helping secure for her. She's very vague on the details, but I'm too distracted to ask for more.

After prayer requests and prayer, Chase instructs us to turn to the first chapter of Mark where he reads verses four and five.

"And so John the Baptist appeared in the wilderness, preaching a baptism of repentance for the forgiveness of sins. The whole Judean countryside and all the people of Jerusalem went out to him. Confessing their sins, they were baptized by him in the Jordan River."

Pausing to take off his reading glasses, Chase begins, "How many of you here tonight hunger for God?" Hands go up everywhere along with quiet amens as he scans the crowd. "Could you imagine being in the midst of those people in Jerusalem, with their hunger so strong, they were showing their faith boldly by being baptized in the Jordan River? There was an urgency to get their lives right. Today we have these modernized baptismal pools." He motions behind him, drawing all eyes to our fancy baptismal pool that is discreetly tucked behind a half-wall. "Things are easier for us than back then. We don't have to admit our faith in God with worries of losing our lives for it. We don't have to go out of our way to demonstrate our inward change with an outer show of being baptized." People amen. Chase takes the break for a sip of water.

Pacing the low stage, he continues. "It's so easy to make a commitment to God. And we even have *heated* pools *indoors* to be baptized in nowadays. Yet we still drag our feet and make it more complicated than it really is." He gestures toward the door. "How many of you would be willing to take a plunge in those icy depths of the Tennessee River down the road this evening to show your commitment to Christ?"

A snicker wiggles loose and slips out of my lips before I can stop it. Neena nudges me with her elbow. I hear Bode clear the laughter from his voice with a cough, but I don't look at him because I'll completely lose it.

"None is what I would be willing to guess. You'd just about have to be out of your mind to willingly agree to that tonight." People amen.

A loud snort sputters from Bode, causing Chase to stop speaking. Heads turn in our direction, trying to figure out the commotion. I shake my head and roll my eyes.

"You two knock it off," Neena whispers harshly, clearly annoyed. This coming from my little sister sounds too silly and causes me to snicker some more.

Our confused pastor goes on to read verses six through eight, but my eyes are watering too badly to read along and my stomach actually aches from trying to hold in my laugh.

Of all nights for such a comment...

Images of a naked Bode jumping in that river overtake my mind. Giving up, I let loose a fit of giggles with Bode joining in. Other tones of laughter chime in, which I think is one of those domino effects. There's just no stopping it once it's started. Next thing I know, the sanctuary erupts in laughter. Even Chase is grinning uncontrollably while shaking his head at us. His message is clear as well—you're funny, but you need to knock it off.

It's a brief disturbance, with everyone settling down fairly quickly—except for me and my goofy husband. After a stern look from a few elders, we decide it's best to go ahead and slide out the back early so the others can actually listen.

Cranking the car, Bode huffs. "Did you see the looks we were getting from them old folks? They acted like we were naked or something."

A very unattractive snort of laughter emerges from me at my husband's lame joke. I tamp it down and add, "The bare truth of the matter is you clearly stripped away the importance of the lesson tonight with your silliness."

He barks out in a deep chuckle. "Bare and stripped—you win."

"Win what?"

"Being the cheesiest."

Laughing all the way home, I know my stomach will be sore from it tomorrow, but I'll welcome the reminder that I got to witness my husband coming back to life.

Chapter Nineteen

Bode

Love is supposed to be in the air around this time of the year, but there's none to be had around the Calder household. Neena talked Mia into going on an all-girls spa weekend retreat thing, leaving me alone with not even a heart-shaped box of chocolates. Of course, a snarky fuss broke out between us when I pointed that out. My wife threw it up in my face that we hadn't celebrated Valentine's Day in the last two years and she refused to sit around in the den with me one more time.

So I've spent most of my time sitting in this blame den alone ever since Mia stormed out yesterday. While channel surfing, I come upon a marathon showing of Lee Sutton's bike-build show, and for some irrational reason I can't stop watching it.

Three hours in of Lee strutting around like he's God's gift to the world, I've come up with a half-dozen ways to get some payback on that shmuck.

Graffiti his garage.

Toilet paper his garage.

Egg his garage.

Slash his tires.

Dump grease on his bike.

Hack his website and run a surprisingly low-priced sale.

Yes, I could pull off every last one of these dumb ideas, but I won't. I'm mad at him, jealous of him, but I won't act on any of it. There's some satisfaction in just imagining it though.

Shutting the TV off, I wander into the kitchen for a bowl of cereal. I pull a bowl down from the cabinet, place it on the counter and then grab the box of cereal from the pantry and milk from the fridge. Once I have the bowl filled past the point of full, I hunch over it and dig in while flipping through the newspaper. Halfway through inhaling the cereal and scanning the sales papers, my eyes catch on a neon-green flyer advertising a new bike shop in town.

Snorting, I move past it, because even though I despise Sutton, there's no denying the fact that the other shop doesn't stand a chance in the same town as his. Folks go crazy over his bikes and if anyone has the funds to afford a custom bike it would be from him. The more I think about it, the madder I get.

What I do next, I'm not proud of, but for some stupid reason I feel the need to help spread the word for that new shop, so I pull the flyer from the innards of the newspaper and head to the copy store.

Well after dark, I load up and beep the horn as I pull to the curb in front of Maury's house. His little form appears within a few moments. As he meanders over to the truck, I hop out and help get him in.

"I can't believe I let you talk me into heading out on the town close to midnight," he grumbles, pulling on his seatbelt.

"How do you know it's that late?" I ask, heading out of our community on a mission.

Maury feels around his watch face until hitting a little side button. "Eleven fifty-six," a computerized voice declares the time.

"Pretty spiffy watch you got there." I refocus on the road that's pretty quiet.

"What are you up to?" he asks with suspicion, completely bypassing my attempt at changing the subject.

"Just sit back and enjoy the ride, old man."

"There will be no enjoying the ride with me feeling like I'm your naïve partner in crime. I'm not going to jail for you, and I guarantee Mia would only agree to bail one of us out and that won't be you."

"It's nothing against the law, I assure you." I keep driving until we reach the business section of town.

I pull to the curb and hop out. "Sit tight," I tell him before grabbing flyers and a tape gun. Lee's had some flyers all over town lately advertising for some big event his garage is having. It's like I see that punk's name everywhere anymore. Well, I think his flyers have been up long enough, so I hurry down the sidewalk, replacing every one of his with my new ones for the other bike company.

After hitting one side of the street and then the other, I rush back to the truck and take off for another section of town.

Two more stops later, Maury asks, "Why do you keep stopping?"

"Just hanging flyers."

"What exactly are on these flyers that they have to be hung up after midnight?" He looks in my general direction with a deep line creasing his forehead.

Knowing he won't let it go, I confess, "A new custom bike company just opened up. I just thought I'd help spread the word." I reach over and turn the radio up with hopes of drowning out the embarrassing conversation. What I'm doing sounds rather petty now that the words have passed through my lips.

Maury's hand fumbles around until it lands on the radio dials. First he scrambles the stations and then turns it louder before figuring out how to switch it off. I settle into my driver's seat and prepare for the lecture that's sure to follow.

"You know this isn't some spitting contest between two adolescent boys. You're both grown men." He folds his arms.

Maury is my sounding board and my voice of reason, so he knows all about Lee Sutton from some long conversations we've had recently.

"The man gets away with being a womanizing jerk. He's always on top. Always getting the girl. Always winning. It's not fair." My fists slam against the stirring wheel as I glare at the red-light.

"Now you just sound like a whiny brat. Really, son, this is downright silly." He doesn't sound amused, more mad than anything.

"He can't have the girl this time. She's mine!" The cab of the truck turns stifling.

"You've got your focus in the wrong direction. Quit wasting your time and energy on being jealous of that man and focus on the woman who does deserve your time and energy." Maury pauses to inhale deeply and I know he's about to cut me deep. "If you would have been focusing like you should on your wife in the first place, you wouldn't be facing this now."

And there it is. Even though I know I deserve it, the sting of that reality slap still has me reeling and my eyes stinging.

"Wow. Don't sugarcoat it, please." I go to make a U-turn, ready to have this night come to an end so I can work on forgetting this entire inane episode.

"You know that's not my style. I either tell it like it is or say nothing at all."

"Yessir."

"Now, since you've dragged me out in the middle of the night with your foolishness, the least you can do is find me a strawberry milkshake and a fat order of onion rings."

"Yessir." I make a right toward the all-night diner and have us there two stoplights later.

Settling in a back booth, I order us both shakes and onion rings from a young woman wearing a poodle skirt and baby-pink sweater with her hair high in a ponytail. This place seems to really be committed to the fifties theme. I study the retro signs hanging on the walls while Maury happily stares off into the unknown. I'm about to ask him the name of the old song playing through the speakers when he clears his throat.

"Dearly beloved, avenge not yourselves, but *rather* give place unto wrath: for it is written, Vengeance *is* mine; I will repay, saith the Lord," Maury says with the eloquence of a professional speaker.

"Where's that at in the Bible?"

"Romans 12:19. One of my favorite books of the Bible as a matter of fact, and those are some words we all need to heed." He nods his head, sending his hat to flop more to the left.

"Yeah, but why do you reckon some people seem to always get away with stuff? How's that fair?" I strum my fingers against the top of the table, feeling my anger building again.

"God said He's going to handle it and we are to be wise and remember that. Don't doubt His words." Maury leans over the table slightly. "Bode, the world is full of Lee Suttons. You're God's child, set apart, so you need to show yourself as one and not pay that man any attention."

"What if Mia... What if..." I can't bring myself to say the words out loud.

The waitress drops off the shakes and onion rings, but my gut is starting to churn and taking my appetite for a nauseating ride.

"Son, you also need to remember you and Mia are not your mom and dad. Their mistake doesn't have to be yours, too. Mia's a good girl, but she's lonely. Don't let someone swoop in and show her the attention you're supposed to be giving her."

Staring at the melting pink shake, I mutter another, "Yessir."

We don't arrive back home until close to two in the morning. I head straight to bed, but do nothing but toss and turn. Maury is right as always. No good will come out of me allowing my jealousy and anger to fester over Lee.

I roll over and steal a deep inhale of my wife's scent from her pillow, wishing she was here with me so I could give her the attention I've neglected to show her for way too long. Flipping back over, I punch my own pillow a few times for good measure and settle on my side of the lonely bed while coming to terms with the words Maury shared tonight.

Sleep edges me out before I make peace with the mess I've made.

*****

A pounding at the front door wakes me, but I could have sworn I just closed my eyes. It takes more effort than I've got to slide out of the bed and pad downstairs, but I eventually make it to the door and see that my early morning company stands dressed in his Sunday's best.

Maury doesn't wait for my greeting. Instead, he pushes the little button on his watch. "Seven sixteen," the annoying robot voice announces.

"Sounds like we've got just enough time before church to go grab up all of the marked down leftovers from Valentines."

I scratch the scruff on my chin as I squint at him. "Didn't know you had yourself a sweetheart."

"I don't, but you do, so go put some clothes on and let's get to it." He waves his hand in a hurry-up motion.

This little determined man won't take no for an answer, that's for certain, so I do as he says. He somehow makes his way into my truck by the time I dress in a pair of slacks and a henley. I load up and crank the truck.

"Where to, old man?"

"The superstore, so we can get everything in one shot."

"Sounds like a plan."

We head in to the relatively empty store and let the big clearance hearts lead us to the right section. Pain slams into my heel for the second time before we get to the right aisle.

"You run into me one more time, and I'll be forced to take your cart driving privileges away." I grasp the front of the cart and lock my arm to keep it on course and away from my legs.

"Get behind me and there'll be no problem."

"Then you'd be running into everything else. Remember, if you break it you buy it."

We make it to the right spot and are overwhelmed by the choices. My eyes eventually land on a monster-sized box of chocolates, so I wedge it into the buggy along with a couple bags of heart-shaped sweet tarts.

"You see any of those fruit flavor filled chocolates?" Maury asks while his hands skim the shelf carefully.

"You're the only person I know who actually likes those nasty ones."

"I like chocolate and fruit together." He shrugs.

"Those are the ones you find abandoned in a box with a single bite missing." I keep harassing him while trying to unearth a box for him.

By the time we've completed our shopping excursion, I've earned a bruised heel and a massive amount of discounted Valentine's gifts for my wife.

Mia finally makes it home late in the evening. She comes to a halt as soon as she enters the kitchen and her eyes go wide.

"Looks like Valentine's Day threw up in here," she mumbles, perusing the room filled with three dozen slightly wilted roses, several shiny helium heart balloons, and a counter covered in candy paraphernalia.

"Aw shucks, honey. You're welcome."

Giggling, she drops her bags and rewards me with a hug and quick kiss. "Thank you."

"Let's have a chocolate supper," I suggest, handing her the big box.

"Sounds good to me." She breaks the seal and fishes out pieces for both of us. They are her favorite and admittedly mine, too. You just can't go wrong with pecan, caramel, and chocolate.

"Remember that time Kaisley and Addison found the box of chocolates I had hidden to give you and ate the entire box?" I pop a second piece into my mouth, savoring the gooey goodness.

She snickers. "Yeah. They were just little ole things. Those little stinkers felt pretty bad after you were done getting ahold of them."

"It was sweet of them to fill the box with an IOU for every piece they ate." I abandon the chocolate and move to my second course of sweet tart candies.

"Every time Mom or Dad took them to the store, they would bring me home a candy bar and swap it for one of the IOU's. They did that until each stolen piece of candy was repaid."

"You definitely came out on top of that deal with full-sized candy bars in place of tiny chocolates." I give into temptation and run my fingers through her soft hair.

"Sure did." Her smile softens and those stunning blue eyes flood with tears. "They are two incredible people, aren't they?"

"Most incredible," I agree, wiping the spilled tear off of her cheek. "How could they not be when they have such an incredible mom?"

"You're a great dad, too, Bode. Never doubt that."

Right here in this kitchen glittering with sweetheart gifts and tears, I want to drop to my knees and beg her to give me time to straighten myself out, to get back on track with my life so I can be the husband she deserves. My mouth opens, but my jaw hinges back shut before any words spill out. Instead, I pretend there are no real problems between us, and go back to eating candy.

Mia seems to be on the same page, so for the rest of our chocolate dinner, the mood lightens up with her telling me about her weekend.

"Got my nails and toes done." She flutters her fingers in front of me to show off the pink and red nails shining with some sparkly stuff. "And I got a massage."

"Sounds like you had a good time."

"I did. The speaker was a Christian comedian named Cherie. I've never laughed so hard in all my life. She was a riot." Mia laughs. "How about you? Did you get into anything interesting while I was gone?" She nibbles another chocolate, waiting for my answer.

"Spent it on the town with wild-man Maury. We went shopping, out to eat, church, and some other stuff I'm not allowed to ever speak of again. I made him behave, though." I don't tell how sorry of a weekend I had, and I certainly don't share with her about my asinine lapse in judgement. I don't admit how jealous and hurt I am.

She laughs like I knew she would. We keep up the light banter for the rest of the candy feast. Even though I go to bed with a slight belly ache and the sugar high jitters, it's one of the better nights we've had in a long time.

Maybe it's not too late to get us back on the right track. Each time her beautiful face lit up by something I said, I saw a sliver of hope. I've just got to remember to keep my eyes focused on my wife and not my problems. Easier said than done.

The sugar could be to blame, but I know better. This is one of those nights that keeps stretching on and on with no gift of sleep in sight. To have a break from my racing mind...

Not being able to get settled, I roll over and study Mia with the bright moonlight's assistance. Sleeping peacefully, it seems she's found the secret to not allowing her worries and cares any farther into the room than the doorway. I wish she would share that secret with me, because worries and cares crawl right into the bed with me each and every night.

There's one certain way that has always helped to shut my worries off and lull me to sleep. Or it has in the past. It's been a good long while since we've done that, so I'm not even sure it would work anymore. The feeling of unworthiness has put a stop to me asking this of her. My norm now is to get up and pace the dark house. But it's never settled me like Mia can.

Unable to doze off, I watch the subtle rise and fall of her chest, the way her hands gently clasp together and rest on her stomach. A soft grunt slips out as she shifts in her sleep. I slide my hand across the space between us and try to summon my voice to call out to her, to beg her, to explain I need her. But nothing comes out and before my hand touches her arm, it cowardly recedes back to my side of the bed.

The echo of the grandfather clock from downstairs keeps reminding me that there's only so much night left and the opportunity of sleep is slipping away. More minutes pass before I try again.

"Mia," I whisper. Clearing the trepidation from my throat, I try again. "Mia."

"Hmm?"

I reach over and lightly tap her on the shoulder. "Mia, I can't sleep."

There's no hesitation on her part as she automatically stretches her arm out to welcome me over, and I happily go to her. Resting my head on her chest, I snuggle close and can't help but moan when her fingers begin a delicate rhythm of weaving through my hair.

"I want you to take me canoeing," she murmurs on a yawn.

"Yeah?" The word comes out hoarsely. She knows exactly what I need in order to shut my mind off—a change of scenery. I inhale her sweet scent and allow the scene she's painting to replace my worry and cares.

"Yes, but not until it warms up. I want to be able to stop at our favorite spot for a picnic," she whispers into the dark while her nails gently graze my scalp.

"I'd really like that, too."

The world settles as I knew it would. This woman knows me well and has taken a happy memory and offered it as a dream gift. My body relaxes and my eyes finally grow so heavy there's no prying them back open as she keeps playing in my hair and describing our canoe trip...

The canoe slices leisurely through the dark river water while a flock of Great Blue Heron squawks in our direction, their sound reminiscent of a bicycle horn. My hand reaches down between paddle strokes and tests the temperature of this brown water that has always looked like brewed tea to me, discovering it to be refreshingly cold. Even though it's murky and some consider it unclean, I find it cleansing. Mother Nature must have spent too much time with God the day He decided to create me. There's no doubt that river water runs through my veins and mud lubricates my joints.

A sweet laugh draws my attention to the back end of the canoe. Looking over my shoulder with a grin splitting my face, I notice the sunrays playing through her brown hair, giving her the golden glow effect of an angel. Shoot, she is my angel, sunrays or not. And we are surrounded by my heaven on earth.

Chapter Twenty

Mia

March boldly marches in with all sorts of change hot on its heels. Surprisingly, Bode was the one to set it all in motion, yet each decision has directly affected me as well.

Quitting his job.

Buying a business with every penny of our savings.

And now, the biggest change is the selling of our house.

Hands on my hips while looking up at this monstrous house, I can't help but feel sentimental. It is the home where we raised our children with the grand walls holding in all of the milestones of our life together. Once the sign was erected on the front lawn, the reality of those changes kicked me into a state of panic. I went through every reason why we shouldn't move, with the biggest being Maury. That took care of itself without any help from me. Maury's daughter has finally talked him into moving in with her. Of course, I had a grand crying spell over that. He's family and I'm going to miss his warmth and wisdom. Friends like Maury are rare and if you ever find yourself blessed with one, *hold* on to them.

Our realtor scurried through a few weeks back, informing us of issues needing to be taken care of before our open house, and that is next week. Sadly, the list is nowhere near complete. I've only had time to tick off a few repairs, and Bode has done zilch. Nothing new there, but boy is it getting old.

I stomp into the garage and eye the paint supplies, wishing the paint would magically make its way to the trim of the house. I grudgingly toe the gallon of *Vermont Cream* exterior paint. The supplies were purchased and neatly displayed here over two weeks ago, so all Bode had to do was paint. Of course, he's put it off, and I'm done nagging him about it.

Lugging the mess to the backyard, a nice, warm breeze meets me. We had a bitterly cold winter and it seems a switch was flipped overnight and demanded the cold to retreat. It feels decadent to be in shorts and a tank top today. Once I wrestle the can of paint open and select a brush, I set out to find my painting groove. Here's hoping one is to be found. The first dip and brushstroke happens unceremoniously, slowly leading to several more.

An hour later, I've managed to knock out five first floor windows. My gaze fixes on the second floor in concern. How am I supposed to reach those? Or maybe I can just leave them be since the power-washing worked some awesome magic. Tilting my head and squinting my eyes, I think that sounds like a plan.

"Whatcha doing?"

Looking over, I find Bode making his way out of the back garage door. I lift the paintbrush and give him a *duh* look.

"I was going to—"

"Don't even say it." Shaking my head, I gather the supplies and scoot over to the garage back windows. My plan is to knock the side windows out next and then move to the front after a quick lunch break.

"You know I've been busy getting the Lodge ready to open for the season." Bode tries grabbing the brush out of my hand as I pass by. "I'll finish."

Yanking it from his grasp a little too harshly, I'm rewarded with flecks of white paint splattering along the front of my pink tank top. "Ugh!" I really liked this one.

"Serves you right," Bode says in a growl, causing me to see red. The nerve of him! He reaches his hand out. "Hand over the brush."

"Serves *me* right?" I point the brush toward the house. "I asked you two weeks ago to take care of this. Two weeks! But it's like everything else around here. You put it off intentionally because you know I'll get fed up and do it myself. I'm not stupid, Bode!" I slap the brush against his chest, leaving a thick splotch of white paint on his dark T-shirt.

Bode's thick brows knit together as he frowns at the mess I made on his shirt. I toss him my paint rag as a white flag, but cringe when he bats it away. *Oh sugar!* In a blink, he snatches the extra paintbrush and, with a flick of his wrist, delivers a shower of white to rain down on me.

My fingers fly up to the side of my head where they meet wet globs dripping from my hair. "You got it in my hair!" I grit out through clenched teeth, hoping I'm pulling off my deadly voice. His lips twitch, and that just ticks me off even more, so I move forward and swipe my brush along the side of his aggravating face. I step back and admire the paint dripping from his earlobe, feeling right proud of myself while he stands there looking offended. "Serves you right!"

"Why you gotta be so stubborn!" He bats the dripping paint from his ear with one hand while delivering another spray of paint with the other.

"Argh!" The growl rings out of me as I reload my brush. Bode takes off in a run, but I still successfully catch the back of his neck before he gets out of reach.

"Dang it, Mia!" He turns back around to face off with me.

"If you wouldn't dilly-dally with every blame thing, I wouldn't have to be so stubborn." I take a step back, but he's already retaliating.

"If you would just chill!" His brush strikes out and paints my forearm white.

War breaks out after this as words mix with splatters of paint, both flinging out until we are practically covered with paint and exasperation.

"I have to do everything around here!" I yell.

"You nag me about everything!" Bode yells back.

"I'm sick of making all the decisions!" I redirect my aim from his head to the exposed strip of skin at his hip when he raises his arm to shield his head.

Bode bats the brush away, coating his fingers in white. "I'm tired of being miserable!"

"It's your fault!" I dance out of his reach.

"It's always my fault!" He stabs me in the chest with the paintbrush.

I turn to run after delivering a blow of paint to his cheek, but Bode manages to trip me. Latching on to his wet shirt, I take him down with me. We wrestle around in the yard, but give up after becoming breathless. Resolving into a fit of giggles over our absurdity, the tension evaporates in the breeze. I really have no energy left to hold onto it at the moment, anyway. Bode rolls on top of me and pins my arms over my head. With my hands clamped in his grip, Bode pries the brush out of my hand and tosses both brushes out of reach.

"What a mess," I whine on a pant.

Bode chuckles, wiping a paint-soaked curl away from his forehead. His flushed face hovers over mine, close enough that our breaths mingle. Finally, my paint-soaked husband rolls off of me, making me instantly ache with losing the contact with him. Tilting his head in my direction, a smirk tugs the corner of his lip up. "You know, I did mow the lawn this morning. That was on the list…" He trails off dramatically.

Glancing side to side, I realize he did and can't help but be impressed. Or I am until I notice green speckles of fresh-cut grass now accompany the paint on our bodies. "Ugh. What a mess."

"We might as well finish the trim." Pushing off the ground, Bode pulls me to my feet.

"Might as well," I agree, wearing a smile.

Hours later, the first floor window trims gleam from their new coat of paint, leaving me totally spent. Bode offers to put the supplies away and he doesn't have to say it twice. My skin is tight and itchy from the now-dried paint. I head straight to the shower to begin the tedious task of ridding myself of the unwanted artwork.

I'm scrubbing my face when I hear the shower door open and close, and then feel a large body wedge into my space. I rinse my face and ask, "What are you doing?"

"I could use some help getting this mess off." Bode gestures to the mess with a boyish grin that makes me melt.

Sometimes, like this moment, I'm struck unexpectedly at how much he still resembles that teenage boy I fell hard for way back in high school. My heart does a skip and my belly flips as he scoots closer to me.

I allow him under the spray of the shower and take a moment to enjoy the trails of water along the sculpted slopes of his body. Directing him to kneel, I grab the shampoo with hopes of releasing the paint from his curls. And they are such lovely loose curls.

"This mess is your fault," I mutter, working the lather through his hair.

"I beg to differ. I recall you starting it," he says mockingly. He leans his head against my stomach and releases a deep moan, vibrating through my core. I forgot how much he loves for me to wash his hair. It's been quite a while...

I pull the showerhead down to rinse away the suds. Working my fingers along his scalp to aid the process, I feel several stubborn bits of paint clinging on for dear life. Replacing the showerhead, I reshampoo his thick hair, focusing on the stiff spots of paint. Bode's hands begin roaming over my legs, scraping paint off along the way. Running my hands over his broad shoulders, my chest tightens with an ache of longing. I just want everything to be set back right between us, but I'm not exactly sure how to do that.

After rinsing once more, Bode stands and seems to completely fill the space with his heated presence. Steam clouds the air as we silently watch each other scrub the paint from our bodies. Every so often, he reaches out and rubs away a spot I've missed with me returning the favor to him. Pulling his head down close to me, I try to dislodge a clump of paint just inside his ear. He holds on to my hips for balance with his thumbs drawing circles along my side.

Once all signs of paint have been removed, we continue to linger in the shower, apparently not wanting this moment to end just yet. His gaze is intense, and I have no doubt he needs to say something. He clears his throat, trying to release the trapped words. When he finally is able to do so, those words undo me.

"You've fallen out of love with me." His voice sounds hoarse with hurt. It's not a question, but a statement. I shake my head no all the same.

"Bode, you know I love you," I say, hoping to dismiss this conversation. The emotions are nearly stifling in the confines of this shower stall. I set my gaze over to the shelf lined with shampoos and soaps, not wanting to face his accusation.

Bode gently cups my chin, coercing me to look at him. "Loving and being *in* love are entirely different." He wraps me in his arms, keeping our gazes connected. "I want us to fall back in love."

"We aren't the same young naïve kids we were when we fell in love. You've changed... I've changed..." His lips part to interrupt, but I move on, needing to get this out. "But I see us making progress... And this man who is finally allowing himself the freedom to live his dreams is very appealing." I cling to him tighter in hopes of forcing our broken hearts back together.

"My resolution this year is to be a better man for you. I want to be better for you."

"Bode, you've always been a good man. The best. It's just that you wandered off from me. I just need you back... come back to me."

The only sounds over the pelting water are sniffles from two fragmented souls. I've not felt whole since the decline of our marriage and wonder if he feels the same. When did we allow ourselves to get so off-track? How did we carelessly lose something so precious—each other's love?

Words can be empty, and so I decide to convince my husband with actions. I need to convey how much I want us to fall in love again. Turning the shower off and grasping firmly to Bode's hand, I lead him to our bed and show him for the first time in nearly four months how much I love him.

Chapter Twenty-One

Bode

Heaven. I wake up in pure blissful heaven. My wife's warm natural body lies loosely on top of me and it's blissful. Allowing my hand to move through her silky wild hair splaying all over, I focus on her calm breaths brushing along my neck where her face is rightfully tucked. She shifts in her sleep, aligning her heart closer to my own, and I feel its steady rhythm reach mine.

With nothing between us, nothing has ever felt so right. This is exactly how we used to sleep in the beginning of our marriage—skin to skin with her sprawled on top of me. I can't think of a better way to wake up. Life put the barriers between Mia and me both figuratively and literally. Then modesty took precedence with the arrival of our children, and then our own self-doubts got in the way, pushing us apart.

My blissful heaven starts to slip away with these thoughts until Mia's sweet body begins to wiggle against me—informing me she's awake. I let those doubts go and focus on keeping the barriers at bay as my hand roams along her smooth back, feeling satisfied when a shiver meets my touch. Mia nuzzles closer, and I'm a happy man when her soft lips press lazy kisses to my neck.

Slowly rolling our bodies until she's tucked underneath me, I begin this promising morning by making love to my wife. *Love.* Not sex. Love, just as God intended this gift to be enjoyed between a husband and wife. It's giving selflessly and taking gratefully. This connection with my wife is so visceral... So right...

Somewhere between the paint fight and this very significant moment, something between us has been mended. Deep inside my soul, I feel this vital part heal. Confident, I know with time and effort, I can convince my wife to fall back in love with me.

*****

I leave Mia in bed to doze a while longer and head to the kitchen to start the coffee. We totally bailed on church this morning. *Forgive me God.* I was *wrapped* up in my own worship service... Anyway...

Watching the coffee slowly percolate, my stomach lets out a mean growl, reminding me we also bailed on supper last night. It was absolutely worth it. Quite frankly, I've worked up an impressive appetite. Grabbing my keys and wallet, I leave the coffee to brew and run out to grab my wife's absolute favorite breakfast.

Thirty quick minutes later, I'm easing back into the kitchen with a warm box filled with cronuts. These babies are better than any donut I've ever put in my mouth. Fried glazed goodness with cream cheese filling. Yeah, donuts hold no candle to them.

Before I fill two cups with coffee, my sleepy-headed bride staggers in.

"I smell them. Where are they?" Her voice is scratchy with sleep, making her tempting in just a little nightshirt.

"Tell me the color of your panties and I might share with you?"

She laughs me off, like I'm joking. I'm not.

Snatching the box and holding it out of reach, I arch an eyebrow. "Tell me."

"Bode Calder, you're impossible." Mia holds her hand out for the box expectedly, but I don't give. "Teal," she finally answers with an eye roll, before popping me in my empty gut.

"Show me."

Hands on her hips, she glares. My morning bear is getting riled up. "Now you're pushing it."

Don't I know it, so I relent and hand over the box. I grab the two cups of coffee and place them on the table before taking a seat. I'm surprised when Mia chooses my lap instead of a chair. Yeah. Life is good.

We eat the entire box of cronuts. They practically melt in my mouth, so it was of little effort for them to disappear with a pot of coffee. High on sugar and love, we spend the rest of this Sunday in bed. *Amen!*

Chapter Twenty-Two

Bode

It's a great day to be on the river. The rain showed up earlier and threatened to put a damper on things, but it finally relented. The clouds have parted and allowed the sun its chance to shine. And man, is it gloriously filtering through the canopy of trees as we carry the canoes to the landing.

There are three full-time river guides in total: me, Fred, and Anthony. Earlier, Anthony and I flipped a coin to see who would have to be stuck taking this bunch of fraternity kids out today. I lost.

Each of the five kids has a very serious water gun strapped on their backs. Yep. The things are that big. Told them the only way I was agreeing to that is if I get one, too. Fair's fair and all.

I set my end of the canoe down on the bank and adjust the neon-yellow soaker strapped to my back. My partner, a kid they call Ox for obvious reasons, does the same with the rest taking our lead, three canoes in all. Here's hoping all three make it back.

"We've already gone over the safety spiel back at the lodge. You all say you've canoed before so you know nothing is in a hurry. You act the fool and flip your canoe, that's on you. Just get it turned back over before all your stuff drowns. Have fun. Get back in one piece and I'll make good on that discount for tomorrow's white water rafting excursion."

They all hoot and holler and seem ready for the adventure. This bunch is staying in one of my cabins, so I thought it fitting to keep them happy in hopes they don't trash the place. All in all, they seem like good kids. Looking around the group of fresh-faced kids makes me miss my own two children. Addison's spring break is next week. I reserved us a cabin for the week so we can use it when we can squeeze it in. I'm not sure how much of that will happen though with everything going on. Mia's parents are driving Kaisley home the following week for her break. She's agreed to hang out with me during the day, but was adamant about sleeping in her own bed.

Her bed. That thought alone tightens the hold on my gut even more. If the text from our realtor Sean is any indication, her bed will be relocated by then, but that's a focus for after work. Right now, I have to focus on keeping these kids safe on the water.

"These boats don't magically get in the water by themselves." This sets them in motion and I take the distraction to douse each one down with my gun, causing a war to break out before we even hit the water.

Soaked, I toss the now-empty gun in the canoe. "All right, you punks, let's get on with it." Ox and I slide our canoe in first, with the other two boats following. Setting the pace, I slice the water with my oar and allow myself to relax into the glide of the river.

Three hours later we make it back to the landing, slightly sunburned and damp. All three canoes ended up being flipped with one kid losing both his shoes and another one drowning his hat. But the boats and all six of us make it back intact, so I call that a success.

"Dude, you gotta go with us on the rapids tomorrow," the kid named Jonas says with a crazy amount of enthusiasm.

"Yeah, man. That'll be epic to have you with us," Ox declares, with everyone else adding vigorous head nods. They all look like drowned rats and I can't help but laugh at them.

"We'll have to see," is all I'll say to appease them.

I flipped a coin with Fred on that one. He lost.

After the canoes go through a quick inspection—all's good—I head into my office to change into some dry clothes. The office is more of a hangout room with a comfortable seating area and a large desk surrounded by chunky leather chairs. There's also an attached bathroom, making it easier to change out of my almost daily damp clothes. But my favorite part of the space is the absence of any kind of computer. Those devices have plagued me long enough in my career, so they are only allowed in my assistant Blythe's office. She thought it was quite an odd mandate, but she's easygoing and has gone along with it.

Donning a fresh pair of cargo shorts and the Lodge logo T-shirt, I take a moment to call Mia.

She answers on the first ring. "Hey, you."

I lean beside one of the tall windows, watching a group pass by on mountain bikes. "Hey yourself. You busy?"

"Between patients. You didn't drown any of those boys today, did you?" I hear papers rustling and someone whisper something to her.

A wide grin pulls at my lips, making me feel like one of those goofy kids from earlier. "Nah. I was tempted once or twice. But I behaved." I turn away from the windows and plop in the seat behind my desk.

"Good. What's up?"

"Can you skip the gym today?"

"Yeah." There's no hesitation in her answer, and it means a great deal to me.

Blythe zooms in and hands me a revised schedule. Giving her a head nod in thanks before she disappears back out the door, I pull my glasses on and study it. I'm not surprised to find it booked solid. Neena got a wild hair to write an article for the local paper about me being the new owner. She talked me into allowing her to include Dave's letter, but not before I got Linda's blessing. Then Neena spread the article to her Facebook page as well as her website. The next thing I knew the phone started blowing up and it hasn't slowed down since.

Tossing the schedule on the cluttered desk, my focus turns back to the conversation. "Good. We can grab a quick bite to eat. Then I've got something to show you."

"What is it?"

"You'll have to wait and see, babe."

"Seriously?"

"It'll be worth the wait, promise."

"Bode Calder, aren't you being quite mysterious."

"Keep teasing me in that flirty tone, and I'll show you erogenous, too."

"Promises, promises."

Pulling the phone away, I inspect the screen. Yep. It confirms I'm talking to Mia Calder aka The Wife. I place it back to my ear and boldly say, "Baby, I can make good on those promises. I'll see you later. Love you."

I deliver those words with as much seduction as I can pull off—not sure I managed anything but sounding hoarse—and hit END before she can respond, hoping I give her something to think about the rest of the day. That woman has me feeling like an infatuated teenager.

And I like it.

*****

Mia's playfulness from our conversation earlier has vanished. As soon as she walks in the house, I notice it.

I gather her in my arms, wondering how many times in the last year or so has she arrived home like this and I didn't bother to notice it. There's nothing I can do about that now, so I focus on Mia before me now and ask, "What's wrong?"

"Bad afternoon."

"Why?" I hold her tighter.

"A patient came in showing some odd signs. And…" She trails off and starts sniffling.

"Shh…" I don't know why I just shushed her while rubbing circles over her back. Why do people do that? I feel stupid, so I cut it off.

"How can people intentionally hurt their children?" Mia manages to ask between sobs and it's gut-wrenching.

I press a kiss to the top of her head. "I don't know, baby. It makes no sense. What happened?"

She pulls back and my heart plummets at the defeat in her glassy eyes. I guarantee she's holding the weight of this, thinking she failed the child in some way. That's Mia. Whole heart. Nothing less.

"I had to get him separated from his parents, so I sent Renee over with the little guy for x-rays and convinced the parents to just wait in my office. I called DSS from Dr. Roger's office." She pulls in a jagged breath and shakes her head. "It's the second time he's arrived all banged up. Last time the excuses were plausible, but today… Today I knew." Her head bows forward, making her thick hair blanket her face.

Reaching over and tucking it behind her ear, I ask, "Is the little guy okay?"

"He has a broken arm with some deep bruises and minor abrasions. They have him in custody and his dad is in jail for the time being."

My jaw begins to ache from clenching my teeth. "Someone needs to beat the crap out of him."

"My thoughts exactly." Mia steps back and I reluctantly release her. "Can I take a quick shower before we go?"

I give her a onceover, thinking her wrinkled scrubs look as tired as her. "We can put it off until tomorrow."

She rubs her eyes. "No. I need a distraction."

I swallow my nervousness over said distraction and send her toward the shower. Here's hoping my news will cheer her up and not add to her stress. If nothing else, it will definitely give her mind a detour for a while. But I know Mia. The situation with the little guy won't be far from her thoughts until she knows he'll be okay.

Alone in the kitchen, I drop to my knees and beg God to heal the child and put his parents' hearts under conviction. Then I pray that He will lift the burden off my devastated wife.

Twenty minutes later, Mia returns, freshly washed and dressed in jeans and one of those frilly tops that show off her collarbones. I can't resist leaning down and skimming my nose over one of my favorite spots on the roadmap of my lovely wife, taking in the soft sweet scent that belongs only to her.

It takes a great deal of effort to move away from her and head toward the truck instead of dragging her back inside. I catch her giving my truck a curious look when I open the passenger door for her.

"What?"

She motions toward it. "It's muddy."

I glance at the mud and then back to her with a shrug. "We can take your car." I'm about to move over to the car when a genuine smile lights her beautiful face, stopping me in my tracks.

"No. I like the mud." As she scoots by me, I hear her murmuring, "Sexy."

Well now. That one little whispered word leaves optimism in its wake that tonight won't be a total bust.

The log cabin is tucked so deep in the thicket on this hefty mountainside that it only shows itself after the truck makes the last bend of the curvy driveway.

"Whoa," Mia leans forward to peer out the windshield. "I was beginning to worry you were driving me out here in the middle of nowhere to dump me."

"No. Nothing that extreme." I chuckle. "Just wanted to show you our new home."

The sassy smile falls as her wide eyes shoot to mine then back toward the cabin that's put together in a combination of thick logs and stonework. It's probably half the size of our colonial, but it has everything we need. And more importantly, it fits our new, tighter budget.

She finally unsticks her tongue and asks, "It's ours?"

"Only if you give it your approval. Sean agreed to meet us at your office in the morning to sign the papers." I climb out of the truck and move around to the other side just as Mia opens her door. I reach in and pick her up.

She giggles when I start walking with her still in my arms. "Put me down."

"No ma'am. No can do. I gotta carry my bride over the threshold." With purpose in my stride, I walk up the flagstone path leading to the wide steps of the deep porch. No fancy garage is included here. All is rustic and homey and feels right.

"I'm not your bride. That's over twenty years past. I'm just your old woman now."

"You'll always be my bride. Now quit mouthing off." I give her an impish grin as I adjust her in my arms. "Now how's about you reach inside my left pocket for the keys. And try to behave yourself, young lady."

After taking a little longer than necessary—I'm not complaining—she produces the keys and unlocks the dark-green door. Pushing it open, I catch the astonished gasp she releases.

"Bode... It's... It's lovely."

A waft of hardy cedar and spice rushes over and welcomes us, and the clarity that this is home hits me just as strong as it did the first time I entered here with Sean the other day. I seriously hope Mia feels the same way. I set her on her feet in the living room. With the absence of walls, it shares the space with the kitchen and dining area. A massive fireplace, dressed in river rock, takes up most of the eastern wall. Mia walks by it, testing the texture of the stone with her fingers.

Following behind her, I attempt to repeat the spiel Sean gave me on the cabin earlier in the week.

"Two bedrooms and two baths on this floor. Upstairs is a closed off loft. The entire space makes up the master suite."

She nods her head as she walks into the kitchen, studying everything thoroughly as she passes.

"Brand new stainless steel appliances that have never been used and new granite counter tops."

Mia smooths her palm along the swirls in the gray and brown hues. The stone is warm in tones and complements all of the woodwork adorning the kitchen. My favorite characteristic of the whole space is the copper range hood. It overshadows the six burner range Mia is inspecting.

"The owners had to move overseas unexpectedly and are anxious to sell. It's been recently remodeled." Shoving my hands in my pockets, I nervously wait for a response. She says nothing, so I push on with my sales pitch. "Furniture is included. All we really need to worry about bringing is our mattresses. They're the same sizes as the bedframes. Bonus, right?" My voice comes out a little high with optimism. She has to love this place. It's so us. The other house seemed to be a façade we hid behind, but this place will simply allow us to be who we are supposed to be.

Mia pauses while inspecting the inside of the double-door fridge to look over at me. "Why don't we just bring our own bed sets?"

I reach out for her hand and lead her to the loft. "Sweetheart, you've just got to see it to understand."

Opening the door, I see she gets it loud and clear. Firmly planted on the wide-planked pine floor sits a hand-carved log poster bed. It's king-size and quite impressive.

"Oh my…"

"Exactly." I let her roam around the room for a while before trying to sell her on it some more. "Our mortgage will be cut in half."

"I like it, but we still need to sell our house first." She eases over to the window and I join her there to take in the view. It's a spectacular sight to see the tops of trees instead of the trunks. Up this high, it's like living in a treehouse.

"We got an offer today. They've agreed to pay full asking price, if we handle closing costs."

She keeps her sights set toward the treetops. "Wow."

Wrapping my arm around her waist, I press a kiss to her head. "Mia, we've been through some kind of trial the past year or so… It's been rough and I'm really sorry for causing it, but now that we've gotten past the worst of the storm, I feel like God is rewarding us." She turns to me, so I take advantage of it and wrap her snugly in my arms.

"I'm to blame just as much as you. And I'm thankful God has faithfully seen us through." Her smile is genuine and reaches well past her cheeks and eyes. This woman just lights up my world. "This is really our new home?"

I nod. "We have to get the paperwork signed and finish up the packing as soon as possible. I'm taking the next few days off to get it all done."

Grabbing ahold of my face, she seems to be trying to see past my eyes. I let her look as I indulge in the feel of her soft hands against my stubbly cheeks.

Moments strum by before she finally asks, "Who are you and what have you done with my procrastinating husband?"

Chuckling, I answer, "The idiot finally woke up."

"Good. 'Cause I sure have missed him."

And all I can do is agree. I've missed him, too. More importantly, I've missed us.

Holding her firmly against me, I whisper roughly in her ear, "I'm *completely* awake and don't feel like putting off christening our new home. Whataya say, sweetheart?" I graze my lips along her elegant neck and can't help but growl in satisfaction when she responds with a soft moan in agreement.

"Okay." The word is barely audible, but it's all the permission I need.

Chapter Twenty-Three

Mia

Days shuffle by with me trying to grasp the idea of living somewhere new for the first time in over two decades. Whether I'm ready or not, that goes down in just days. Luckily Addison is home, helping alleviate some of the moving burden. He's already begged Bode for a summer job as a mountain trail guide. It took very little arm twisting for him to secure the job.

Between sorting through and packing up the house and testifying at an emergency hearing for my patient, the past week has been quite overwhelming.

I'm stressed about it all, so Bode encouraged me to hit the gym and work off some of the tension while he and Addison knock out some of packing duties. I cram the earbuds in and crank up the music, hoping for no distractions. Normally people are respectful when seeing the earbuds in place. I've learned it's a gym sign that means *do not disturb* and it generally works.

No such luck for today. My insides tense up when out of the corner of my eye, I see an intimidatingly muscular form take the spot beside me. His large hand waves in front of me, so there's no way not to acknowledge him now.

Without removing the earbuds, I mumble, "Hey." This is all I offer before studying the treadmill dials. I've gotten pretty good at sidestepping Lee's attempts at hanging out with me, but not today, I suppose. I bump the pace up to a light jog as I notice another familiar albeit out-of-place face breeze by. I pop my earbuds out in surprise.

"Hey, babe." Bode offers this with a wink. *What?*

My lips twitch, but I hold them together, because my first response isn't so pleasant. I decide to go with another mumbled, "Hey."

I watch cautiously as my husband blatantly sizes Lee up by giving him a onceover full of arrogance. Lee seems to be unfazed. Bode gives him one of those chin jerks full of attitude as a way of greeting.

Oh sugar. *Please don't embarrass me.* Please!

"What's up, man?" Lee says coolly. He's clearly not impressed.

"Lee, this is Bode. Bode, Lee."

"Ahh... The husband," Lee says matter-of-factly. Disdain shows up in his tone and is deeply set in the scowl creasing his forehead.

"That I am. And just who exactly are you?" Bode asks this like he doesn't know the celebrity motorcycle designer. His clipped tone clearly broadcasts that he doesn't care either.

Well, well, well. Bode the actor is portraying an arrogant jerk who is above the likings of Lee Sutton.

He has an eyebrow raised to accompany his steely gaze.

"I'm your wife's gym *buddy*." Lee laces a challenge into his words—one that he has no right throwing out there.

My eyes dart toward Lee in shock. I want to deny I'm any such thing to him, but he seems to be over the little confrontation by securing his own earbuds and facing forward as he picks up his pace in a dismissive manner.

Bode steps onto the treadmill on the other side of Lee. After a few tense minutes creep by, I notice Bode has his treadmill really moving. I catch Lee bumping his speed up as well. Of course, Bode challenges by bumping his up even faster. I'm silently praying that my husband doesn't go flying off the back of it.

This is clearly one of those testosterone-induced battles I want no part of, so I cram my earbuds in with hopes of drowning out these two idiots' pounding feet with my music.

At about a mile and a half, my pace is set and I'm all but forgetting my company until I find Bode standing between my treadmill and Lee's.

Popping out one earbud, I ask, "You already done?"

Bode reaches over and dials down my speed without permission until it glides to a stop. "Yeah. Three miles are no big deal." *Clearly.* He's not even winded. I guess he has over two decades of conditioning to thank for that.

I want to ask him what exactly he's doing here, but Lee is still zooming on the treadmill beside me, so I figure it's best to keep my query to myself. Instead we have one of our silent conversations.

As my head tilts slightly, my eyes open a little wider with lifted brows. *What are you doing?*

His eyes cut over to Lee before locking back to mine with a sneer gracing his lips. *You know exactly what I'm doing.*

"I'm going to hit the weights and then grab us some supper. That sound good, babe?"

When did I become his *babe*? "Okay."

Bode surprises the heck out of me when he reaches over and firmly grabs hold of my backside as he plants a significant kiss on my shocked lips. Well, it's obvious Mr. Macho just marked his territory. I'm relieved he didn't choose to pee on the side of my treadmill. I let out a small snort while watching him saunter off. Since when did he learn to *saunter*?

I'm still trying to figure that one out when I hear the whirling of Lee's machine shut down. Looking over, I see him climbing off. Good. Maybe I can get two more miles in with no more awkward interruptions.

Once Bode is out of earshot, Lee says, "Looks to me the husband hasn't forgotten you, sweetheart."

"Yeah. Well, he's just remembering." I can't take my eyes off of the husband as he begins a set of bicep curls with some hefty-sized weights.

I barely catch Lee mutter an expletive and then, "Lucky guy," as he walks away, finally leaving me alone.

Popping the earbuds back in, I scroll through the bank of songs until Trisha pops up. Yep, I'm in the mood to listen to one of my old-time favorites all of a sudden. Hitting play, I restart the treadmill and try my best not to sing out loud about how much I'm in love with my boy. The grin won't stop over his little stunt here. I absolutely love being claimed by Bode Calder.

After leaving the gym, I swing into the grocery store for a few things before heading home. I place everything on the kitchen island and head into the den where I hear the guys talking. Bode and Addison have their backs to me and are wrestling the humongous flat screen off the wall, both in baggy shorts barely grasping onto their lean hips and T-shirts clinging to their shoulders. The only way I know who's who is that Bode is slightly wider in the shoulders and his skin tone is darker from all of his recent outdoor activities.

"You two gonna scratch it, if you don't watch it," Maury speaks, drawing my attention toward him where he's sitting in Bode's chair.

"All of my favorite guys in one room. What more can a girl ask for?"

Bode grunts out, "Hey, babe." There he goes calling me babe again. And again, I like it.

"Hey, Mom." Addison also grunts his welcome as they set the seventy-two-inch behemoth down onto the floor.

"Maury, I'm gonna steal some sugar off your cheek," I warn before leaning down. I feel his cheek lift in a grin under my lips. "Are you supervising these guys, Maury?"

"Somebody has to keep an eye on them," he proclaims.

This little man has been the one true constant in my life for the past twenty years now. My throat thickens and nose stings as my mind plays a quick reel of all the milestones. We watched as his youngest went off to college. We were guests at his daughter's wedding. He and Dorothy were there at the hospital to congratulate us after both of our children's births. We stood by his side when his lovely wife died of a massive stroke way too young, and also helplessly watched him mourn her over the years.

The slideshow of recollections continue to flash before me on a nostalgic reel as I watch Maury apparently watching Bode and Addison disassemble the electronic gadgets littering the entertainment center. It's a long memory lane and I'm a blessed woman to call it mine.

After blinking a few times, I ask, "How about I make y'all my fish tacos?"

Maury and Addison are quick with head nods in agreement, but Bode groans out in mock-protest.

"As long as you find Maury a bib. He can't eat a taco without making a pure mess," Bode grouches.

My brows arch. "I guess I need to find a bib for you, too, because you're just as messy." After teasing my husband a little more, with Maury and Addison adding to it, I head into the kitchen to prepare the last meal I'll ever cook in this house.

Chapter Twenty-Four

Bode

Life is trucking along. A good bit of our stuff is now crammed into our new home. Tomorrow will officially be our last night in the colonial, but more than that is occurring. All of a sudden, I'm not so sure I'm ready to face it. Maury's daughter picks him up tomorrow and Kaisley heads back to school.

A few lessons have been learned as of late...well, a lot of things to be exact. I'm learning that change is something you can't avoid. I tried and it almost did me in.

"Daddy?"

I glance over and see Kaisley giving me an odd look. "Yeah?"

"Where'd you go? I was telling you about the summer mission trip and you grunted like it hurt you."

I didn't even realize I grunted out loud. I shake the mood off and smile, working on being back present in the conversation my mind wandered from.

"A mission project lasting all summer, huh? I'll really miss you, but I think it's great." I pat her on the shoulder.

"I believe it's where I need to be this summer."

"Well, I'm quite honored you felt this is where you needed to be today." I playfully tap the bill of her hat. "I enjoyed you spending the day here at the lodge."

"Me too."

We hiked two trails earlier with a small group of tourists, and the way she handled things, I'd say the mission work will be better suited than her working here alongside me and Addison. I can't help but chuckle.

"Now you're laughing. What's so funny?" She cuts me a look.

"Snake," I whisper in a tease, earning me a slap on the chest.

"That wasn't funny, Daddy!"

Earlier she totally freaked out at the sight of a garter snake sunning on top of a rock we passed. The whole group started bolting down the trail in a tizzy, so I grabbed the harmless snake and commenced to explaining about the species. They eventually settled down enough and some actually took turns cautiously touching the reptile. Not Kaisley. Miss Priss wrinkled her little nose in disgust and kept her distance.

We stroll along the riverbank, watching the last canoe group glide in. The grounds crew just finished mowing so the fresh cut grass perfumes the air in one of my favorite scents. Taking a deep inhale of it, I lean my head back to feel the sun on my face and just revel in the moment. This is the life and I can't believe I finally figured out a way to claim it as my very own.

"Daddy?"

"Yes, sweetheart?"

"Add and I will be home in just a few weeks."

"You know he hates you calling him Add." I nudge her in the side.

"That's exactly why I call him that. Duh." She sasses, sounding just like her mother. We both laugh.

I lift my hand and wave at the boat just as it passes us, and they return the gesture. It's a family reunion canoe trip with a total of ten boats. Now that is a pretty cool way to spend a reunion. "Is there something else to go with that statement?" I ask, turning my attention back to my daughter.

"We thought maybe we could put the Christmas tree up and have a proper Calder Christmas once we're home."

The unopened gifts now sit in wait on shelves in the utility room at the cabin, and every time my eyes land on them a pinch of remorse hits me. "You know, I think that's a perfect idea. Your mom and I should have the house unpacked by then."

She weaves an arm around my back and gives me a side hug. "Awesome. Thanks, Daddy, for fixing whatever you and Momma broke."

Now that right there deserves a proper hug. I forfeit the side hug and pull her in for a good ole bear hug.

Obviously, Mia and I aren't completely fixed—we may never be—but as long as she is by my side, I don't mind the imperfection we call our marriage. I've realized I'd rather be broken with her than whole without.

Later tonight, I push through Maury's door with a plate piled with thick slices of lemon pound cake in hand. Knowing this is the last time I'll ever do this does something really weird to my gut. Leaving that peculiar feeling by the door with hopes it'll vanish before I leave, I hurry in and find him sitting in the den, in the dark. After flipping a light on, I go and plop down beside him on the couch.

"I see you have finally come by to bid me goodbye."

"You're seeing wrong, old man. I'm merely here to bid you *see ya later*."

"That works better for me."

"You know the offer still stands. We can transform the shed out back at the cabin into your very own bachelor pad. It shouldn't take any longer than a month to have it finished. Addison won't mind you borrowing his room till then."

He shakes his head and laughs like I'm joking, but I'm dead serious. I'd build the little guy a new home beside the cabin if that's what it would take to get him to stay. Never have I grown as attached to a friend as I have him and it hurts to have to let him go.

"You're going to be living on the side of a mountain. I'm not so sure it's a sensible place for a blind man to live."

"Why not?"

"More than likely, I'd end up falling to my demise."

"Nah. I'll hook you up with a harness and lead line. You'd be just fine." We both chuckle.

I give up on talking him into staying and peel the plastic wrap off the plate. The moist piece of Mia's homemade pound cake crumbles a bit as I scoop it up. It's still warm and makes my mouth water. I wave it in front of him.

Maury sniffs the air. "Hmm... Lemon." He holds out his hand, so I place the thick wedge of cake in his waiting palm.

"Your favorite."

After Maury enjoys his first bite, I swipe me a piece and we munch in silence for a spell.

I look over at him and notice he's wearing pale yellow crumbs down the front of his blue shirt. I pick the specks of cake off and deposit them on the plate in my lap. There's a few on my shirt as well, so I add them to the little crumb pile. Maybe Mia's right about us both needing bibs.

He breaks the silence after a while. "Iron sharpeneth iron; so a man sharpeneth the countenance of his friend."

"Ah. You're quoting Proverbs again, I see."

"Yes. It's good stuff. You and Mia have been the dearest of friends to me." He pats around until he finds my arm, grasping it.

"Mia says it's because you're too darn cute and we can't help but be your friends."

Maury chuckles, dabbing at his eyes. He didn't laugh hard enough to produce tears, and that in itself makes my blame eyes water up too.

"Do me a favor," he says, looking vaguely in my direction.

"Sure. Anything."

"Never forget Mia again."

"No worries there. Lesson learned the hard way." A deep sigh pushes free from my lips. "Any more wise advice before we part ways?"

"Leave your clothes on the shore next time you decide to go skinny dipping."

Plopping my head on the back of the couch, I snort out a quick laugh. "Mia told you about that?"

He's laughing and crying wholeheartedly now. "Too funny not to tell," he finally gets out between wheezes. "Sure wish I could have seen that."

"You're a riot, old man. No, you would not have wanted to have witnessed my stupidity that day. I'm gonna pretend it didn't actually happen."

Maury waves off my idea. "You've made my life interesting, young man. I'm quite grateful."

I set the plate down and give him a hug. I try to stay tough, but my throat closes off with sentiment anyway. Clearing it away the best I can, I say, "See ya later."

"See ya later, my boy."

*****

A day that will never be forgotten lights my thoughts as I pack up all the stuff scattered around the garage. Only being a few years into our marriage, my young wife and I moved into this grand house. Man, was I proud to be able to provide such a grand house to start our family in.

"Last box," I announce, grunting as I set it down.

Mia looks around the garage while tightening the red bandana holding her hair away from her face. It's evident that the mountain of boxes won't be conquering her today.

"We don't have to knock it out all in one day," I reassure her.

Mia smooths her hands down the front of her jean shirt, barely giving away the subtle hint of her small rounding belly. My cheeks pull way up with knowing my son is resting just inside her sweet body. Just that glimpse wasn't enough, so I move to stand before her, burning up for a better peek than that.

"Bode, what are you up to?" Mia asks with a twinkle in her eye, knowing darn well what I'm up to.

I take my time with unfastening the snap buttons and spread the shirt wide to expose her baby bump. I smooth my palms over the soft, warm skin of her rounded belly. Glancing up, I catch the attractive blush tinging her cheeks.

"Never have I seen you more beautiful than right now." I close the distance and press a kiss to her lips.

"I see we have a young couple as new neighbors," someone says near the garage door, producing a little old man with rich brown skin, leaning heavily on a walking cane.

I scramble to cover my wife and am about to defend her by laying into this peeping scoundrel when I realize his eyes aren't focused on anything.

"Sorry, sir. We didn't hear you come up."

"I suppose you were preoccupied." He's wearing one of those cat-that-ate-the-canary looks and there's no denying the humor lacing his tone.

We shuffle over to him and take turns shaking his hand and introducing ourselves. We fumble a bit with meeting his hand, making it perfectly clear that our new neighbor is blind.

"My wife is baking you one of her famous chicken casseroles for supper. How about you come over in about an hour to fetch it, Mia, so you can meet her."

"I'd love to. Thank you, Mr. Jackson."

"My father was Mr. Jackson. I go by Maury."

"Yessir," she says, grinning. She's smitten with the little guy already.

He reaches up and adjusts his tweed hat in a parting gesture before turning to leave. He says over his shoulder, "My wife and I always lock the doors before we make out. You young'uns would be wise to learn to do the same." He leaves on a quiet chuckle.

Moving over to load up the next box, a chuckle bounces around the nearly empty garage as I think about that day. What a way to be introduced to such a man as Maury. He only moved a few days ago, but missing him has already taken deep roots.

I offer a prayer of thanksgiving for having such a fine mentor in my life as I move the boxes out.

Chapter Twenty-Five

Mia

The overwhelming emotions of the day threaten to get the best of me, so I swallow them down continuously as box after box exits through the front door. This is supposed to be a good thing—a step forward in our life—but I want to stay glued to the spot for a little while longer.

Bode took charge earlier when it became evident that I was incapable. He's been breezing through each room with the movers as I numbly hover around the edge of the activity. There is just no forcing myself to participate any further than this. Instead of helping in a more productive manner, I spend my day watching my lively husband. He can hardly contain his excitement—talking animatedly with the moving guys and unable to sit his fine butt still. He reminds me of a kid about to embark on the adventure of a lifetime. I've never seen my husband so carefree. I hadn't noticed just how severe the chains of discontentment had weighed him down until witnessing them alleviate recently.

Sitting on the only spot left to sit, the fireplace hearth, I rest my chin in my palm and stare at the bare walls. Bode rushes in the den, pauses long enough to lay a loud popping kiss on me that echoes in the empty space, and grabs an unused box before bustling back out of the room.

He's worn the polished appearance of suits, neatly trimmed hair, and a clean-shaven face exquisitely well over the years. But when he pulled on the casual wear, shaggy curls, and unshaven look, he became stunning. It's like my Bode showed up and peeled off the figment he tried so hard to become. I'm glad he's free to step out of that and just be his true self. He wears it incredibly well.

I have no idea how long I stay planted to this brick stoop, contemplating everything, until Bode rushes back in and declares it done. Tears wash over my vision with this declaration.

He comes to a halt and guardedly watches me. "You okay?"

"I just... It's harder than I thought..." I forcefully sniff back the tears, worrying I'm about to completely fall apart.

"But you like the new cabin, don't you?" He closes the space between us and kneels before me.

"It's not that." I toy with the frayed hem of his cargo shorts. "It's all the memories..."

"Oh, baby..." He presses me into his chest as I begin to cry in earnest. "You need to dry it up."

What?

Well, that works, because the sadness is replaced with anger. Pushing off his chest, I smack him in the arm for his insensitiveness. "Gee, thanks for letting me have a moment." I use the shoulder of his shirt as a tissue to dry my eyes.

Bode chuckles. "You can't help me pack up our memories if you don't stop this crying." Standing and pulling me up with him, he ushers us out of the den. "Come on. There's a lot to pack."

We don't get very far, only to the banister of the stairs, before he comes to a halt. His hand goes directly to the twelfth spindle and gives it a good shake to show off its looseness. "Let's pack this one." He looks at me with a boyish grin.

"You want to remember our son breaking his arm?" I ask skeptically.

"No, I want to remember that ten-year-old daredevil going whole hog with thinking he could ski the stairs." He points to the front door. "Addison timed it perfectly with me coming home from work so I wouldn't miss his stunt. He nailed it until the ski caught that spindle and sent him crashing," Bode tells me like I'd ever forget that day.

Bode hurries us up the stairs, saying over his shoulder, "I have the perfect memory to pack with that one."

We pass a recently added memory in the hall that I can't help but pack—Bode going all caveman on me. Maybe it shouldn't be a memory worth keeping, but I still enjoy visiting it. His eyes land on the same wall he pinned me against, so I guarantee he also tossed it in the box as we passed by. We come to a stop near the end of the hall. The dent in the wall is on perfect display now that the picture hiding it is gone.

"That one? Really?"

"Oh yeah. No way can we leave the memory of our first real fight behind." He runs his fingers along the indentation. "Who knew a baby bottle could do so much damage." He tsks.

"I think it was a weak spot in the plaster," I defend as the memory washes over me. "I was so tired that day. Kaisley was colicky and I don't think either one of us slept a wink the night before. You came home that afternoon with your selective hearing turned on. It set me off when you ignored me asking you to go reheat her bottle."

"I was tired that day, too."

"Humph."

"I was. While you tended to her all night, I was crammed in a toddler bed with Addison. He had a nightmare and so I endured kicks, punches, and even hair pulling all night before heading to work the next day. I was a walking zombie and don't have a clue how I made it home."

"I didn't know that." That's the thing with memories, I suppose, you only store your personal parts of it. "I was so ugly to you, only wanting that blame bottle warmed."

"Yep, and it almost hit me upside the head."

"I guess we were already flunking in communications way back then."

Bode moves a little closer to me and leans down. "You want to know the part I want to pack up the most from that memory?"

"What?"

"Little Kaisley was perched on your hip during our entire heated exchange. As soon as we shut up, she let loose the loudest burp I had ever heard. How that manly burp came out of that tiny baby still baffles me. We both laughed until we cried and you gave me the sweetest kiss in apology. Then all four of us crashed on the couch." He gives me a sweet kiss now. "I love that memory. It goes with us."

"Thank you for packing it."

Bode tips his head and recollects my hand. "Come on. We have a lot more to pack."

For the next hour or so, we wander room after room, collecting our memories. We pause long enough at the laundry room for Bode to shake his head and move on. That memory by the dryer is where he stood with me as I loaded a laundry basket, discussing something about Addison going to camp, when his phone began ringing in his pocket. That phone call brought my husband crashing to his knees—it was his aunt informing him of his mom's passing. I don't blame him for wanting to leave it here, but I'm no fool about the memory game we are playing. Even though he has no desire to pack it, his mom's death will always be a part of the package.

By the time we've covered the entire house, another moving truck could be filled to the top with all of our memories. We have them in abundance and have neglected appreciating them way too much.

"We almost forgot one," Bode says as we reach the front door. Pulling the coat closet door open, he hurries us inside.

"That was the best rainy day hide-and-seek game I've ever played." I giggle

"It was quite stimulating," he teases, drawing me close in the dark space.

We sort of got carried away in our own game that day as we waited for our two children to find us. Luckily, they never did.

Snuggling in his arms and skimming my nose along his warm neck, I say, "Bode Calder, you surprised me today."

"How so?"

"The memory packing. Such a romantic notion, sir."

"I can be romantic," he whispers close to my ear.

"You most certainly are." I sigh like some lovesick teenager as my husband nuzzles into my neck.

Pulling back, his eyes go from playful to serious. "Mia, just remember one thing. These memories are ours, and we can take them anywhere we go. They belong only to us. You get that, right?"

"Hmm... Just like you only belong to me." I can't help but swoon.

"And never forget that. Now..." He trails off as his lips brush along my neck.

"You wanna make out?"

"Baby, I'm always up for that," he murmurs, ridding himself of his shirt.

And so we do just that and pack up one last memory to take with us to our new home.

Chapter Twenty-Six

Bode

Moving day turned into one of our best memories, and I'm stoked with the promise of a lot more to come. It's all I can do not to daydream about it as the canoe glides along the river. The clouds covering the sky have me close to lethargic and my eyes beg to drift shut. Somehow, I manage to keep them open and guide this group back to the landing.

Back in my office, a dainty knock taps my door before opening to produce Linda.

"It's about time, young lady." I round the desk and wrap her in a hug. She sniffles, so I tighten the hug.

Linda pats my back after a while so I let her go. We eye each other—me watching her dry her tears and her looking like she's seeing a stranger.

"I knew it," she finally speaks, her voice warming up.

"Knew what?" I ask patting my hair down and standing straighter from her scrutiny.

"I knew this place would be your rebirth." Her trembling lips kick up into a smile.

"Rebirth?"

"Bode, you were like some zombie roaming aimlessly the last few years. I'll have you know that Dave and I were quite worried about you."

"You were?" My brows draw together.

"Yes. We prayed for you many nights. I'm just glad I got to see you come back to life." She hooks her arm in the crook of mine. "Now, how about show me what you've done with this place."

"The place was nearly perfect as it was, we just spiffed it up a bit."

We spend the next hour or so with me showing her some of the changes. They're minimal with just adding some new equipment and renovating the cabins, but she's interested all the same. Linda's approval is important and it was clear in her comments and smile before she left that I've got it.

Between the canoe ride and trail guide this morning and the surprise visit from Linda, I'm ready to clock out for the day and head over to the gym to work out with my girl. It's a new routine, with me popping in once or twice a week. It doesn't hurt to let it be known there's a living, breathing man in her life.

I pull in to the parking lot, but don't see Mia's car. She's probably just running behind, so I head on in. My phone goes to pinging as I hit the workout floor. Digging it out of my pocket, I have to hold it out and squint until the words make sense—*Patient emergency. Not going to make it.*

Shoot. After sending a quick *okay*, I decide to get some weights in before heading back out. Selecting the thirty pound weights, I begin a set of bicep curls and notice Mr. Motorcycle Jerk sidling up next to me.

"The *husband*. How's it going?"

His cockiness makes my hand want to punch the smirk off his face.

"That's me. Everything's great." I angle slightly away from him, hoping the man takes a hint.

He picks up the fifty pound weights and starts curling them like we're workout buddies or something. Well, there's nothing chummy about us. Far from it. The tension is already heavy in the air. I finish the first set, drop the thirties, and grab up the fifties to show the sucker I can handle them, too.

"Where's that sexy wife of yours?"

"Patient emergency." I cut my eyes to his reflection in the mirror before us and notice him looking way too smug. I know I shouldn't and fight against the urge, but I'll be danged if I don't go right ahead and size him up. The mirror shows off the blatant fact that he is one big, tatted-up dude. The thought bugs me that maybe this is what Mia finds attractive. I wonder if she would like me with tattoos... Great day, I sure hope not. I'm freaked out by needles.

The punk catches me staring and has the nerve to flex, showing off huge, bulging biceps. I glare at him before directing my focus back on my form. Lee may have me in the muscle bulk department, but my gut is a lot leaner...

STOP! I silently yell, reminding myself I'm not in competition with this creep. I already won way before he crashed into our lives. Mia's mine.

"Tell Mia I miss seeing her lovely self around here."

Pausing between sets, I say in the most menacing tone I can deliver, "Maybe you should find yourself an available woman to be missing."

He laughs like I made a joke. Ignoring him, I knock out the last set and head over to the weight bench. The son of a gun follows me and sets out to spot me. *Really?*

"One sixty? That's all you're benching? You can handle more than that, can't ya?"

"I rowed a boat all day." *Why am I explaining myself to this punk?* "Besides, I have nothing to prove to you, man," I add for good measure.

"Relax, man. If I wanted Mia, I'd have already had her by now."

I'm off the bench standing toe to toe with my nose close to his before my actions even register to me. Fists balled solid to my side, I grind the words out through clenched teeth, "My wife is off limits. Take care to remember that."

He grins with a cold glare. "Men like you take your pretty wives for granted. Then have enough nerve to go huffing and puffing when your ladies come running to guys like me, who have no trouble tending to their *needs*."

My hand twitches, but the very same words I shared with my son warn me—*never allow someone enough power over you to push you to react stupidly.*

Taking a few deep breaths to calm down, I say, "You know what, man? It's pretty pathetic that you can't get a woman unless it's one playing with you as a second choice."

I back off and head out, knowing it wouldn't take much for me to ignore my own warnings. He may be a bit beefier than me, but my rage would more than make up for that. It wouldn't take much for me to turn around and collide my fists into his smug face, but I remind myself Lee Sutton isn't worth it.

I head home to tend to my wife. She's well worth it.

Chapter Twenty-Seven

Mia

Walking into this new place we now call home, the comforting scents of cedar and cinnamon welcome me. Everything conveys warmth and coziness, and I have the undeniable feeling that we are just finding our home after two decades of searching. I place my bag on the dining table and head into the kitchen where Bode stands at the counter, putting together what I'm hoping is supper.

I comb my fingers through his damp hair and deliver a kiss to his neck. The fresh scent of freshly showered male engulfs me.

"Hey, you," he says, voice sounding a bit distant. "Sandwiches okay for supper?"

"Sure." I wrap my arms around his waist and hold tight. "Is everything okay?"

"How about the patient emergency?" He didn't answer my question, but I let it go for now.

"Oh. Our little daredevil Jordyn decided to try her hand at flying this afternoon. Problem with that was her dad's very pricy remote control plane couldn't bear her weight."

"You have the most bizarre patients." He lets out a quiet chuckle, not sounding exactly like himself.

"Jordyn and the plane took a leap of faith from her treehouse, earning her a broken ankle. I stayed long enough to help her choose neon green for her cast."

"I bet you're beat." He picks up two plates of sandwiches and mounds of potato chips, so I let go of his waist and follow him to the dining table.

"You seem tired, too. Or is something bothering you?"

"Yeah. Long day. All's good now that I'm home with my woman." Offering a wink, he then bows his head and blesses supper.

We eat in amicable silence with me trying not to worry about his mood. Maybe he is just tired, but I have a nagging feeling something else is going on.

After a long hot shower, I climb into our cozy bed beside Bode as he watches SportsCenter. I simply cannot look away from him—rumpled T-shirt, boxers, hair tousled in careless disarray, and glasses perched on his handsome face with the shadow of beard stubble highlighting his defined jaw.

He glances at me then back to the sports broadcaster. "What?" he mumbles.

"I really like those glasses."

He snorts and rolls his eyes, clearly not believing me.

"I really wish you would wear them… and *only* them." My fingers itch to test the locks of hair curling around the edge of the glasses. I give in and twirl one around my index finger.

Well, this gets his full attention. Whatever had him despondent is now forgotten, and a wicked grin lights his face as he powers off the TV.

"Oh, baby, I think we can make that happen." Hopping off the bed, Bode struts over to the dresser where his iPhone is conveniently docked in the speaker. He plays with it a few minutes before Right Said Fred starts crooning out "I'm Too Sexy" from the speaker rather loudly. I haven't heard this song in years and hearing it now cracks me up.

Still facing away from me, his hips start swaying in an exaggerated figure eight! How does this man even know how to work his hips like that? *Oh sugar!* I bite my lip rather hard to hold back a giggle. Only Bode Calder would be able to pull off being downright sensual and silly at the same time.

"Take it off, baby!" I squeal out, bouncing a little in excitement.

Looking over his shoulder, hips still swaying to the beat of the music, Bode slowly lifts the hem of his holey T-shirt. The tease is silly yet incredibly hot as the long toned expanse of his back and then shoulders come into view.

"Such a tease!" Needing closer access to the show, I crawl to the end of the giant bed and have a seat.

Bode shakes his fine tush in sync with the lyrics of the song before turning to face me. He eases the shirt over his head and twirls it around in the air several rotations before flinging it across the room.

"You're killing me!" I hoot and holler, playing it up for the pure fun of it.

My saucy husband rewards me by undulating in such a yummy way, causing the muscles in his abdomen to ripple as he smooths his hands down his chest.

The dancing continues until the boxers join the shirt somewhere on the other side of the room, leaving my hot stripper in nothing more than those sexy glasses.

I'm learning all kinds of new things about this man. My husband not only knows how to properly saunter, he also knows how to pull off one sexy striptease…

*****

"Why do you keep giggling like some teenage girl this morning?" Renee asks as she places a file on my desk.

"Nothing," I mumble through a grin.

She rolls her eyes before disappearing out the door. I start skimming the folder, but my mind goes back to my husband. I feel like a teenager, too, and have the silly urge to doodle his name on top of the folder.

After last week's striptease, I thought that was treat enough. But then I came home a few days later to find Bode folding a load of laundry while *only* wearing his glasses. That was quite the welcome home. I still can't decide what was sexier—my husband naked with only those glasses on or that he was folding laundry.

Laughing again, I clear the memory away the best I can and focus on the day's schedule, but then my phone rings.

I pluck it out of my coat pocket, read the name flashing on the screen, and answer, "Hey sweetie."

"Hey, hey. How's my favorite sister?" *I'm Neena's only sister.*

"Good. You?"

"Great! I want to hang out with you tonight."

"Sounds good. You want to go to step class with me?"

"Heck no! But I'll agree to go out to eat with you." There's laughter in her voice.

"Okay. Where?"

"That new Thai place?"

"Curry?" It's a new hotspot downtown. The local papers declared it hip and trendy.

"Yes. That's it. Seven?"

"Sure."

"Fantabulous!" Neena sings before the phone cuts off. My little sister is such a nut.

Laughing, I place my phone back in my pocket. She sure seemed excited about something. My laughter cuts off immediately and I plop my head on the desk. Oh no. She's got another assignment...

I arrive at the restaurant the same time as Neena. She's looks carefree as always—white blouse, worn jeans, and boots. Her light-brown hair seems a bit more voluminous than normal, like maybe she played with an electrical outlet. Who knows what that one has been up to today.

As we grab a booth near the back, scents of ginger, coconut, and spice waft through the air, sending my mouth to watering.

"We need to try the five-spice noodles, and some coconut curry shrimp," Neena insists.

"Sounds good." I glance back at her as the hostess walks away, too curious not to ask about the bouffant. "Okay. What gives with your hair?"

Neena pats it down. "Is it that bad?"

"Umm... It's a bit *poofy.*"

Neena keeps patting it down, but it's a lost cause. "I spent the day on the back of a Harley." She grins, seeming so proud of herself.

"Really?"

"Hello ladies," a young waiter interrupts.

We order the spicy noodles and shrimp with iced waters and he kindly brings a pitcher of water to accompany our spicy fair.

"How's Nerd?" Neena asks, taking a sip from her glass.

"Nerd is turning into a Neanderthal, I'll have you know. A sexy one at that." My grin widens as I take in her frown.

Covering her ears, Neena whines, "I don't want to hear that part. Ugh. He's like my brother." She drops her hands. "What I want to know is if you two are happy?"

My shoulder lifts in a shrug. "For the most part, yes. We're still licking a few wounds, but we've gotten back on the right track."

"Good. That's all I want for you both. Just be happy." Neena smiles and points a finger at me.

The food arrives shortly after this and my nose already stings from the heavy spice.

"What were you doing on the back of a motorcycle all day?" I ask while fishing a shrimp out of the giant bowl of noodles.

"I'm writing a feature on this group of motorcyclists who ride around the country doing home missions. They call themselves 'Cruising for Christ' and are absolutely the best group of guys I've ever met. They find out about people in need—whether they need a roof on their home, a car fixed, or simply need someone to rally around them in a health crisis. These guys are the epitome of altruism."

"Altruism?"

Neena crams in a mouthful of noodles and seems to find the hot dish not hot at all. My mouth is on fire and I've already had to refill my glass. After she swallows, she answers me, "It means selflessness."

I smirk. "Word of the day?"

"It was one of them a few weeks back, but that's a known word. Not odd enough." She crams another bite.

Neena is a rarity. I've sat on a beach with this girl and while I would devour a chick lit novel, she would be engrossed in a Thesaurus. She has these apps on her phone that deliver words of the day. She's in love with words. Too bad we can't find a man for her to be that passionate about.

Giving up on the overwhelmingly spicy dish, I munch on a piece of sesame bread and watch this lively woman polish off her entire plate.

I know I need to ask, but don't really want the answer. Taking a deep breath, I ask anyway, "Where's the assignment?"

She looks up from her clean plate, so I push mine over to her and she gladly sets into it, too.

"How'd you know?" she mumbles around a mouthful.

"I know *you*."

Neena shrugs a shoulder, but still dodges my question. "Let's get some mango sorbet for dessert." She flags the waiter down and orders without waiting for my response.

This isn't good...

"Neena."

She looks anywhere but at me. "I'm heading to Afghanistan in a few weeks."

I almost drop my glass of water. "No."

"No? Yes. Dad pulled some strings and got me an exclusive with this top-secret special ops group. Sorry, but that's all I can say about it." She gives me a stern look.

"Please tell me Parker is going with you."

She shakes her head. "No. No photos are permitted, and I'm the only one approved for clearance to go. He's not happy about it either, just so you know."

"It's too dangerous. There's plenty of stories that need to be covered right here in the U.S. Why can't you just stay put?" I'm getting upset, so I take a few breaths to calm myself.

Neena finally puts the fork down. The passion flickers in her eyes, and I know right then and there, she won't be changing her mind.

"I've been praying diligently about it for the last several months. It's an overwhelming pull calling me to go. Mia, you should read these letters some of the soldiers sent me. They are extraordinary men, and I have to meet them."

I want to applaud her bravery, but I still need to try to talk some sense into her. "Dad really agreed to this? And it makes no sense for civilians to know about secret military groups. Aren't those guys supposed to be like ghosts?"

We pause as the waiter places the petite bowls of sorbet in front of us. My stomach is churning too much with worry to even sample it. Not Neena. She happily shovels in her serving.

"It took several months for Dad to get on board. He's not thrilled about it, but I told him I would do it with or without his help. One of his biggest fans is in the know, so that's how he's helped me get in on this."

I slump against the booth seat. "How do you even know about it?"

She shakes her head. "I'm not at liberty to say."

"You can't expose them, Neena. I think it's best you just leave this group alone." *Please, dear Lord, let me be getting through to her.*

"These guys risk their lives. Our country is oblivious to what these groups sacrifice for our freedom. We take it for granted. I plan to expose nothing. I simply want to walk a week or two in their lives and shed some light on their gallant sacrifice. Do you realize most of these soldiers have no personal life? They give it all up for us. We have no clue."

"Just please be careful." I reach for her hand that is balled tightly in a fist on top of the table. "I'm so proud of you."

"I promise to be as careful as I can be." She places her other hand over her heart, emphasizing her vow. I'm not comforted by it at all.

"Why don't you settle down and think about allowing one of the guys chasing you to finally catch you? I'm sure Parker wouldn't mind having the opportunity. Don't you think it's time to look at the idea of getting married?"

Neena giggles. "That was one silly statement. I don't have time for that. Plus… What could I possibly have to offer a husband?"

I squeeze her hand before letting go. "You're a complete package—beautiful, successful journalist, big heart, great sense of humor…"

"I'm lacking in one major department. I could never offer a child to celebrate a marriage." Her smile falters, and then vanishes completely.

I know this is why Neena runs the exuberant race she continuously endures, all the while keeping any man at a distance.

"There's so much more to a marriage than that. Plus there's adoption."

"A potential husband may not see it that way." Her eyes flick around the room, avoiding me once again.

"You won't know until you try."

A hard line forms along her lips and I know it's coming.

"I have my family, a respected career I love, and most importantly Jesus as my Savior. I. Don't. Need. A. Man." She punctuates each word through gritted teeth.

"I'm not saying you need a man to be happy. I'm just saying that having a companion to help you celebrate everything you just said wouldn't be so bad."

With a shrug of her shoulder, Neena launches into an animated discussion about a mission project she's working on with the youth group of our church—efficiently shutting down the husband discussion. I let her, knowing she won't budge until she's ready. I just don't want my sister to feel she lacks self-worth due to not being able to get pregnant and birth a child. She's so much more than that.

We spend another thirty minutes lingering over cups of coffee before I head home. Tired and not feeling the best, I call it an early night.

As I pull up to the cabin, my headlights illuminate the front porch and spotlight Bode rocking on the porch swing. He seems so lost in thought, he doesn't even look up. Exiting the car, I go over and join him in the swing and wait for him to share whatever it is that's bothering him. I promise myself not to get up from here until he does—even if that means the mosquitos get to make a meal of me first. I swat one away as an owl hoots from a nearby tree.

Ten solid minutes creep by with my stomach churning. I'm seriously not feeling so hot and I'm not sure if it's the spicy food or my husband's shift in demeanor all of a sudden.

"Bode, what is it?"

"I just... I need to know, Mia. I need the truth." He takes a deep breath and mine seizes in my chest.

"What do you need to know?" I whisper.

"I need to know what happened with Lee Sutton. The truth."

Guilt washes over me even though I know no lines were crossed. "Nothing happened."

"There was no missing the way he was looking at you that day at the gym. It wasn't friendly. Closer to predatory and he has no business even thinking he could claim you. I swear I've tried to brush it off and forget about it, but I can't. I'm going crazy thinking that creep laid his hands on you."

"I promise nothing inappropriate happened." The one incident I felt Lee took too far was when he grabbed my hand and whispered in my ear, but I pulled away. I stopped it, so why is guilt taunting me?

I use my foot to stop the swing, so I can turn and face him. "You checked out a few years back, and I've been so lonely. Yes, I was naïve, thinking he could be my platonic friend—to fill the void of missing you, missing us... I'm sorry for that. I distanced myself when I realized he was after more."

"This is my fault. It's what I deserve. I didn't take care of you." Bode plops his head in his hands.

"Bode, please." I push him up and wiggle my way onto his lap, holding him with all my might. "It was a stupid, attention-seeking thing. He showed me some and I know that was wrong. I should have never looked anywhere else for attention, but from you. Lesson learned. You can bet I won't be letting you not see me again."

"I'm so sorry," he mutters.

The words I shared with Lee flood my mind. Those words were intended for my husband and now the urge to share them overtakes me.

"Promise not to forget about me again. Don't forget I'm a human with needs. Don't forget I'm special. Don't forget to surprise me. Don't forget to steal kisses from me." I pause to steal one for myself. "Don't forget why you fell in love with me. Don't forget to simply flirt with me. And please never forget how much I need you."

Clearing his throat, he whispers, "Promise."

"And I promise to do the same."

He finally smiles and I can finally breathe again. I've never been able to handle this man hurting. It actually causes me physical pain.

Picking me up and ushering us into the quiet house, Bode heads straight upstairs to our bedroom.

"Never doubt that you are the rightful and only owner to this old girl's body." I kiss the words along his neck before he lays me on our bed.

He slowly traces his fingers along my temple and trails them down my neck, leaving tingles in their wake. "This body is mine. *Only* mine. And my body is yours. *Only* yours," he declares before leaning down and reverently caressing my lips.

We spend a good long time putting actions to those declarations, making it perfectly clear how much we belong to each other before dozing off.

Waking up this morning is rough, to say the least. I feel the bed dip down just as a faint wave of nausea passes over me.

"Good morning, beautiful."

I force my eyes to open and find Bode peering down at me, sweat trickling along his temple. "Hey. Good run?"

"Oh yeah. The inclines around here are a challenge. Want to join me for a shower?" He waggles his eyebrows playfully at me.

I try to scoot up on the pillow and grimace. "I better not. That spicy food from last night didn't set well with me."

He runs his fingers along my forehead. "You've got a fever."

I notice the slightly elevated temperature of my body, too. "I think it's just low-grade."

He studies the clock on the nightstand. "I'll call the office for you when they open."

"No. I'll probably be okay once I get a dose of Tylenol in me." Another roll of nausea pitches in my stomach. "I think it's that meal from last night. I wonder if Neena is sick, too."

"I'll call and check on her after my shower," he says as he heads out of the room and not to the shower.

I'm too weak-feeling to question it. Instead, my eyes ease shut with hopes of blocking out the pain. I'm about to doze back off when he reenters with a glass of water and two pills. Placing them in my hand and a kiss on my cheek, Bode now heads to the bathroom. I pop the pills and swallow with a big gulp of water before rolling to my side. The shift shoots pain all along my abdomen. I immediately shift onto my back, but the ache won't ease up. Maybe I need to get up and move...

Climbing gingerly out of the bed, I decide to join Bode. Hopefully, the combination of medicine and the hot water will soothe some of this ache away.

Bode is in serious mode and only helps me wash while encouraging me to stay home. I know the lineup for today and Dr. Brock is on vacation, so there's really only one choice—work it is.

The morning goes by in a blur of agony. Nausea and dizziness accompany me while I meet with patients. Bode's called a few times to check on me.

The fever is gone, so I don't think it's a bug. I'm pretty much convinced it's food poisoning, but Bode checked on Neena and she's just fine and dandy. Her gut is ironclad, so it doesn't surprise me the food poisoning was no match for her. Unlike me, I guess.

Renee finds me in my office during our lunch break with my head resting on the desk. The nausea and pain are starting to escalate again.

"Mia, are you sure you don't need to go on home?"

I try to answer, but a sharp pain slices through me and captures the words. She hurries back out and returns moments later with Dr. Rogers in tow.

"Mia, you think you can stand up for a moment and let me get a good look at you?" he asks.

My head is still resting on the desk, so I roll it to the side and peer up at him. Concern is etched along his long face with his thick, white brows pulled close together. Renee starts rambling off my symptoms, so I guess that makes me the patient for a change. Odd…

Dr. Rogers helps me out of the chair. "Renee, bring that stool over here."

The next foggy thing I know, they stand me on top of it and are asking me to jump off. That may sound like an odd request, but the puzzle clicks together before I jump off and wither on the floor in acute pain—appendicitis.

Once I'm able to breathe again, Renee helps me into a wheelchair and whisks me across the street to the emergency room. Excruciating pain ripples through me every time the wheels catch a bump.

Looking up through bleary eyes, the emergency entrance doors slide open, and then everything begins moving in a sluggish haze until all goes dark.

Chapter Twenty-Eight

Bode

The view is glorious this fine morning with the water producing a foggy mist hovering mysteriously above it. The sound of vigorous river water rushing by has the blood rushing in my veins. The wet rocks gleam in the early-morning sunlight, showing off everything in a fresh way. The verse, *this is the day the Lord has made, let us rejoice and be glad in it*, echoes through my thoughts, producing a satisfied smile to my face. It's the verse Maury has shared with me many a morning over the years as we often bumped into each other while starting our day.

Chatter from the buses draw my attention to today's assignment. I glance over and watch a lively youth group unload while eagerly taking in their surroundings. They're here for a long weekend, staying at the cabins and exploring all that the mountains have to offer. Everyone gathers around me by the riverbank with their helmets and water vests on, waiting for me to give them the go-ahead.

"Everyone grab a paddle and man your rafts." I've already gone through the safety procedures back at the lodge, but once we are on the landing, I give a little spiel. "This adventure is five miles of continuous white water. It's mostly class four and five with only a few short stretches of calm."

"What's that mean?" A teenage girl asks. She reminds me of Kaisley with her nose scrunched up in apprehension.

"It means you won't be bored," I say with a wink, causing everyone to chime in with a laugh. "Any more questions?"

There are only shakes of heads. Everyone seems ready to get this show going, so I lead my seven-member team to the edge of the landing and instruct them to climb in. I give us a push off and the immediate force of the water yanks the raft in a quick motion down the river. Hoots and hollers ring out as we get on our way.

The adrenaline high kicks in and I'm on cloud nine. Now this is living!

The jarring motion is continuous and we are soaked through immediately as the raft slams into a wave. It's already hot, so the icy water is refreshing and no one seems to mind. Two miles in finds us teetering on the edge of tipping over. I instruct the group to paddle backwards on the right, causing the raft to catch in the current, pulling off a rapid three-sixty. All's cool with us managing to keep it from overturning.

My group gets the rhythm of white water rafting fairly quickly. We glide past a few overturned rafts along the way, and we tease with shouts and waves as we continue on.

By the time we make it back to dry land, the teenage girls all moan about their arms hurting from paddling and the boys all groan about being starved. All I can do it grin at this, wishing my own two teenagers would hurry up and get home. I even miss them griping with one another.

As soon as the rafts are loaded and secured on top of the bus, I check my phone. Nine missed phone calls—three from Mia's office, two from Neena, and two from Mia's mom… My heart seizes at the last two missed calls—Valley Medical Hospital.

*****

Running into the hospital with shoes squeaking against the floor, I search for Neena in a panic and find her in the waiting room. She looks up from her iPad and smiles with nonchalance. Nothing ever seems to overwhelm her.

"Where is she?" My voice comes out a bit harsh.

"Calm down, nerd. She's in recovery."

Her calmness is raking my nerves, so I storm out of the waiting room and go seek out the lobby receptionist.

"Are your clothes wet?" Neena calls from behind me, but I ignore her. There's not even an ounce of patience I can summon for my sister-in-law right now.

As quick as my feet will carry me, I approach the redhead at the desk and ask, "Ma'am, my wife is Mia Calder. She's in recovery from surgery. Aren't I allowed?" I sputter the words out in a rush, but I can't help it. I feel close to losing it. I know recovery is the better end of surgery, but I need to see her for myself to make sure she's alright.

The receptionist taps the keys of her computer. Seconds later she gives me directions and I take off. Somehow, I actually end up in the right place and discover my sleeping beauty looking too vulnerable. The look doesn't suit her at all. Relief washes over me all the same.

She's here. She's okay. I still have her. She's still mine.

Kneeling beside the small bed, I run my fingertips along her cheek, just below the oxygen tube. "Mia," I whisper.

Her eyes flutter open before slamming back shut. They seem so weighed down, probably from the anesthesia. I chastise myself as I watch over her. I should have never left her this morning. I had a peculiar feeling that it wasn't something simple going on with her, but there's nothing I can do about that now.

A nurse eases up to the bed and quietly takes Mia's blood pressure and temperature.

"Ma'am, is my wife okay?"

The nurse gives me a warm smile. "She's doing great, just seems to be one of those sleepyheads."

"Is that normal?" I feel my own pulse rising as I listen to the machine tap out the rhythm of Mia's.

"For some patients. Don't be alarmed. Just keep her company, and I'm sure she'll wake up soon."

"And the surgery, how'd it go?" I ask while stroking the top of Mia's hand.

"Mia's appendix ruptured during the procedure, but we were able to get her squared away."

I turn to find the man who just spoke. He's about my age in blue scrubs. "Doctor?"

He offers his hand. "I'm Dr. Jennings."

I rise up and shake it back. "Bode. Mia's husband."

"She's been talking about you in her sleep." The nurse giggles.

I glance around to give her a questioning look and catch the blush warming her cheeks.

"She... umm... really likes your glasses."

I snort in laughter at this—thankfully the nurse didn't elaborate any further than that. From that bright blush, I have no doubt my lovely wife said much more.

The doctor clears his throat as he jots something down in Mia's chart. "Normally this is an outpatient surgery, but we had to perform an open appendectomy, so I'd like to keep her overnight for observations."

"Open?" My heart goes back to pounding.

He pats me on my shoulder to tamp down my concern, but it's not working. "It means I gave your wife a new two-inch beauty mark on her lower right abdomen instead of the usual, much smaller laparoscopic incisions."

"Oh." It's all I got. I can barely hear over the roar in my ears.

"She's fine, though, and is actually peeping at us." Dr. Jennings points at Mia.

Turning my attention to her, I see she's weakly watching us. "Hey, you." I lean down and place a kiss on her forehead.

Mia licks her lips several times with trying to get them to work, I'm guessing, before she speaks. "Why are you here?" She sounds really raspy.

"You're here. Where else would I be?"

Her eyes drift back shut, but she manages to reopen them. "Why am I here?"

"Appendicitis."

"But... I thought we were home... and you were wearing just your glasses..."

I hear a quiet giggle from the nurse. I choose to ignore them both. Really. How to address that? Nope. Not going to.

"Mrs. Calder, can I get you something to drink?" the nurse asks as she scoots close to Mia's other side.

Mia's wobbly eyes seek her out. Licking her lips again, she mumbles, "I don't drink." Mia turns her attention back to me with pinched eyebrows. "Bode, am I drunk?"

"Nah. It's just the anesthesia. It hasn't worn off completely yet." I smile at her encouragingly.

"Oh..." Her eyes flutter.

"How about a can of soda?" the nurse offers.

"Sure," I answer for my tipsy wife. My poor woman is loopy. She's never had surgery before so this is all new to us. She definitely can't hold her own against anesthesia meds. A lightweight for sure. I'll tease her about it one day.

About an hour later, we are settled into Mia's hospital room for the night. Neena brought me a fresh set of clothes, for which I'm grateful. With the anesthesia finally worn off, my tipsy siren has been replaced with my growling bear. Yep. She's hurting and she's not happy. At. All.

Chapter Twenty-Nine

Bode

Two weeks feel like a lifetime when you are served a swift reality check. It all feels like a nightmare I want to completely forget about. They say in a moment of crisis, your life flashes before your eyes. Mia's crisis sent my life with her flashing before my eyes, but I could only see the parts where I failed her.

I've done all I can do to show her how much she means to me. In the process, I'm pretty sure I've gotten on her last nerve. She's a caregiver by nature and hasn't taken too kindly to being on the other end of this. She's growled at me a few times, and in those times, I've backed away slowly to avoid riling her up any more.

A month ago, Chase talked me and about twenty other guys into meeting at our favorite BBQ joint. We packed the place out. Over pulled-pork sandwiches and mounds of fresh-cut fries, Chase led us in a discussion on being the head of the household. He shared two sets of verses with us.

"*I am the good shepherd. The good shepherd lays down his life for the sheep.*" John 10:11.

Chase explained that Jesus is the ultimate shepherd and we are to live by His example on how we take care of our families. Jesus loves us with an absolute love. So fierce that He died for us. I get that, too. I'd lay my life down any day for Mia, Addison, or Kaisley and not think twice about it.

I was totally on point with that verse, but the second verse slapped me in the face. He shared 1Timothy 5:8.

"Anyone who does not provide for their relatives, and especially for their own household, has denied the faith and is worse than an unbeliever."

Chase stated that we are directly ordered by God to take care of our families, but more importantly, we should want to do it without so much as a thought otherwise. I put myself before my family without realizing it. I let depression and self-doubt shackle me down in my den for the last few years. So much so, I couldn't stand up and be the head of my house. People may think the verse talks about financial provisions and I'm sure it does, but more importantly I think it means not a day should go by that I'm not tending to my family's needs.

Mia and I were mending what we messed up, but that Bible study helped me to open my eyes to *my* wrongs. I shoved Mia into the position of taking care of my divine duty. I forced her hand and it nearly cost me everything.

That health scare happened and I can tell you this much—I'll *never* get over it. In turn, for the last two weeks, I've done my part as well as my wife's, and I am willing to take it all on for the rest of our days if God allows me to keep her. Laundry, housework, bills, dealing with Kaisley's transfer to University of Tennessee since her homesickness never improved... You name it and I've taken care of it with no resentment.

More importantly, I've started paying attention—diligently looking for ways to make my wife's life easier. All those miniscule things that I used to overlook—oil changes, fixing the leaking kitchen drain, taking out the garbage. These tasks take very little of my time to knock out, but it alleviates a tremendous burden off my wife.

Parking beside Neena's little sports car, I grab up our supper of chef salads and head inside my home. Neena's been hanging out with Mia a little during the day this week so I can get some work done.

"Hey, twerp."

Neena looks over the top of her laptop screen. From the looks of it, she's transformed my dining table into her desk. "Nerd."

"Where's my wife?"

"Shower," Neena replies and starts packing up all of her mess that's strung all over the place.

"How was she today?" I place the bag on the now-cleared table.

"Irascible."

"Ira-what?"

"Cranky," she says slowly with an exaggerated eye roll.

"Why didn't you just say that to begin with?" I huff, not being in the mood for a word-lesson.

"I've got a late meeting with my editor. I'm out." She shoves on her boots in one of those impatient hopping around maneuvers before heading to the door.

"Here. At least take your supper with you." I fish her salad out of the bag and hand it over.

"Thanks, dork." She backtracks to place a quick peck on my cheek.

"Irascible to dork?"

"You pronounced it correctly. I'm so proud!" Neena claps, almost losing the container in the silly process, and breezes out the door.

Laughing off our ridiculous exchange, I jog up the stairs to check on Mia. I took her to the post-op appointment yesterday and they finally removed her stitches, so I bet she's glad to wash properly.

Knocking once, I push into the bathroom and find Mia standing in front of the mirror, wrapped in a towel with tears streaming down her face.

"Baby, what's wrong? Are you hurting?" I ask in a rush as I step closer.

"I don't understand why we're together?"

My knees buckle, landing me in a pile of panic in front of her. "You're all I want."

Shaking her head, Mia motions toward me. "You look incredible..." She sniffs. "And I..."

Relief washes over me with the realization that this is about her insecurities and not actually about us. Well, I can handle that. Motioning her forward with a wave of my hand, I give her a stern look. She seems hesitant and a bit confused, but obeys. Remaining on my knees, I gently tug the towel away from her body and toss it behind me.

No words are needed for now. Instead, I scan her body and watch her fidget slightly under my scrutiny. The woman has no clue what she does to me.

"This body... it intimidates me." Shaking my head, I give in and skim my fingertips softly over her new pink scar. This is a point that needs to be made with no rush. Taking my time, I move on to the very faint stretchmarks. They're barely noticeable, but Mia is mine, and I know every inch of this body.

She tries to pull away, but I don't allow it. With one hand firmly holding onto her hip, I lean forward and brush a kiss against the new scar and then along her bellybutton where most of the miniscule stretchmarks reside. Her body quivers against my lips.

"I've never gotten over how your beautiful body grew two perfectly healthy humans, and witnessing this strong body birth both of them... Mia, you blow me away." I lean forward and rest my head against her abdomen and wrap my arms securely around her waist, overwhelmed by my own emotions.

Her fingers thread through my hair as I hold her. Bowing down before this woman, I thank God again and again for allowing her in my life. I beg Him and her to forgive me for taking this gift for granted.

I don't know how long we remain in this bathroom, but I'm in no hurry. I just want to reassure my wife of my devotion to her and take all of her insecurities away. She eventually speaks and the world feels right again.

"Bode, make love to me."

I gently pick my wife up and respectfully do as I'm told.

Later in the night, I produce the copy of our marriage vows and have Mia place a check by *in sickness and in health*. It amazes me how God has revealed the significance of these words to us in the last few months. I'm not going to lie—I had no idea what I pledged to that day of our wedding. All I knew was that I wanted that woman to be mine and mine only. I would have pledged to shave my head bald that day and done it with a grin, if I got the girl.

I place the worn paper back on the nightstand, leaving the rest of the puzzle for another time. Wrapping my bride back in my arms, I focus on her.

Chapter Thirty

Mia

I've heard it said many times throughout my life that if things are going smoothly, something is going to show up unexpectedly and wreck it. Sitting in the waiting room at Valley Medical, that stupid omen taunts me and I'm forming quite an aversion for these hospital walls. Three difficult visits to this place in less than a year's time are just too many.

I've also heard storms come in threes. Clutching Bode's hand for dear life, the weight of the third storm has rendered me distraught. I keep thinking we've gone through the worst this life can dish out, but keep being slapped with a harsh reminder that I am wrong. Very wrong.

Murmurings and activity out in the hall continue on the edge of my peripheral, but my heart and soul is in that operating room with my son.

"How long has it been," I mutter, rocking in my chair. My entire body is wired, prohibiting me from sitting still.

"Shouldn't be much longer," Mom says instead of answering my question. She pats my free hand. "It's going to be okay... Addison is going to be okay."

"How can it be okay, Mom? My son almost died today." My throat closes as more tears stream down my cheeks.

Bode's head lifts from praying. This is what he's done pretty much since we arrived who knows how long ago. Thank goodness he is, because the only thing I can mutter to God at the moment is, "Help him. Please help."

Sniffling comes from the other seat beside him. He squeezes Kaisley closer. "Addison is tough. The doctors just need to patch up his leg and he'll be good as new." Thankfully, Bode is stepping up as our strong tower, doing what I'm unable to—lending comfort to our scared daughter.

"He's a brave young man. Swerving in such a way to take the worst of the collision, so his little friend would be okay," Dad speaks proudly.

All eyes ease over to Addison's little friend, aka Ashley. Thank goodness she walked away without so much as a scratch on her pretty little self. She looks miserable like the rest of us, though.

"How about the other driver?" Mom questions, still coddling my arm. "Is he okay?"

"The idiot sustained a concussion. Hopefully it knocked enough sense into him to never text and drive again," Dad answers in a harsh tone.

"Richard, we've all made our fair share of stupid mistakes," Mom comments.

"Yes, Claire, but you can't hold it against me at the moment for being livid with that man for his irresponsible mistake. His dumb choice hurt my grandson."

My parents bicker a little more before moving quickly on to apologies. Everyone is so riled up and upset with feelings running amuck. I wish Neena was here. She's great in these stressful situations, but of course my strong-minded sister is somewhere in the world doing what she does best—drawing out a poignant story and shedding light on it. I just hope she makes it back in one piece, but I can't worry about that right now. All I have room for at the moment is Addison and his wellbeing.

Sighing deeply, I rest my head on Bode's shoulder, only to pick it right back up when the doctor finally appears at the door.

"Addison is out of surgery. Everything went smoothly with repairing his leg, although he will now sport hardware inside of him for the rest of his life." He smiles weakly, but I don't return it in the least. "He'll be in a cast, toe to thigh, for at least eight weeks. It'll be a tough road to recovery, but with physical therapy, I'm confident he'll fully recover mobility."

Bode releases me and Kaisley to rise and shake Dr. Truett's hand. He's an orthopedic surgeon, and I'm so thankful the hospital was able to get him in so quickly.

"Thank you for taking care of our boy," Bode says hoarsely, allowing some of his bravado to slip.

"You're welcome. They're settling him in recovery as we speak. I'll have a nurse come get you and Mia soon."

"Thank you, Dr. Truett," I whisper through tears.

"He's going to be fine, Mia. Promise." The doctor squeezes my shoulder before leaving the room.

I'm close to breaking, so I pull Bode out of the room and down to the prayer room. As soon as he shuts the door, I collapse on him, bringing us both to our knees.

"We've been so... stupid. So careless. What on earth has been wrong with us? What were we thinking? Just taking for granted what we have... God gave me you, and Addison, and Kaisley..." I'm freaking out—all out sobbing with my chest heaving.

"Shh... It's okay, baby. Addison is going to be fine. We're all going to be fine."

His arms are strong and secure, so I sink into his comfort even more and allow him to rock me while he continues to pray until I can pull myself back together. This happens rather quickly with the nurse peeping in the door moments after we enter, but it's enough for me to get it together before we go see Addison.

I come close to collapsing again when we enter the recovery room and find Addison looking like a sleepy young man with only a cast marring his perfectly healthy body. No bruises... Not even a hair on his perfect curly head is out of place. Pure relief washes over me when he squints his brown eyes open at us and smiles weakly.

"Ashley?" he mumbles.

"There's nothing wrong with the boy, Mia. He still has girls on the brain." Bode chuckles, but I ignore him.

Pulling my son's hand in my own, I answer, "She's fine, thanks to your quick thinking. You are her hero, I do believe."

Addison lets out a long breath. "Thank you, God."

"She's in the waiting room. Once they settle you in a room, she'll be allowed to visit."

"Can't I go home?" he rasps. "I'm fine."

"Tomorrow." I smile warmly at this fine young man I've been blessed to raise. Such a big heart.

"Son, if you didn't want to work with me this summer, all you had to do was say so. Great day, man." He motions to the cast. "This is a bit of a dramatic way for getting out of it."

We all chuckle, which effectively breaks the tension. The laugh helps me refocus on the fact that my son is going to be just fine. We are all going to be just fine. *Thank you, Lord.*

*****

The next few weeks ease painfully by for my boy, but we all rally around him. His newly claimed girlfriend Ashley has been his biggest cheerleader. I think him protecting her in that accident the way he did totally sold her and her family on him. They're good people, so I'm good with it. Ashley is here more than not, tending to Addison and keeping him company. I've only caught them with locked lips a few times.

When I whined to Bode about it, he just laughed, saying, "They've got to figure out if they make a good fit."

That earned him a pop in the shoulder. I bet he would have a different response if we were talking about his baby girl Kaisley being caught kissing a boy.

I glance over at Addison reclined in Bode's chair, which Bode relinquished his ownership of it until the cast is off. Ashley has a chair pushed close and is holding his hand while she's telling Kaisley about a song she's learning to sing. Leaving them be, I return to preparing supper.

My thoughts drift to Neena while I finish up the tossed salad. Thank the good Lord, she's back on U.S. soil. The impact of this latest adventure seems to have changed my sister. I don't know what happened over there. Every time I ask, she is quick to point out that she's not at liberty to discuss it. She's too quiet and reserved for Neena. You can see the weight of her thoughts pressing down on her. They say war changes a soldier, but I'm wondering if it's true for journalists as well. Maybe after a little time has passed, she'll get back to normal.

I remove the heavy pan of lasagna from the oven and place it on the stovetop just as strong arms wrap around me from behind.

"Smells good." Bode moans.

"Lasagna, my two guys' favorite."

"I'm talking about this sweet neck." Teeth playfully nip along my neck, sending a shiver to race along my shoulders.

The next thing I know, my mountain man has me hoisted on top of the counter, claiming my lips. Now this is one delicious hello.

A throat clears dramatically from the den, breaking our spell. We look over and find the three of them staring at us in amusement.

"Eww, Daddy. Put Momma down. We're sitting right here!" Kaisley's nose scrunches.

"Yeah, you two. Mia, I do believe we've had a talk recently about controlling our *urges*." Addison's booming voice is full of authority and heavily laced with sarcasm.

"Eww!" Kaisley whines again and the rest of us crack up laughing.

"Well, it's you two punks' fault." Bode points to our children in deliberate sternness. "You said fix what we broke. We fixed it, so now you're just going to have to deal."

Chapter Thirty-One

Bode

What have I gotten myself into this time? I'd rather go skinny dipping in the dead of winter again than to have a needle anywhere near my arm. I must really love my wife to agree to this, or I've completely lost my flipping mind. Either way, I'm doomed. Agreeing to this is pushing me way too far!

"You gotta hold still, man," the guy reminds me once again. His grasp on my arm tightens in warning.

I turn away from him and the needle and look around the wildly colored space for some comfort, only to find my sister-in-law smirking at me from a chair beside mine.

"Pansy," she whispers, her lips curling in a wicked grin.

"Why are you even here? Go away." I reposition in the leather chair, not being able to get relaxed. Nothing is working. The roar of my pulse is pounding in my ears like an out-of-control jackhammer.

"I signed up, too, and I'm next." She looks over at the guy with the big needle. "I promise not to be a baby about it like him." She nods her head in my direction and the both of them laugh... at me!

"Shut it, Neena." A burn takes over my arm while I try giving her my death glare. "Ouch, man! I think you hit bone!" I yank my arm out of his gloved grasp.

"Sorry about that," he mumbles, coming back at me again with the needle.

I close my eyes and try focusing on the music they've got playing. It's supposed to be soothing, but it's doing nothing for me. The burning in my arm reappears, sending my eyes flying back open in a flash. "Ouch!"

"You promised Mia. Now, suck it up," Neena nags. Her hair is a frizzy mess. I have the overwhelming urge to pull it.

"Go away, clown," I grouch at her before I address this butcher with the needle. "I'm not feeling so well. Maybe we shouldn't—"

"Stop being such a malingerer," Neena snaps.

"A what?" I snap right back.

"You're being pusillanimous."

"That's not ringing any bells either. Plain *English*, woman!" I growl.

"A coward trying to get out of his promise to his wife," Neena clarifies, causing the butcher to chuckle.

"I can't do this..." Sweat beads on my forehead and upper lip. I love Mia, but this is going beyond my comfort zone by a hundred miles.

"We're halfway through. Hang in there a little longer," he reassures me, but it does nothing for me.

Moments pass and all of a sudden my vision starts sporadically checking in and out. I know I'm in trouble when my body starts tingling. Fight or flight kicks in and sends me out of the chair, but I don't get far before spots cloud my sight. Then everything turns completely black.

*****

"Hey, mister."

I keep hearing this over and over, but am having a hard time prying my eyes open.

"Hey, mister."

Something probes my eyelid, making me flinch away from it.

"Hey, mister."

My eyes finally decide to crack open slightly. Looking up, I see a young boy staring down at me. Light shines from behind him, making his outline glow.

"You an angel?" I croak out.

"No, sir. My momma calls me her little devil, though."

"Little devil?" I want to ask if I am in hell, but he pokes at my sore arm before the words make it out.

"Yep."

He reaches out to poke me again, but I jerk away from his touch. "Stop that... What's your name?"

"Gatlin," he answers with an outstretched hand.

Shaking it, I look around and see that I'm still in the jungle themed room with this little guy of maybe ten years of age. He's standing on top of the chair Neena occupied earlier.

"What are you doing in here? And standing in that chair like that?"

"I was told to keep an eye on Mia's baby." He nods his head, seemingly proud that he kept to his assignment.

Sitting up slowly to ward off the dizziness, I ask, "Is that what she called me?" A smile spreads across my face.

"No. It's what Neena called you. She said for me to take care of the big baby who is scared of a little needle."

My smile vanishes. "Word of advice, kid, stay far away from that weird woman." My hand lands on all kinds of oddness on the front of my shirt. Looking down, I discover a sea of get-well stickers covering it. "You do this to my shirt?" I scowl at him.

He gives his head a brisk shake. "No, sir. The weird woman did it."

This kid is pretty cool. I ruffle his dark hair and chuckle. Neena must have pilfered about a year's worth of Mia's sticker supply for this little stunt.

"You got one on your face, too." He points.

Feeling around the scruff of my cheek until my fingers land on it, I peel it off and find a yellow smiley face sticker grinning back at me. I start peeling the rest of them off my shirt with Gatlin helping me.

"Our sleepyhead is finally awake," Mia says, coming through the open door while shoving her hands into the pockets of her purple lab coat.

"I could have thought of a million less painful things to do on a Saturday than this." I motion to the bandage in the crook of my arm. Gatlin rids me of my handful of stickers and tosses them in the trash. He's pretty handy to have around.

"But you did it for a great cause. I know our Pipsqueak would have been tickled to see such a handsome man as yourself face down his fear of donating blood to honor her memory." She places a kiss on my cheek, soothing the stinging in my arm some.

The pediatric office is hosting a blood drive in Sophie's memory today. Mia organized the whole thing. Yep. I'm proud of her.

"Where's your aggravating sister? And why'd you let her in here to pick on me the entire time they drew my blood?" I look up just as she skips inside the room. "Speak of the devil and she shall appear, carrying cookies and a juice pouch."

"Here, big baby. This will help you get over your little fainting spell." She hands over the offerings and I grudgingly accept them.

Now that the terror of the needle has passed, I can actually form the question I wanted to ask my goofy sister-in-law earlier. "What's up with your wild hair, Neena? Played with an electrical socket?"

"A sweet little girl asked to do my hair while we waited earlier for her mom to donate blood. How could I resist?"

That's our Neena. We may give each other a hard time, but I couldn't have been blessed with a better sister-in-law. She's pretty great, but I don't tell her that often. No need in giving her the big head. It's frizzy enough...

I take my time chomping on the chocolate chip cookies as Neena shows off her prick spot to Gatlin. The little kid looks all about it, too.

"Say, who's this kid? Neena didn't steal him, did she?" I ask Mia, hearing Neena snort.

"He's not stolen. This is Gatlin," Mia answers before her sister comes up with something snarky, I'm sure.

I don't correct her on the fact I've gotten that much already. "And he's here because?"

"Oh, he's our honorary host today. He and his twin brother are patients of mine. His brother, Gavin, is kicking a rare disease's butt as we speak, but sometimes the poor guy needs blood transfusions. So Gatlin is here representing his brother and showing his family's gratitude to the participants."

I shake the little guy's hand again. "You've been a great host, sir. Thanks for taking care of me in my time of need." His freckled face lights up with a wide grin. He's one of those who smile with their entire face.

"Come on, Gatlin. I think your work here is done with this patient. Let's go see who else might be in need." Neena holds his hand and they vanish out the door.

Swinging my legs off the edge of the chair and planting my feet firmly on the floor, I slowly stand but wobble a bit.

Mia wraps her arm around my waist to help steady me. "Whoa, big guy."

The vertigo seeps away after a few minutes. "I must be madly in love to agree to shed blood for you." The smile feels weak on my face.

"We're wrapping up the last few donors, so it should only be another thirty minutes or so." She starts to lead us out the door, but I stop her.

"Mia, I wanted to talk to you earlier but…" I pull in a steady breath. "I think maybe there are some things we need to go discuss with Chase soon. Remember I mentioned it the other night, and we really can't put it off much longer."

Her brows pinch together. "I just don't know if I can go through with it."

She told me the other night she didn't think she could, but there's no way around it. Some things need to be taken care of before it's too late. I don't say anything else about it, choosing to text Chase and request a meeting. She'll have no choice but to go along with it.

I bump into Gatlin in the hall as I head out. "Hey, kid, where's your mom?"

"I didn't do nothing!" His eyes go crazy wide. "Neena did it!" He points down the empty hall.

"It's not about that. I want to invite your family on a boat ride if your brother is up to it."

Relief floods his round face before it beams with a huge grin. He grabs my hand and rushes us up front in the waiting room where he introduces his mom who is manning a welcome table.

"Momma, Mr. Bode says he wants to take us on a boat!" Gatlin interrupts before I can explain. She looks at me skeptically.

"I'm the owner of Tennessee Valley Outdoor Sports Lodge." *Boy, that's a mouthful.* "If Gavin is up to it, I'd like to invite your family out there for a day on the river. We just purchased a brand new pontoon boat, so there's plenty of room."

"He's Mrs. Mia's baby. He's good," Gatlin reassures his mom.

"This is true," I agree.

Mia joins us. "I can vouch for him, Nichole."

Nichole nods her head. "I think both boys would really enjoy that. Thank you, sir."

"No problem. It'll be my pleasure."

We exchange numbers before I head home with promises of getting it lined up soon.

The following weekend, we make it happen. With the pontoon stocked with snacks and a cooler full of those kids' drink pouches, I stand patiently on the dock for the Jones family to arrive. Minutes tick down as a van comes into view, followed by a motorcycle.

"What's that jerk doing here," I grumble under my breath as I hesitantly head over.

Before I can get to the van, people pile out with Nichole and Gatlin being the only two familiar faces in the bunch. They head over to the bike and hug its cocky owner.

"No way, God. You have got to be kidding me. This ain't even funny." I mutter some more under my breath, wanting to wrench my fist toward heaven and yell, *why me*!

The smirk on Lee's face says he thinks it's hilarious.

"Mr. Bode, this is my Uncle Lee," Gatlin introduces, always the polite little dude. We nod our heads, barely acknowledging each other.

Uncle. Perfect.

"Lee is my stepbrother. The boys had a fit for him to join us. I hope that's okay," Nichole says as she helps another little boy out of the van. He looks similar to Gatlin with dark hair and freckles except the roundness in his face is missing.

"More the merrier, right?" I say, keeping my eyes averted from Lee. The tone of my voice sounds fake to my own ears. "You must be the little devil's brother." I hold my hand out to the puny boy.

"I'm Gavin," he says in a slightly frail voice. There's no mistaking that his health isn't where it should be. I'm really glad I sucked it up and donated blood now. Putting a face to that need is an eye opener.

"Well, Gavin, it's mighty nice to meet you. Shall we set sail?" I motion toward the boat.

"Yes!" both boys say in unison.

An older couple comes from the back of the van carrying bags and another cooler.

"This is my mom Karen and my stepdad Thomas."

We shake hands. "I'm Bode. It's nice to meet you."

After loading everyone up, Lee helps me grab a few other things from the van.

"Well, well, it's a small world," Lee mumbles as we head back to the boat.

"Too small." I take a deep breath and choose to be the bigger man. "This is about the boys today. Not us, so let's just leave our differences here on the shore."

"Agreed."

The day stretches on with me giving the family a guided tour of the river. I talk about the wild life found on the water and some of the history with the kids seeming quite interested. Lee, not so much. He stays to himself, barely interacting with the boys, and glued to his fancy phone the entire time. Each time Gatlin mentions it, Lee scoffs about having important work to do. It makes me wonder why the kids even bothered with inviting him, if this is how he interacts with them.

It's clear the boys hero-worship the undeserving jerk, but he seems oblivious to it. At one point the boys ask him to flex his muscles. Of course, he puts the phone away long enough to do this.

Lee snatches his shirt off and flexes like a fool. I turn back to the boat controls, effortlessly ignoring them until Gavin yanks on the hem of my T-shirt.

"Mr. Bode, you got any tattoos like Uncle Lee?"

Before I can answer, Gatlin does it for me. "No, Gavin. He's scared of needles."

The bark of laughter from Lee is clearly overdone. I keep disregarding him and say to the boys, "*My* woman doesn't care for tattoos, so I don't mess with them." That's stretching the truth just a little. I doubt Mia cares one way or the other with tattoos. She's one who looks deeper than the outward appearance of people. Tattoos are cool, but not for me. No way could I ever sit that long with a needle jabbing my skin.

I think about it for a beat, before adding a little more than my two cents. "My wife's happiness is most important. You boys be mindful to remember that. And also remember that girls are special and should be treated with respect." Yes, my mouth is shooting solid advice/warnings to their dumb uncle and not them, but I deliver it anyway.

"You're Mrs. Mia's baby," Gatlin says adamantly, and I could kiss him for it.

Instead, I ruffle his hair and laugh. "You're absolutely right."

Gavin shrugs. "I don't want a tattoo. I get tired of needles."

Clearly he's still stuck on the tat conversation. Poor kid.

"I bet you do, but I hear you're a champ about it." His little mouth downturns, making my gut ache. "Say, you ready to captain this boat for me for a while?"

When his lips automatically make a U-turn to form a grin, I know that was the right conversation detour. I take a step back and beckon him to stand in front of me. We go over all of the functions of how to steer with him and Gatlin pretending to be pirates. A continuous echo of *argh* and *me thinks* and other pirate gibberish sounds along the river as we make our voyage. They make me a deckhand and I'm completely okay with it, as long as they get to just be two boys for a while with no health problems plaguing them on this ship.

The best part of this awkward day comes when we are almost back to the dock. Gatlin gets a little rambunctious as he runs by Lee, who is leaning over the side of the boat, and knocks the big man right into the water head first.

Now don't try to tell me God doesn't have a sense of humor. I guess revenge is His, but it was nice for God to let me get a little taste of retribution today with Mr. Ego being brought down a humiliating notch or two and losing his phone in the river.

Made my day!

****

Lost a canoe today along with two oars and a whole lot of patience. Luckily, we didn't lose the two idiots who thought it'd be funny to drown my boat. The two idiots in question are sitting in my office dripping all over the place while signing the incident report. These guys are closer to my age than not and it's rubbing me wrong that they still haven't learned the lesson of respect. Needless to say, they won't be allowed back. If they were kids, I might overlook it, but late thirties... No. Not overlooking it.

Shaking my head, I ask in sheer bafflement, "How on earth did y'all manage to sink three items that *float*?"

These jerks have enough nerve to shrug their shoulders like two dumb kids. They know how they did it. My head won't stop shaking in frustration, and the pen nearly goes through the paper when I add my signature to the bottom of the incident report.

"You're eighty-sixed. Get out of here and never come back." I don't yell, but really want to let them have it. Biting the inside of my cheek, I point to the door, where Fred is waiting to escort them off the property. He gives them a stern look as they walk by him.

As the door closes, my phone pings with a new message. I readjust my glasses and read it.

The Wife—*Meet me at the bridge at 7.*

Hmm... she's being cryptic. I play along and send—*what bridge?* She doesn't respond. She knows I know. The clock only reads three and that's too long to wait—especially after the banner day I just had. I try focusing on some paperwork to get the time to hurry up.

Fred walks back in after a while and plops down in one of the soggy chairs. "You ready to throw in the towel on us?"

I chuckle. "It'll take more than a sunk boat to sink me. I'm home here, and I seriously doubt y'all got any chance of running me off. Face it, you're stuck with me."

Fred smiles. "That's what I want to hear. You handled those idiots well. Dave would have done the same thing. No doubt, he'd be proud of how you're running things."

"Thanks, man. That means a lot."

"So, you wouldn't want to hit the rapids this afternoon?"

"Heck no. We flipped a coin. You lost. Fair is fair." We both chuckle.

Admitting defeat, Fred heads out. Now, if I could get another hour or two to hurry up. I'm ready to see what my bride is up to.

Walking along the woods behind the school property, faint music seems to be drawing me closer to my destination. It's an old pop song, but there's no recalling it at the moment. I pick up my pace, weaving between thick red maples and ancient oaks that have hung around all these years, until I make it to the secluded bridge and it's like I've just stepped back in time. Slowly blinking, I readjust my eyes to be sure this isn't an illusion.

Standing before me at the foot of the bridge is that sweet girl I fell hard for—wearing my old track jersey from high school over her tank top, jean shorts, and all of that hair pulled in a cute side-ponytail. I'm struck dumb, and feel like that seventeen-year-old boy wanting nothing more than to grab hold of his girl tightly and never let her go.

A warm breeze rustles through the air and seems to propel me forward until my hands find their rightful place on her lovely hips.

"You look killer," I say, wasting no time claiming her lips in a lazy kiss.

Mia pulls back and eyes me. "We need to talk." She tries to move away from me, but I won't let her.

"What's up?" I ask as my lips move along her inviting neck. There's no holding back the growl when I feel the shiver dance along her body. After over twenty years, I can still get her to react like this... yeah... I want to beat my chest and growl out, MINE!

"The marriage vows. We've been dilly-dallying with them long enough." Her tone is wobbly. It's beyond satisfying to know I'm evoking this response.

"Baby, you can dilly my *dally* any time." This earns me a pop on the shoulder.

Mia pushes hard on my chest, so I reluctantly look up.

"I'm being serious." Her gaze is stern.

I return it with a grin and hooded eyes. "Me too."

"I need to tell you something. Please be serious for me."

Taking a deep breath, I say, "Okay."

Mia tries protesting, but I pick her up and walk us over to the bridge rail. Balancing her on the edge, I step close between her thighs and *try* to pay attention.

"I'm sorry," she whispers.

I'm about to respond, but Mia stops me by placing her hand over my mouth.

"Bode, we've almost gone through all of the vows. It's not slipped my notice that you've claimed the blame for most of it, but I'm at fault, too."

We stare at each other in silence and I'm finally able to place the song she has playing on an ancient boom box. "Cherish" by Madonna. The pop queen is declaring she'll never leave, and I sure hope that's the message Mia is conveying.

"Something happened to you a few years back... Maybe even longer than that. I should have stood by your side and helped you through it. Instead, I was too mad to care about whatever it was you were wrestling with. You needed me to be supportive, and I let you down."

The shake of my head is fierce, but she banishes it with her hands that are entwining through my hair to hold me still.

"I promised to be there for you in the better or worse. Instead, I resented you for the worse. I'm sorry. It's a lesson I've learned the hard way, and I'm here before you now with the promise to *love* and *cherish* you." She leans in and offers the tenderest kiss I've ever received.

To love and cherish is the last part of our vows.

I'm ashamed of the depression and self-loathing I went through, knowing my family had to endure it, too. Man, I just can't get over the fact that this woman still loves me anyway. And her promising to love and cherish me, right along with all my short-comings, just blows my mind.

"I have something to show you," she whispers against my lips.

I reluctantly release this amazing woman and allow her to hop down. Leading me to the bank, Mia points to the side of the bridge where fresh graffiti dominates all of the old art.

Mia Cherishes Bode

Rubbing the tears from my eyes, I look to this incredible woman and back to the declaration. The words are painted in bright white and are surrounded by vibrant red hearts. The woman just stole my own heart again and much harder than she did way back when. I don't even know how that was possible, but she most definitely pulled it off.

I tug her close to me and start dancing until we are back to the middle of the bridge. "You know, there's one thing I really wanted to do with you way back then that I wasn't allowed." My eyebrow lifts in challenge as I give her an exaggerated once-over, leaving no doubt as to where my thoughts rest.

Mischief flickers through her blue eyes, so I know she gets my drift. My fingers find the hem of the jersey, and I take my time removing it. Talk about a teenage boy's fantasy finally coming true after waiting over two extremely long decades...

Chapter Thirty-Two

Mia

Before going to bed last night, I opened the window to allow the trees to fan fresh mountain air in. Thoughts of the summer ahead lulled me into a peaceful sleep, but this morning I'm met up with such oddness that I think I slept through a few seasons.

With the window now closed, the summer breeze has disappeared and has been replaced by spicy hints of cinnamon and nutmeg undulating around the room. Those scents are out of place, but the sounds are even more so. I could have sworn I heard Christmas carols. Without opening my eyes, I cock an ear out from under the blanket to listen. Sure enough, "I'm Dreaming of a White Christmas" croons from downstairs. Blinking a few times, I toss the covers off and go find out what on earth is going on.

The cozy glow of lights twinkling from a tree placed by the fireplace makes me do a double-take.

"A Christmas tree?" I scoot over to it and test a branch, finding it to be real. Looking around, I discover our Christmas decorations nestled throughout the space. How did they do this within the night? Am I dreaming? The air conditioner kicks on, letting me know I'm not. It's June. Not December.

I abandon this part of the puzzle and follow my nose to the kitchen where all three loves of my life are hunched over the open oven door, inspecting a pan filled with fat cinnamon rolls. Rumpled pajamas and bedheads define the trio and never has a sight been more comforting.

Addison shifts on his crutches and eyes Kaisley. "Well?"

"You think they're done?" Bode asks her. She's obviously the one they've deemed in charge of the baking.

"I don't know. Poke at it like Momma does and see if it feels done." She shrugs, scratching the side of her head.

Bode gives the dough a tentative poke while Addison mirrors his action. Both guys look at each other with uncertainty.

"How long have they been in the oven?" I ask.

All three clear the ground with Addison coming close to losing his crutches. He knocks Bode in the leg with one of them. There's no holding back the laughter bubbling out of me from startling them so severely, but I hush as soon as I notice Bode shaking his hand in the air.

"You're not supposed to be up yet," Bode rasps, before pushing his knuckle into his mouth.

"Let me see it." I hold my hand out palm side up, so he places his burnt one on top. The angry red mark will surely blister. "I'm sorry I caused you to burn your hand." I place a gentle kiss near it. "Kaisley, will you grab the Silvadene from the medicine cabinet?"

"Sure thing, Momma." She zooms out of the room and is back in a flash with the little jar of ointment.

After I place the ointment on the burn, I say, "All better."

Bode leans in and presses a kiss to my lips.

"Yuck. Don't start that mess again. We've got Christmas to celebrate," Addison bellows as he and his sister firmly separate me from their dad.

Kaisley nudges Bode's Bible into his hand. "If we are doing a Calder Christmas, we're doing it up right."

He starts flipping to Luke as we follow him to the living room. The morning is in no rush as he shares the true meaning of Christmas—our Savior's birth. Later on, I finish up the cinnamon rolls with a thick slathering of cream cheese icing while Bode serves up coffee.

Once we have settled around the tree, Bode divvies out the abandoned gifts.

"I don't even remember what I bought y'all, it's been so long." I laugh, wiping the dust off the top of the shoebox shaped gift Bode just handed me.

"I remember that one and have come close to unwrapping it and giving it to you a few times," he admits, pulling his hand through his messy curls. "Open it."

I place the gift between my legs on the floor and rip into the snowflake wrapping. Nestled inside the shoebox is a gift that instantly gathers tears into my eyes. With a quivering lip, I pull the glittery nurse clogs out and show the kids the fairies fluttering about them. "Pipsqueak would have loved them," I whisper hoarsely.

Bode wraps me in his arms, so I lean into him for support. "I'm so sorry she never got to see them."

Sniffing back the tears, I smile appreciatively at the lively shoes. "I know a lot of other patients who will love them just the same. Thank you." I place a kiss on his scruffy cheek, beckoning a proud smile out of him.

Kaisley and Addison tear into their stacks of gifts next, mostly being clothing items they won't be able to use until next winter. Games and make-up and perfume and cologne round out the mix. I'm so wrapped up in enjoying them open their gifts that I've just realized Bode hasn't touched one of his own yet. Watching him grin while he observes the children tearing into the presents is a gift in itself. Bode Calder has always been a selfless man, a unique quality rarely found in people nowadays.

"Open yours, Bode." I nudge his leg.

He shrugs his shoulders. "I have everything I need already in this room."

"Me too, but open them anyway." I point to the stack teetering beside him.

He opens several before reaching mine. If I'm going to be honest, the gift I purchased him was done out of sarcastic spite back in December, but it'll actually be an appropriate gift now.

His face beams when he pulls the hefty mud flaps out of the box—each proudly displaying the Volunteers signature T.

"Oh, Dad. Those are sick!" Addison scoots closer to Bode to check them out.

"They are. We'll put them on later today." My husband leans over and rewards me with another solid kiss. "You've always been the best at gift giving. Thank you." He goes back to kissing me.

"That's it! Addison, get ready. I'm taking us to see Aunt Neena. I've had enough of this kissy stuff." Kaisley points sternly at us in reprimand.

After they bustle out the door, Bode scoots us closer to the tree and starts swaying our bodies to the carols still singing about.

"Now that we finally got rid of those punks, there's one more gift I would really like to unwrap," Bode says, nuzzling along my neck.

"Okay, my naughty Santa."

*****

Back to the principal's office. Ugh. It's no more comfortable than last time. Something about being on the opposing side of a desk while an authoritative figure looms from the other side causes me to squirm in my seat.

Bode slaps the paper down on the desk and jabs it with his index finger. "We've got a bone to pick with you about these vows."

Glancing up, I see Chase's face is turning red. I can't look him in the eye, so my gaze averts back to my lap where my hands sit clasped together.

"But... I thought the two of you were doing better?" His tone is questionable.

"We've gone through each part, just as you requested. Man, I'm going to be honest with you, I had no clue what I was getting myself into way back then." Bode lets out a long sigh.

I can't even look over at Mr. Dramatic. I'm still learning things about this one. No... on second thought, I already know he has a flair for the theatrics. Flashes of him darting in the house naked clearly remind me of this. I can just imagine him dancing around that riverbank buck-naked as he tossed his poor suit in the water, piece by piece. I wonder if anyone found his discarded wardrobe washed up on a shore and was scared to death a body would wash up next.

A snort of laughter sounds in the room. I look up and find both Chase and Bode staring at me. Oops.

"Mia, we're here to discuss the state of our marriage, and you're over there daydreaming and giggling." Bode scoffs and flicks a hand in the air.

"I'm sorry." Redirecting my focus on Chase, I say, "Sorry. Bode's right. You should really consider making a pamphlet with the vows broken down and bullet points under each part. People need to know what they're getting themselves into."

A sidelong glance in Bode's direction confirms I've done my part when he nods his head in agreement.

Bode huffs. "Those vows should be null and void since we didn't know what we were actually agreeing to."

My eyes timidly glance over to Chase and I nod my head. "Bode's right. Again. For the last six months we've been on a crazed rollercoaster with trying to figure them out."

Chase scrubs his hands over his face in clear disappointment. "What are y'all getting at?"

"We don't think the commitment we made should count," Bode says sternly.

"Divorce isn't that simple," Chase mutters, growing flustered.

"That's why we want a marriage vow renewal ceremony on our twenty-third wedding anniversary next month," I pipe in, thinking Bode has baited our poor pastor long enough. I can't help but be quite impressed with our improved acting skills. We had our friend going there for a moment.

Chase's shoulders fall back to normal position and a smile slowly spreads across his face. "You two think you're comedians."

Bode roars in laughter. "You should have seen your face!"

"That wasn't funny." Chase declares this even though he's laughing right along with us.

"Seriously, man, thank you for pointing us in the right direction with getting our marriage back on track." Bode shakes his hand and gives him one of those manly half-hugs.

I give Chase a hug. "But you should seriously think about the marriage vow pamphlet idea with bullet points."

Epilogue

A wedding anniversary is a gift of remembrance and celebration of a precious promise. It's acknowledging the day a man and a woman stood before each other and before God to commit their lives together. It's a promise not to be taken lightly, yet sadly most lose their way. But never doubt the gift of rediscovery is always waiting to be claimed. It's up to the husband and wife to reach for it and grasp hold of the treasures God has in store for them.

> *To have and to hold from this day forward,*
> *For better or for worse,*
> *For richer, for poorer,*
> *In sickness and in health,*
> *To love and to cherish;*
> *From this day forward until death do us part.*

The bride walks over in her favorite hot-pink and lime-green scrubs while sporting sparkly fairy clogs. She grasps her groom's hand. He is dressed in his favorite T-shirt and cargo shorts. Both proudly acknowledging who they've become—individually as well as together. No pretenses. No naivety. Only a clear foundation of the commitment they want to declare to each other before God.

Surrounded by friends and family outside at the Lodge, Bode and Mia Calder recommit to simple words that hold a significant meaning. A significance they admitted to taking for granted.

It became clear to the both of them the important need *to have and to hold*. They are partners in this life and need support and compassion from one another to make it through the obstacles presented along the way.

The understanding that being there through the *better or for worse* is a big part of it. Every life has seasons spent on the mountain tops as well as the valleys. The Calders finally understand you have to celebrate on those triumphant tops and mourn in those valleys—together, not separate.

Money and status are not keys to true happiness. Understanding *for richer or for poorer* led them to seeing life can be abundantly lived without material possessions. Life can be rich in love and happiness if you focus on your blessings. It can also be a poor existence when taking these gifts for granted.

Living doesn't come without bumps and bruises. *In sickness and in health,* loving continues and will only flourish when divvied out selflessly.

To love and to cherish should be a given once a couple understands and commits to the vows preceding. Remember, appreciate, and live it out.

The Calders came to many understandings during this valley in their marriage.

Bode is not perfect.
Mia is not perfect.
Their home is not perfect.
Their family is not perfect.
Their life is not perfect.

But there is no denying the love and respect they have discovered is perfect. They said 'I do' a long time ago, but didn't get it right until now.

Until I Do Playlist

"Lead Me" by Sanctus Real
"Just Give me a Reason" by P!nk
"First" by Lauren Daigle
"I'm too Sexy" by Right Said Fred
"I Bet My Life" by Imagine Dragons
"Mess is Mine" by Vance Joy
"Broken Together" by Casting Crowns
"She's in Love With the Boy" by Trisha Yearwood
"Cherish" by Madonna
"Courageous" by Casting Crowns

"Broken Together" was the theme song for this book. We are none perfect. All are flawed. How beautiful could our lives be, if we accept those flaws together instead of casting stones at them? Remember the good, celebrate it, and seek more of it…TOGETHER!

If T.I. isn't writing a book, she's reading one. She's proud to be a part of a tiny town in South Carolina where she is surrounded by loved ones and country fields.

For a complete list of Lowe's published books, biography, upcoming events, and other information, visit www.tilowe.com and be sure to check out her blog, COFFEE CUP, while you're there!

She loves to connect with her reading friends.
ti.lowe@yahoo.com
www.facebook.com/T.I.Lowe

Made in the USA
Columbia, SC
17 April 2025